Button String Bride by Cathy M.
Unexpectedly orphaned and all alone in an untamed world, Charity Davis is ordered to combine wagons with widower Ethan Cole. Ethan needs help with his children; she cannot care for her oxen and pull guard duty. United as a team, they may continue with the train; apart, they must both drop out. Can a rich young woman and a poor, widowed carpenter fall into step and become equally yoked?

Wedding Quilt Bride by Colleen Coble
Faith, club-footed and withdrawn, is visiting her grandmother in Johnstown, Pennsylvania. Daniel is also visiting town to check on the dam. His fears about the dam's stability are confirmed one May day and now his new love may be swept away.

Bayside Bride by Kristin Billerbeck
Jo has left home to escape her new stepmother. The mansion where she finds work cleaning hides a "speakeasy" during Prohibition. Two men will vie for her attention until she discovers where God wants her to be.

The Persistent Bride by Gina Fields
Carly longs to use the heirlooms passed down to her, but she feels she is aging too fast for Mr. Right to catch up. As a hospital social worker, Carly meets a new patient. Mitch is angry at the world. Can Carly help him? Could this bitter man be the one for her?

MOTHER'S WEDDING DRESS

*Four Romantic Novellas
Linked by Family and Love*

Kristin Billerbeck
colleen coble
Gina Fields
cathy Marie Hake

BARBOUR
PUBLISHING

Published by Barbour Publishing, Inc., P.O. Box 719, Uhrichsville, Ohio 44683, www.barbourbooks.com

Our mission is to publish and distribute inspirational products offering exceptional value and biblical encouragement to the masses.

ecpa Member of the
Evangelical Christian
Publishers Association

Printed in the United States of America.
5 4 3 2 1

mother's WEDDING DRESS

BUTTON STRING BRIDE

by Cathy Marie Hake

Dedication

Dedicated to two of my greatest joys,
Kelly Eileen and Colin James.
May you each wait on the Lord
And seek His choice for you—in life and in love.
Whatever joys or trials lie ahead on the path,
Walk with the Lord and let Him light the way.
Love,
Mom

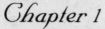

Chapter 1

"Miss Davis, the trail master ordered us to combine wagons if we want to continue on to Oregon. Otherwise, they'll leave us behind when we reach Fort Laramie." Ethan Cole shifted his weight more firmly into the heels of his scuffed cowhide boots as he broke the news. "We'll try to make the best of it. A single lady like you shouldn't be stranded among all of the soldiers, and to be perfectly frank, I need help with my young'uns."

Miss Davis wet her lips and whispered, "I'm willing to watch your children, Sir. I just don't see how you can do more. . ."

From the way her voice trailed off, Ethan knew she didn't understand exactly what the order entailed. He cast a quick look to the side. Banner Laswell had come along to lend the soothing support of her presence. She stayed silent, so he softened his voice and strove to break the news gently. "The plan is for you to put your essentials in my wagon. We're to leave your rig behind." Every speck of color seeped out of Miss Davis's cheeks, and he feared she might keel over from the revelation. Ethan cupped her elbow and coaxed her to sit on a nearby log.

Other than knowing her ma was the first to die on their trek due to a snakebite and her pa's heart gave out a few nights ago, Ethan knew virtually nothing about Charity Davis. He'd been too busy with his own troubles to mind anyone else's business. For a few moments, he silently studied her and tried to take her measure. Most of the women set out on the trip in simple, full gowns made from calico feed sacks; but quality bolt goods draped artistically over Miss Davis's hoops, and her outfit boasted more frills and doodads than any gown he'd ever seen. Small and fine-boned, she looked hopelessly out of place in this wilderness. All it took was a bit of bad news, and she was nigh unto swooning. Ethan barely disguised his grimace. He feared he'd been saddled with a temperamental, helpless female.

"I'll mind your children." She wrapped a fancy shawl about herself more tightly. "If you hunt for us, I'll do all of the cooking and still keep my own wagon. Wouldn't that suffice?"

Something in her voice tugged at him. *Poor gal. She's lost her folks, and now she's losing everything else.* Sympathy replaced his concerns. It felt wrong to hover over a vulnerable woman, so Ethan hunkered down to stay at eye level. "Miss Davis, we set out knowing each wagon had to be self-sufficient. Betwixt the two of us, we can't drive both wagons, care for all of our beasts, do our fair share of guard duty, and mind the kids. By leaving behind one wagon, we'd halve several obligations. We're both in a fix, and the council ruled we either join up or fall out. I can't go on without your help."

Though he paused to allow her an opportunity to speak,

she said nothing. Ethan cleared his throat and added, "I know it's an awkward situation, but I'll bedroll beneath the wagon, and you can sleep inside with the kids."

Tears glossed her wide blue eyes, but she didn't shed a single one. He had to hand it to her. Though both shocked and embarrassed, she didn't indulge in an emotional show. Instead, she looked at Banner and quavered, "I can't pack tonight. It's my turn to stand guard."

Banner quietly offered, "One of the other men is covering for you tonight. I know you're heartsore, but Mr. Cole is a fine man. The council felt it was for the best. For what it's worth, I agree."

"I see." Charity smoothed back a strand of fiery hair with an unsteady hand. "Please let me know who took my guard shift. I don't want to be beholden to anyone."

Ethan grabbed her wrist and turned her palm toward the flickering campfire. No calluses dared mar her dainty hand, but a prime crop of new blisters showed she'd done hard work—man's work—in the past few days. "Do you have salve for these?"

"Yes, Sir." She slowly pulled her hand free and rose. "Please pardon me. I have a lot to do before morning."

"Best thing you could do right now is turn in for the night, Miss Davis. The train is staying put tomorrow so some of the men can go hunting. We'll have a full day to do what needs doing." He paused, then softly added, "Come morning, you'll see the wisdom of this."

She gave him a woeful smile and shrugged. Tired, aghast, and heartbroken as she was, he figured he ought to be glad Miss Davis wasn't sobbing or pitching a fit. *Poor thing's so shaken, she probably can't react,* he thought. He offered her his arm. "I'll walk you to your wagon."

"I thank you for the offer, but I need to be alone." After whispering those timid words, she fleetingly squeezed Banner's hand, then walked toward the edge of the campfire's light to reach her wagon. This would be the last night she'd spend in it.

Ethan watched her go. Banner Laswell filled a chipped enamel cup with scorched coffee and handed it to him. "Don't fret. She's got a lot of polish, but that gal is pure hickory straight through."

"No one told me her age," he said grimly. "She looks young."

"Small, but not young," Banner corrected. "Charity's nineteen. Don't be fooled by appearances. She's shouldering heavy grief, but she still managed to keep up with us all. Give her the night to let this news settle. Come mornin', things will be better."

Banner's words echoed in his ears the next morning. *Things will be better. . .* It was going to be a rough day. Wagons measured all of forty inches across and ten to fourteen feet long at the base. The sides flared upward to permit ease of movement and make them float boat-style if fording a river became necessary. He'd built his to the maximum specifications, so he had a bit of room in his for Miss Davis's things. Still, he reckoned she might be unreasonable about wanting to haul too much. He whispered a prayer for wisdom, then rapped on the side of her wagon.

She peered down at him. The moisture in her eyes didn't bode well at all, but he acted like he didn't notice. "Good morning, Miss Davis."

"I've started sorting through things." She gingerly handed him a brand-spanking-new Colt patent rifle. "Careful. It's loaded. Banner said you're a crack shot, so I presume you'll want all of the ammunition and arms."

"I'll bag you some fine meals with this, Miss. Before you start handing more down to me, it might be best if you come look at my wagon. It'll help us decide what to take and what to leave." He added on, "Gracie Adams said she'd watch the kids for us today, but they're hoping to meet you first."

A timid smile lit her face. "I'd like that. Thank you."

Ethan set aside the rifle and reached up to help her out. The tentative way she set her hands on his shoulders told him this gal wasn't accustomed to a man's touch. He braced her tiny waist and swept her earthward. Yards of petticoats whispered—a sound he'd just about forgotten after three years of being widowed. She'd left off her hoops and donned an apron today. Did that indicate she possessed a streak of practicality? He sure hoped so. A hint of flowers swirled in the air, and since she barely came to his chin, he realized the fragrance came from her hair. In daylight, the red and gold strands blended together like a fine piece of carved cedar. Half a dozen faint freckles sprinkled across her finely chiseled nose. A fetching pink suffused her cheeks, and she shyly dropped her lashes. "Thank you kindly, Sir."

He picked up the rifle and fought the urge to caress the sleek walnut stock. He'd seen fine Colts like this in a mercantile, but they were far too costly for a simple carpenter to own. "I'll pull my wagon alongside yours in a while. It'll make transferring things easier."

She gave him a perplexed look. "I thought I was just to bring essentials. Food, clothing, my Bible, and a quilt."

Ethan settled his free hand on a wheel spoke and looked into eyes bluer than the sky. Her unwavering acceptance of the necessary sacrifices came as a complete surprise. "Miss Davis, I'll do my best to help you take as much as possible. You're going to need more than that to set up a home once we reach Oregon. We'll work on it."

Charity thanked him, but she tried to quell her hope. She hadn't yet seen his wagon and didn't know if he had any space at all. She walked beside him to his rig. Two bedraggled children sat on the seat. Both had their daddy's deep brown hair and eyes. From the way the little girl wiggled, Charity knew she was excited. Charity opened her arms, and the tike leaped at once. After all of her grief, an armful of love felt heaven-sent. She cuddled the waif and looked up at the boy. "Hello."

"This is Tad." Mr. Cole set the rifle under the wagon seat and lifted down his son. "He's eight. This is Catherine, but we call her Cricket. She's three. Kids, this is Miss Davis. You are to obey her at all times."

"Yes, Pa," they said in unison.

"We'll get along just fine," Charity declared. She shifted Cricket onto one hip and touched the button string around the girl's neck. "You sure have a pretty collection of charmglass started. My gracious, what a big girl you are!"

Mr. Cole took his daughter and unlooped the string over her head. "She has thirty-one buttons already. Cricket, I told you you're not to wear this 'cept for Sunday worship. If you lose the buttons, you'll never collect enough to be a married lady when you grow up!"

"Gotta have a thousand buttons to marry a beau," Tad said. "How big is your button string, Miss Davis?"

"If you'd like, I'll show it to you later, Tad. It has 982 buttons." Like so many of her friends back home, Charity's parents started her collection on the very day she was born.

An exquisite assortment of buttons, all carefully corded on her string, lay nestled in her trunk. She'd earned buttons for spelling bees and gotten them as gifts. She'd traded with friends, too. . .all with the understanding that someday a very special man would follow the custom and give her the last button—the thousandth—then ask for her hand in marriage.

"Son," Mr. Cole said, "we've got plenty to do. You take Cricket and go off to Gracie Adams. Take the milk with you."

Charity turned her attention to the wagon. She knew Mr. Cole was a carpenter. He'd made his own wagon, and folks said it was the finest in the train. The tar seams promised it would be watertight. He patted the side and said, "I'm hoping to fasten one of your water barrels here and balance it with a flour barrel on the other side. We'll try to work in a fair share of your goods. Let me lift you in so we can get to work."

Charity suspected he tried hard to be gentle. The breadth of his shoulders and the strength in his hands made it clear he was a powerful man. Brawn like his would mean protection—something she appreciated after the last few days of feeling terribly vulnerable and alone. The fact that he kept a sheathed jackknife on his belt instead of wearing a holstered pistol reinforced the fact that this man, though reputed to be a marksman, preferred preparation to violence. He followed her into the wagon and winced.

"I didn't pay much mind. I fear it's a mess."

"We've both had more important things to tend."

Clothes cluttered the floor. A trunk and wooden crates lined the walls. Food storage looked haphazard, at best. A lumpy straw mattress rested atop a square of wood. When he shoved the ticking out of the way and flipped up a hinged lid, Charity's nose twitched.

"Cricket is too tiny to sleep outside. The kids sleep safely on this makeshift bed, and I built storage boxes below it. The other side has my tools. Over here, there's a section for each kid." Two sections each held a few things, but the third lay conspicuously empty. "That space was my nephew, Sam's. My sister-in-law, Lydia, wanted to make a new life for her and little Sam, but she didn't bargain on travel being so hard. They turned back with the Wilsons and Chroners when we reached Chimney Rock. Things fell apart when she left."

"I'm not managing any better on my own," Charity confessed. "I've had to have men see to my oxen and do guard duty for me."

"We need each other, Miss Davis. I give you my word, I'll provide as best I can and do all it takes to keep you and the kids safe. I know you must feel uneasy, but I'll continue to observe the same proprieties I did when Lydia was with me."

At least he was sensitive to the more delicate aspects of combining their wagons. His words gave the reassurance she'd prayed for. Charity promised, "I'll tend the children diligently and do my best for you. Would you mind if I worked in here a bit so I can determine what essentials to bring along and how to combine our food?"

"Not at all."

Charity knelt and surveyed the contents of the children's boxes. She rocked back on her heels and thought for a moment. She needed to say some things, but they weren't easy subjects to bring up. The last thing she wanted to do was offend him.

"I can see you're struggling to be polite. We may as well speak plainly between ourselves, Miss Davis. Tiptoeing around is liable to cause us more problems than being outright."

"Your daughter is still young. She's not gotten up enough at night." She didn't want to dwell on the problem and chagrin him, so she hastened to solve the difficulty. "We need to dispose of the mattress and bring one of mine over. The quilts are in need of attention as well. I have a length of waterproof gutta-percha we can put under her in the future."

He nodded curtly. "My sister-in-law took the length we kept under Sam and Cricket. I should have thought about that." Relief mingled with embarrassment. This gal was already seeing to the housekeeping and food supplies. Could it be that God had blessed him with a truly remarkable travel partner?

"With everything else we need to do, I'm not sure salvaging the quilts is a good use of time. Do you object to leaving some of them behind and bringing more of yours along?"

"I have plenty. As long as you don't care. . ."

"The only one I'm particular about is the wedding ring quilt. My Justine made it our first year, and I hold it dear."

"I'll see to it."

Ethan waited at the end of the wagon while she separated the quilts. He'd posed the question tentatively, but after it was out, Ethan was glad he'd asked. She actually almost smiled. He should have realized how hard it was for her to give up most of her possessions. Women were, as a rule, quite proud of the quilts they spent hundreds of hours making.

He looked at her ruffled day gown and glanced at the elegant way she'd styled her hair. It stretched his imagination to picture her cleaning, cooking, and minding the kids for more than a day or two. "Miss Davis, the trail is only going to get harder. It's best you know from the get-go that I'm a man who isn't fancy in the least. I reckon things are going to be difficult betwixt us because you're a lady, and I'm a common man who lives by the sweat of his brow and the swing of a hammer."

She gave him the sweetest smile. "I cannot imagine better company. Jesus was a carpenter, too."

Chapter 2

Ethan Cole grinned. "You mentioned your Bible earlier. Am I to take it you're a sister in the Lord, Miss Davis?"

"Yes." The way he phrased that let her know he was a believer, too. "Undoubtedly, our faith will ease things between us." She drew a breath to bolster her gumption. "Mr. Cole, my father was about your size. You should go through his things and have first call. I don't mean you any offense; but you've been without a wife, and my father had two women to care for him. His breeches and shirts were all newly made for the trip and should last you a long while. Whatever fits, you're free to claim."

"That's very generous of you, Miss Davis." His compassionate brown gaze didn't waver. Between his neatly trimmed mustache and beard, a warm smile tilted his lips. "In truth, I could use a few things."

"While I see to combining our sugar and cornmeal supplies, maybe you could go through Daddy's things. There's a crate holding his ammunition and pistols, too. I'm sure you'll want those."

He stepped over a box and went to the front of the

wagon. "If you stay put, I'll roll this rig next to yours so we can set to work."

As he got the oxen from the rope-fence enclosure and hitched them, Charity cast out the mattress and three spoiled quilts. Once done with that, she untied the edges of the double-layered, homespun wagon cover and rolled up the sides. Air wafted through as she carefully examined each article of clothing. If space permitted, Charity quickly determined to bring along more of Mama's clothing. The fabric in one of the wool skirts would yield a couple pairs of britches for Tad, and Cricket needed flannel nightgowns and another frock or two. *Poor motherless children!*

Charity's father bought whatever he felt necessary. A restless man, he'd come just for the sake of adventure. After Mama died, they discussed going back, but Charity declined. He had wanderlust, and she knew he would never be happy being tied down. Luckily, his inheritance had been enough to support them in whatever his whim happened to be. He'd spared no expense in outfitting them well with clothing, food, and trade goods.

Ethan Cole, on the other hand, was a hardworking man of meager means. He'd laid by modest food supplies, but obviously counted more on hunting than Daddy had. His clothing had seen far better days, but he'd gotten a new set for both of his children. The way he prized the quilt meant he cherished his wife's memory, so beneath that rugged exterior, he had a tender heart.

Charity began to tidy the chaos and assess his goods. Clearly, his sister-in-law had taken food and supplies without regard to how it robbed him of essentials. *More soap, a washboard. . .* Charity mentally listed basic things to bring along.

He drove his wagon so close to hers, they nearly touched. She let out a small sigh of relief. It would make her job far easier if she could simply shove things across.

While they'd been gone, Banner and her oldest daughter pulled the heavy cotton bonnet off Charity's wagon and folded it. "You'll need this to make a tent to live in once we reach Oregon," Banner said as she pulled a strip of twine tightly to make the bundle smaller. "You two take a bit of time to work out some details, then I'll be over with breakfast."

"Much obliged, Ma'am," Ethan said as he set the brake. "We'll certainly work up an appetite today." Banner left, and he climbed into her wagon and stood by Miss Davis. In the short time he'd been gone, she'd worked wonders in his wagon. "I'll take the oxen back. Is there anything you want me to do before I go?"

She bit her lip and surveyed things. In an uncertain tone she asked, "Is there any chance we could take along my highboy? I'm using it as a pantry, and I could add your supplies to it."

Ethan studied the walnut piece. *A master craftsman must have spent weeks making this.* He reverently ran his hand across the satiny finished surface, clearly appreciating the fine fit of each drawer and the exquisite carving of a ribbon. He thought for a moment, then nodded. "It'll actually free up some floor space if we empty a few bags and crates into it. I'll need to counterbalance the weight by putting another water barrel out on the other side."

A few men came over to help, and the job was done in a flash. They also moved Charity's trunk across and set it in the corner. One of the men said something under his breath to Ethan, cast a quick look at her, and then left.

Charity started tucking food tins and bags of beans into the highboy. Ethan came alongside her. "Miss Davis, we need to discuss a few matters before we go on. I could see by their mark the Studebaker brothers made your schooner. They're fine wainwrights, and it's a well-built rig."

She stopped working and faced him. "Mr. Cole, even to my uneducated eye, your wagon reflects remarkable workmanship. Due to your talent, it has several extras my wagon can't match."

He felt a surge of pleasure at her words. "It's mighty nice of you to notice. Jed Turvey's getting by with his old farm wagon, but I doubt it'll last the trip. He asked how much you want for your rig."

Her eyes widened. "Of course I'd much rather see one of our fellow families get it than leave it behind. Please tell him he's more than welcome to have it."

"We'll get back to that in a minute." Conducting business with a woman made him feel awkward. Ethan took a deep breath and broached the next subject. "Between us, we have ten oxen. Providing water for all of them will become impossible. Folks are asking about them. I'm of a mind to sell the extra."

She knelt and started to sort through other bags to see what they contained. "Daddy knew nothing about livestock, so I know full well yours are superior. Why don't you choose my best pair to keep and give the other four away?"

"Miss Davis, you can't afford such a generosity. You're going to need every last cent when you reach Oregon. I helped bury your pa. The two hundred dollars from his pocket won't last you very long once you have to set yourself up again."

She dipped her head and tried to blink back tears. "I thank you for your concern, but Daddy didn't leave me destitute."

He made a wordless sound of comfort and squeezed her hand. Neither of them moved for a few moments. She finally took a deep breath to gather her composure. When she looked at him, he tenderly wiped away her tears from her soft cheek with a brush of his thumb. "Mind you, I'm not asking for any specific number, but did your pa really leave you so you aren't too strapped?"

She swallowed hard and whispered, "That was his carrying money. I have more." She ignored his sigh of relief. "Please make the oxen a thank-you gift to the Washingtons for helping me these last days. Rick already lost an ox to the rogue log in the river and didn't replace it at Fort Kearny, so I know money is tight for them. My conscience would trouble me if I took his money—especially since I'm in his debt. As for Mr. Turvey—he's using that old wagon because a new prairie schooner was too expensive. They floated across the river instead of paying the five dollars for the ferry, and I overheard Leticia mention most of their things got soaked. I can't think of anything more shameful or selfish than to deny them a sound schooner."

Ethan shook his head. "I won't argue about the wagon. If the Turveys don't take it, it'll be left behind. Oxen are a different story. An ox costs twenty-five dollars back at Independence. By the time we get to Fort Hall, one will be worth forty, maybe even fifty. Men can't accept something that valuable as a gift."

She lifted her hands in a helpless gesture. "I'd be delighted if the Washingtons took a pair. If pride is at stake, maybe you could charge them five dollars. Certainly no more. Since your oxen will be carrying me and my belongings, it's only fair that you determine the terms of what happens to the other pair. You must promise one thing, though: You'll keep that money to help pay for river crossings and such. I fully expect to cover those expenses since you're kind enough to take me on."

His voice went harsh. "I don't accept charity!"

She arched her brow. "Oh, yes, you have. Charity's my name, and you've taken me on." Sensing she'd dented his pride, she then curled her hand around one of the prairie schooner's rib-like bows. "Please, Mr. Cole, let's not quibble. I'm stranded without your help, so I'm thankful you're willing to let me ride with your family. If I cannot contribute, I'll feel as if *I'm* accepting charity. I'd feel so very wrong. There is so little I have to offer. You must accept what I am able to give toward our eventual success."

"We'll see about that."

Charity pursed her lips. "We have work to do, Mr. Cole."

He rubbed his beard. "We're going to be shoulder to shoulder for the next few months. This formal business strikes me as being ridiculous. I'd rather have you call me by name. I'm Ethan."

"And you'll address me as Charity?"

"Only by your leave." She nodded, and he looked from wagon to wagon, then jumped down. "Fine, then. I won't be gone long. Don't go lifting anything heavy."

During the night, Charity had already repacked her trunk. Dear friend that she was, Banner sacrificed her sleep and had come to help. They'd gone through Charity's belongings and even winnowed through her mama's things.

Charity held up fairly well until they came across a muslin-wrapped length of pure white satin in the bottom of Mama's trunk. Carefully included in the folds was Mama's wedding veil. As Charity began to weep, Banner made a soft hushing sound. She simply placed the bolt at the very bottom of Charity's trunk and started layering in clothes. "Some dreams you don't give up on. Your mama left you that. It goes along."

Charity felt relieved she'd already seen to the intimate details of choosing clothing and packing her personal belongings. She'd have been mortified to have Ethan watch her do so. When he came back, he pitched right in, helping her make decisions; but to his credit, he didn't get nosy. He cleverly determined their washtubs were just an inch different in diameter, so he nestled them together. "We'll both have tubs when we reach Oregon!"

At one point, he caught Charity tracing her finger over the dainty flowered edge of a teacup. "Charity, we're going to have to leave some duplicate things behind. Space is limited. It would gall me if you thought I'd arranged to take you on so I'd have your high-class wares, but since you'll be doing the cooking, it's only fair you keep your better household goods."

She gave him a shaky smile. "You've been most generous. I sensed your reticence last night when you told me the news, and I know you're not a grasping man. Naturally, we both worry about having to replace things once we reach Willamette, so I'll do my best to fit as much in as I can without weighing down the wagon."

He helped her out and watched for a moment as she opened the cook boxes hanging from the tail ends of both wagons. Skillets, dishes, and towels filled them. She whispered, "Please go look through Daddy's trunk while I keep busy here."

When she'd finished with the dishes, Charity climbed back into the wagon. "Can you make use of Daddy's things?"

Ethan looked at her for a minute before answering. "First, sit down."

"What's wrong?" She hesitantly sat on a barrel.

"I need to know: Will it bother you to see me in your pa's clothes or using his things?"

"I've saved many of Mama's clothes to wear myself."

"That didn't answer the question, Charity. They are two entirely different situations. Life has been hard enough on you lately," he said softly. "I wouldn't want to add to your grief."

She looked at him. *He has such kind eyes. A kind heart, too, if he's willing to forgo having clothes he really needs just to spare my feelings.* She felt compelled to return that consideration, and in realizing it, no longer felt the misgivings that flitted through her mind earlier when she'd originally made the offer. "Daddy would want you to have them. I'll try to think of it as him passing his mantle of protection on to you."

The smile on his face made her decision worthwhile.

"Gal, I think we're going to make this work."

Chapter 3

S moke, food, and coffee. Every morning, Ethan awakened to those same scents; but for a solid week they had come from other wagons, not his own. He'd farmed the children off for breakfast and satisfied himself with reheated mush. The aroma of coffee wafted over and teased him. Ethan burrowed in for a second more before he opened his eyes and realized Charity was up already. He hiked off to the shrubs, then ran his comb through his hair and beard. By the time he returned, Charity was ready to dish up his breakfast. Lydia hadn't been half as attentive. He'd needed to awaken her each morning.

"Do you take anything in your coffee?" Charity asked as she handed him a steaming mug.

"I like it black. Thanks. It smells wonderful."

She flipped three flapjacks onto a plate, added bacon, and passed it over. "When do the children wake up?"

"Anytime now." He wolfed down the food and grinned broadly. "Mmmm!" Folks had been kind enough to provide meals for them yesterday so they could finish combining their wagons. This was his first sample of her cooking, and it more than pleased him. "Someone did a fine job of teaching you to cook."

She flipped a flapjack and caught it midair in the heavy cast iron skillet. "Miss Amanda's had a French chef."

"A fancy finishing school?" When she nodded, his heart sank. She didn't just have some of the expensive doodads and trappings of money. She'd been reared in privilege. That would put even greater barriers between them. He muttered wryly, "Imagine that. Finishing schools hold a course on flapjacks."

Charity arched a brow. "Not precisely. I liked the chef. Much to Miss Amanda's dismay, I'd slip off to the kitchen in my spare time. I learned how to make crepes first, then several other dishes. I've had to adjust a few recipes for the trail."

Most of the day, her words played over and over in Ethan's mind. Charity was a lady, born and bred. She'd been trained in all of the finer things. Gals like her were social butterflies. Pretty, bright, and spoiled. Right now, she was playing at a new game. Would she soon tire of minding the kids and cooking? He didn't want to judge her wrongly, but he needed to evaluate the matter carefully. His kids' welfare was at stake.

Her name certainly fit. She'd virtually given away four oxen and a wagon yesterday, and her pa's clothing—everything from shirt to boots—fit Ethan perfectly. She had a bit over two hundred dollars; he, on the other hand, had forty measly dollars to his name. Ethan worried about the finances, but there was no way around it. A man did his best and trusted in the Lord. His family had always been blessed with their daily bread, and the move to more fertile ground would ensure that it would continue. It also meant that there would be some mighty lean years ahead until things were established.

At midday, he pried Cricket away from Charity's side and tucked her in atop the new feather bed Charity brought along. Every last thing Charity owned was grand. To her credit, she'd never once turned up her nose at his things.

Goodness only knew, Charity was blessed with more than anyone he'd ever known. Still, it tugged at his pride a bit when he took off Cricket's sunbonnet and spied a rose-embossed pink satin ribbon in her hair. She smelled dainty, and her skin didn't have any of the little red, rough patches it usually did since Charity used her own violet-scented glycerin soap to bathe his daughter last night, then shared her skin cream, much to Cricket's delight. He'd never had money to buy such fripperies.

It took no time at all before Tad and Charity were thick as thieves. They sat by the fire together and looked at her button string. She'd praised Tad for his new skill at multiplication and let him make marks in the dirt to practice ciphering. *Nine hundred eighty-two. Eighteen to go. Who is the lucky man who will give her the thousandth button and become her husband?*

Charity walked most of the day, but she'd driven the wagon for a short while this morning as he rode out with a few of the men to hunt. Ethan had taken along the new Colt rifle with her blessing and even lent her mare to Steven Adams since his gelding had gone lame. Charity congratulated them warmly on their successful hunt, but she'd turned three shades of green and disappeared when he unsheathed his knife and started to dress and butcher the pair of pronghorns he'd bagged.

A few days later, Tad caught a fine pair of trout. Ethan happened upon Charity as she valiantly tried to gut them. At first, he thought she was simply inept; but then he noted how pale she'd grown, so he simply took them from her and finished the chore. "I'm sorry," she said thickly.

"Gal, no one can do everything. If it makes you queasy to dress out meat, I'll handle it. All you had to do was say so."

She kept her hands clasped in front of her and stared out at the horizon. "I'm so gutless, we ought to serve me for supper."

"You're too hard on yourself." He handed back the fish. As she walked away, Ethan marveled at her. It was the only time he'd seen the fancy lady balk at anything.

The rhythm of trail life continued on—rising before dawn, hitching up the oxen, eating, and traveling until midday. Nooning break for man and beast, then dusty travel until they reached the spot their scout designated for evening. Wagons circled, supper eaten, and men holding watch over the camp and livestock by night. Charity stepped in beat to that rhythm, but she sang in a different range. They tried to be mindful and adjust so harmony reigned. Still, for the first time in his life, Ethan felt discontented. He simply didn't measure up, and the glaring disparity between her polished ways and fine goods and his common holdings made it clear he was second-rate.

Charity knelt in the creek bed as she rinsed out the laundry. The cold water felt delicious after the heat and dust of the last several days. Farther down the creek, men watered the livestock. The captain of the wagon train strictly enforced the rules governing water usage. Whenever they reached a stream, water for drinking was taken from upstream. Once the drinking water was dipped out, folks could fish from upstream, too. Bathing and laundry was at midstream, and livestock drank from downstream. So far, no one had gotten cholera, so the rules seemed beneficial.

"Kids sure do get filthy, don't they?" Banner asked in a cheerful voice as she scrubbed the knees on her sons' britches.

"Yes," Charity agreed. She twisted Cricket's little nightgown to wring out a bit more water. It wouldn't be dry by nightfall, but the little girl could sleep in one of Mama's camisoles. Charity carefully rinsed the rest of the lye soap from each garment. "I'm not much cleaner than the children, though. I'm looking forward to finally washing my hair."

Leticia Turvey squinted at the horizon. "I reckon we'd better hang these things out to dry. I'm aching to take a swim myself, and the boys are so eager to hit the water, the menfolk will be hollering at us to hurry up."

All of the women laughed at the truth in that statement. The routine was practical enough: As the women did laundry, men repaired wagons, saw to the livestock, started fires, and strung temporary clotheslines. Once the women hung up the clothes, they'd take the small children back to the water, scrub them, and send them back to their daddies. The women bathed wearing their chemises for the sake of modesty. If the water was shallow, they helped each other rinse the soap from their hair. The men and boys swam last while the women fixed supper.

Charity hastened back to the fire so Tad and Ethan could have their turn. To her surprise, Ethan squatted on his heels by the fire. He had catfish sizzling in the pan. He glanced over his shoulder. "Go on ahead and comb out your hair. See if you can't dry it a bit with your towel. It's going to be cold tonight, and you don't want to catch a chill."

"Why, thank you." She did as he bade. The whole while she coaxed the tangles from her hair, Charity marveled at how thoughtful and capable Ethan was. Considering all of her misgivings and fears, things had turned out quite well so far.

Ethan bathed quickly after supper, then warmed up with a cup of coffee before he took his turn at guard duty. As he came by on one of his passes, he spied Charity huddled by a lantern. He thought to come closer to see what was wrong but then saw her Bible. She faithfully read the Word each day—most often first thing upon rising. If circumstances prevented that, she made sure to find a time later. The Good Book said it was easier for a camel to fit through the eye of a needle than for a rich man to enter the kingdom of heaven. Ethan smiled to himself. The verse didn't say anything about a rich woman.

Later, Ethan came around again. To his surprise, Charity was still up. She sat huddled in her shawl, close to the fire. Instead of banking it, she'd added a few more buffalo chips. Just as he turned toward her, she got up, went to the wagon, and lifted her arms. Cricket climbed down, and Charity carried her off a short ways. Ethan met them. "Here. I'll take her." He took Cricket and headed back to the wagon.

Rick Washington ambled toward him. "Your shift is over. Sleep well."

Cricket snuggled closely and lazily combed her fingers through his beard. "Daddy—pretty."

"Yes, Princess, you are." He kissed her cheek.

"No, Daddy. See? Pretty." She patted the garment she wore. "Smells pretty, too."

Now that they were closer to the fire, he could see she was wearing a woman's beribboned chemise. It smelled of violets. Men tried their best to turn a blind eye to the small clothes women hung to dry on the laundry lines. As a decent, God-fearing man, he'd tried his hardest to ignore Charity's personal garments. He cleared his throat and made no comment.

Embarrassment colored Charity's voice as she murmured, "I washed Cricket's nightwear, so it was too wet for her tonight. I'll sew her a second gown soon."

"Fine. Night-night, Cricket." He gave his daughter a swift kiss and lifted her back into the wagon. Charity started to climb up the wheel spokes. "Hold it there." He cupped his hands around her tiny waist. "How many times am I going to have to tell you not to scramble up these things when I'm around to help you, Gal? You're likely to catch your hem and fall. I'd hate to see you get hurt on account of foolish independence. You have to take back a bit of help for all the help that you give others. You aren't alone out here." He yanked her backward and set her on the ground in front of him. "Do you hear me?"

Tears glittered in her eyes, making him catch his

breath. "Yes, I am. I am alone, and—" She clapped a hand over her mouth to capture a sob, spun away, and started to scramble into the wagon.

"Oh, Charity," he groaned. Ethan quickly grasped her waist and pulled her back to earth. He twisted her and clasped one arm around her back while using the other hand to cup her head to his chest.

Charity struggled for all of a few seconds, then gave way to her tears. She flooded his shirt with her grief and clung to him like a drowning victim would. He murmured soft, comforting words. The cradle of his arms supported her when she sagged, then he scooped her up and still held her tightly.

Ethan remembered the soul-deep anguish of fresh grief and couldn't fathom the fragile woman in his arms had to shoulder two recent losses. Her sobs tore at him, made him long to lend her his consolation. Holding her made him feel both strong and tender. He gently swayed side to side until she calmed and almost fell asleep. As her damp lashes fluttered shut, he urged, "Go to sleep, Honeygal. Leave your sorrows behind. You'll never be alone again. I promise."

She whispered tearfully, "I'm s—sorry."

"You don't have a thing in the world to apologize for. Now go on to bed." He lifted her into the wagon and listened as she eased down beside Cricket. Satisfied she'd settled in, he went over to the fire and poured himself some coffee. A hand on his shoulder made him turn around. "Yeah, Jason?"

The captain of the wagon train tilted his head toward the Cole schooner. "She's been spoiling for that cry for a good long while. My missus saw her brooding by the fire and said she was due to fall apart. You did right by her."

"Can't do much of anything for her but pray. That poor gal has been through far too much, and you'd never guess it by watching her. She's. . ." He shrugged in want of words.

"She's quite a little woman," Jason said softly. He stayed silent for a time. Finally he pushed, "I'm going to ask, because I am responsible for her, too: Are you starting to have feelings for her?"

"What man in his right mind wouldn't? She's gentle as a spring rain and sweet as honey. My kids have taken to her instantly, and she changed us from a haphazard willy-nilly group back into a family."

"I'm asking about feelings that run deeper than gratitude."

"The way things are is more than enough for the present." Ethan tossed back the last of his coffee. "Charity is a fancy lady; I'm a rough man. Whatever I might feel isn't the issue. She deserves far better."

"Voices do carry. I heard you tell her she's not alone anymore."

Ethan winced. He'd revealed far too much when he'd uttered that pledge. "I was a fool to say so. I'll hope by the morning she takes that as a pledge of friendship. Peasants don't marry princesses."

Chapter 4

Everyone was road-weary by the time they pulled into Fort Laramie. To their dismay, the scout announced they'd only stay overnight. "There's another train on our heels. If they get ahead of us, we'll have fouled water and lousy hunting. The council has voted to take Sublette's Cutoff to spare us more than a week of travel. That means we'll bypass Fort Bridger. This is your last stop to get supplies until we're through most of the mountains, so load up and be ready to go by first light."

Charity climbed into the wagon and reappeared a few minutes later. Ethan noted she'd changed her dress, combed her hair, and put on gloves. A reticule dangled from her wrist. "I'm ready."

"Not yet, you aren't," he said firmly. He needed to set matters straight first. "When we joined wagons, you had a bounty of supplies. Lydia took the lion's portion of my foodstuffs, but you brought a complete pantry, furnished plenty of extras. Expensive extras," he stressed. "Like those Edwards's preserved potatoes and all of the dried fruits and vegetables. There's not another wagon on our whole train that enjoys a fraction of our treats. I'll not have you spend one red cent on a thing."

Charity looked at him and raised her brows. "I seriously doubt you have much idea as to what we do or do not need, Ethan. Furthermore, I saw how you salvaged the main portion of the headboard to my bedstead and situated it beneath the mattress. If I had to have one made to match the highboy, it would cost a minor fortune. Whatever I spend is a pittance in comparison."

"Reasoning with you is hopeless," he snapped. Instead of escorting her to the post store, he turned and hastened ahead. Once he beat her there and placed his order, she'd be sensible enough to defer.

Ethan arrived before the crowd and grimly noted they'd posted a sign that placed limits on nearly everything. He'd assessed their supplies and decided on some basic items. As soon as he started ordering, Charity arrived. She walked directly up to him. "Mr. Cole, your partner asked that you buy the limits of everything and sent this." She held out four twenty-dollar gold double eagles. When he refused to accept them, she placed them on the counter and sashayed off. She'd given him almost half of her money! Ethan planned to serve her a healthy slice of his mind once they were in private.

An assistant came in and asked, "Who's next?"

Charity smiled and handed over a lengthy list. "What are you doing?" Ethan demanded hotly as soon as the storekeeper went into the back room.

She pulled her fan from her reticule and whispered from behind it, "Ethan, the limits are too low. The others won't be able to stock up enough. The limit is per family, and so our wagon qualifies for twice as much. We'll buy everything we're allowed, then our friends can get the excess from us tonight at the campfire."

"I'm eavesdropping, and I'll admit to it. I want to buy some of your extra flour and sugar," Stu Green murmured, brushing past. He went over and whispered to Banner. Banner came over and pled for first call on excess cornmeal, and Mary Pitts put in for the salt.

"You sure can skin a cat nine ways, Charity." Ethan lifted his hands in defeat. "I'll admit when I'm beat."

"Goodness, I forgot baking powder!" Charity cried. She twirled around and headed back to the counter. By the time she was done, she added on another two-pound tin of Ely's fine gun powder, four spools of thread, one pound of gum drops, a paper of sewing pins and needles, and several buttons.

Gracie teased her, "You can't buy buttons for your own string, Charity. That's breaking the rule!"

Charity laughed. "Oh, I know. I got some for a frock for Cricket, and these others will be special treats for her. There are two end-of-day glass buttons on this card. Since no two buttons can be alike on her string, would you like the other for your Priscilla's string?"

"I'll buy it from you."

"No, you won't!" Charity sidled closer and murmured, "Gracie, I feel so beholden to you. How many times have you gently shared your wisdom and advice so I'd be able to care better for Tad and Cricket? A button is nothing—it's a tiny thank-you, and I'd be offended if you didn't accept it."

After Gracie consented to accepting the button, Charity went back to the counter to get a final tally. "Lady, yer order comes to a hundert an' three dollars an' ten cents," the exasperated storekeeper warned. The other pioneers in the store didn't even bother to muffle their gasps.

"Well, then, here we go." She opened her reticule and produced five more double eagles and a five-dollar piece.

The man behind the counter gaped at her.

"Before you make change, how much is that container of marbles?"

"A buck even."

"I'll take it and ninety cents' worth of lemon drops, then."

"Whatever you want, Lady." He shook his head in disbelief.

"Ninety cents of just lemon drops!" one of the women in the background gasped.

"With the prices they've got posted, 'tain't gonna be no bushel of 'em," Jed Turvey grumbled. "Flour's a buck a pint!"

The storekeeper snapped, "It'll be a good gallon, an' then some. She'll be takin' half of my stock of 'em with her, and you won't find sweets again till you reach the Willamette Valley. Iff'n you don't like my prices, you can go without the goods!"

"I do apologize for setting this off." Charity blushed becomingly. "I just felt I'd taken a fair bit of your time and hoped it would simplify things if you didn't have to make change."

"Aw, forget it, Lady. Do ya mind just takin' a gallon jar and callin' it even 'stead of havin' me measure it up?"

"But of course. Would you care if I opened it and offered everyone a few in the interest of peace?"

"They're yers. Do whatever ya want with 'em. Maybe

ya ought to. I'd druther not sell any more to yer train so I have some for the next one. Never thought I'd have to set limits on lemon drops!"

A while later, Charity fanned herself and murmured, "I'm sorry if I embarrassed you, Ethan. I didn't mean to."

"I'll live through the embarrassment, but I'm worried. You have no idea who was in that store. It's dangerous for anyone to advertise they're holding money like that. Stu and Rick are both smart enough to pass the word that you just went a bit trail crazy and spent the last of your money. Hopefully, it'll keep you from being robbed when folks on our train pay you back."

Charity sucked in a deep, shocked breath. "I'm sorry! It never occurred to me. . ."

"Yeah, well, remember that in the future. The other thing is, you can't go tossing your gold away with both hands, Charity. If you do, you won't manage at all once we reach the trail's end. To my reckoning, even if everyone pays you back for what you bought, you'll only have eighty bucks to your name. Gal, that's about four months' wages for a man—and you won't be able to last long on that!"

Charity cast a glance all about her, then leaned close. "Ethan, please don't worry about that anymore. I've not quite spent all of Daddy's carrying money. That was only a small fraction of what he had. The highboy has a false bottom. I have funds. . ." She looked down, then back at him, "*considerable* funds left in it."

Ethan stared at her in shock. He'd almost convinced himself that they might consider matrimony. Even with her fancy upbringing and fine goods, she never acted superior or haughty. Now he knew better. There was more than just a class barrier between them. No self-respecting man married a woman whose wealth eclipsed his to the point of humiliation.

Oblivious to the fact that she'd poleaxed him, Charity said, "Daddy told me to keep it a secret. I owe you peace of mind not to fret about me. I'm sorry I let you worry. I understand now that I acted far less circumspectly than I should have back at the store, but I was appalled at how stingy he was with his limits." She paused a moment longer, then added, "I promise to exercise reserve so there won't be any more awkward moments."

Until now, Ethan hadn't realized he'd let his heart get ahead of his mind. He forced himself to sound conversational when he really wanted to walk off and kick a stump. "I can't believe you bought all of that stuff," he shuffled uncomfortably, "and I can't figure out for the life of me where you put it all."

Charity smiled. "I had it all planned out. Aren't you glad we can give the others our surplus?"

He shook his head. "I'm not sure it's wise for you to give stuff away. Even if you trust them and figure they won't rob you, you need to concern yourself with the fact that folks will feel beholden."

"Nonsense! I owe so many of those people more than I can ever repay." In an instant, her cheerful countenance melted. Tears welled up, and she choked out, "Banner helped me prepare Mama for her burial. Rick took my guard duty. Jed minded my oxen. You helped bury Daddy and took me on. . . ."

"Hush," he crooned softly as he squeezed her hand. "We all help one another, Charity. It's the Christian thing to do."

She turned soulful eyes to him. "Then please don't be

upset with me when I use the money the Lord blessed me with to help others. It's all I have to give. The Bible says, 'To him whom much is given, much is required.'"

A short while later, as Ethan sat whittling a button for Cricket, Tad asked, "Pa, was Miss Davis crying?"

"Yes, Son. She lost both of her folks since we've been on the trail. That is a powerful lot of sorrow to bear."

"Pa, that makes me wonder," Tad asked as he scratched his knee, "why doesn't she cry all the livelong day like Aunt Lydia did?"

"Because people are different. Miss Davis is a very strong young woman, and she seems to be able to bear a big burden without complaining. She mostly does it by leaning on the Lord. Those are qualities to admire, Tad."

"There are lots of good things about her."

"I kind of feel that way myself." Ethan admitted that much, but he said nothing more. As the days passed, his feelings for Charity deepened. All along, he'd known it was unfair for him to reveal the attraction. Tenderhearted and sensitive as she was, she'd probably feel indebted and accept his suit, but he didn't want a wife who married him out of gratitude or pity. Now, staggered by the fact that she could spend such a sum and still possess "considerable funds," Ethan pushed aside any hope of marriage. He knew they'd have to part at the trail's end in the Willamette Valley.

They continued along the north fork of the Platte River. The water supply grew less and less tasty as they traveled on, but the oxen were happy with it. Previous parties had been displeased with the river water taste and tried to dig water holes. The guide warned them not to—much of the water was too salty or plain bad. They made do the best they could.

Their scout seemed satisfied with the distance they'd managed each day. On average, they covered a bit over fifteen miles; but he'd warned once they hit the Continental Divide and traveled through the mountainous terrain, they'd slow down considerably. Fear of not making it through the mountains before winter storms hit motivated them to push onward.

Delays happened—a broken wheel needing to be repaired or replaced, an axle that cracked after the wagon ran over a big stone. Several wagons benefited from Ethan's skills. Never once did he ask to be paid for his expertise. Most of the travelers were lean on cash, so when Ethan fixed a yoke or repaired a wagon, the recipient usually offered to pull his guard duty in return.

Working together and learning to give and take kept the train moving along. On occasion, they encountered an abandoned wagon. If there was anything to be salvaged, the men did so quickly and efficiently. The Laswells had just used their only spare wheel when an abandoned rig was found with two good ones still available.

Everyone gave praise to the Lord for His providence, but their guide heaved a sigh. "Folks, I'm just as grateful to the Almighty, but I may as well use this time when you're all together to give you warning. The going will be getting much rougher. In another month, things will be downright miserable a fair part of the time. Tempers will get mighty short; and if things get bad, I'll suggest that the troublemakers take back a portion of their fee and join up with another train or go on to the California territory instead of heading to the Willamette Valley with us. I don't cotton to backbiting or gossip, but if there's a problem, you aren't to keep it quiet. Come to me or Jason at once. I've seen men get riled up enough to come to blows on several trips, and on two crossings there were even shootings. I'll not abide anything of the sort. Far more men die from fighting with their trail mates than fighting with Indians. First wind I get of discord, I want a full account."

Solemn faces stared back, and heads nodded in slow assent. This was the ugly side of humanity. The crucible of hardship and grief had drawn them together. It sobered them to hear their unity was tenuous.

The evening they reached the Sweetwater River crossing, Jason walked through the train and collected a string of women. He specifically chose them and left others out. Charity felt a twinge of worry when he nodded his head at her and said, "You, too, Miss Davis."

Jason pulled the knot of women off to the side and set his weathered hands on his hips. He gave them a stern look. "I'm not putting up with no nonsense."

Nonsense? What have I done? Charity shot a worried glance at her friends, then focused back on their leader.

"Trail's getting harder. Hotter, too. Them hoops have gotta go. Shuck 'em and leave 'em here." He swung his arm in an arc. "The womenfolk who went ahead of you already did, so I don't want no fuss." Without another word, he paced away.

Abby Legacy started to twitter, and her cousin, Hyacinth, gasped, "Dear mercy! They've hung their hoops from the trees!"

Charity had been busy with Cricket, so she hadn't noticed the strange sight. Months ago, when they set out, she would have blushed at anything half as indelicate. Now, she smiled. "I'll bet the birds here make odd nests." Everyone laughed.

Myrtle looked down at her gown. "I'd best do some hemming. I can't stand to leave a stitch of clothing behind. Guess I'll cut the hoops from my crinoline and shorten all of my things."

"Add some buckshot to your hem," someone said. "It'll keep your skirts weighted down so the wind won't cause you grief."

Daddy had read women did that, and he'd instructed the seamstress to stitch gold coins into the hems of their skirts and gowns. It worked well. Charity determined she'd simply move them. As she walked back to the wagon, she decided to use the fabric she cut off to make Cricket a gown. She turned to Myrtle. "You're right. Wasting fabric would be foolish. Had Jason waited until morning to make his announcement, we wouldn't have time to salvage the fabric. Scraping the ground all day would ruin it."

"I'll save my extra for quilt blocks," Hyacinth decided. "Maybe we could all trade a square and make memory quilts."

"You're forever trading things," Abby said. "I'd venture to say your button string doesn't have a single button on it that hasn't been swapped!"

Hyacinth laughed as she reached up and touched the piece. "They're called memory strings, too. I remember everyone I ever traded with to have these. Each one means something to me!"

Myrtle said, "Back home, we always called them charmstrings because most of the gals had charmstring glass buttons on them. Charity has more kinds of buttons than I ever imagined existed on hers—but it's the charmingest thing I ever did see!"

"Thank you," Charity said. Somehow, the single women and girls on their train had come to the habit of wearing their button strings on Sundays. Life and work was too hard to subject their treasured pieces to daily wear, but it was sweet to bring them out once a week. Leaving friends and family behind was hard; being able to finger a button and remember those loved ones still helped them feel in touch.

Charity smiled. "Ethan is carving beautiful little buttons for Cricket's string. He's so clever with his hands. He uses all kinds of wood. He brought a few corozo nuts to carve so she'll have vegetable ivory, and he has horn he saved to do the same. Her string will surely become a family heirloom. He helped Tad make a leather bag for his marbles last night, too."

Myrtle held her back as the others went ahead. "Charity, are you losing your heart to him?"

"Ethan? Myrtle, I deeply admire him. He's a godly man. He cherishes his children and has been kindness itself to me; but we've both done our utmost to remain cordial and circumspect, so I'd be mortified if anyone thought there was anything improper between us."

"Oh, now, I didn't mean to imply you were chasing after him," Myrtle said as they started to walk again. "He's a fine young man. I've wondered if perhaps he's taken a shine to you."

Ethan remained kneeling by the Jasons' wagon. He'd

needed to replace a cracked doubletree. He hadn't meant to eavesdrop, but Charity's words warmed his heart. It was good to know she held him in high regard. Their relationship didn't fit into any of the usual molds, and he tried to make things easier for her when he could. Keeping things balanced strained his mind at times. Because he could never wed her, he didn't want to do anything to give the appearance that they might be courting, but she deserved special treatment for the countless ways she eased life for him and his kids.

He agreed with Myrtle. Even to a common man's un-discriminating eye, Charity's string held rare and wondrous buttons. Sometimes, she'd tell Cricket a nap-time story about how she'd been given a particular button. In those moments, Ethan learned little things about Charity she'd otherwise never have revealed.

The touch button—her first—was a big, gold military button from her great-great-grandfather's Revolutionary War uniform. Her birthday was in July, which accounted for the buttons that held genuine rubies. A small cluster of buttons commemorated her first formal tea when she turned ten: a pearl, a cameo, two china portraits from Austria, a thumbnail-sized gold teapot from Silesia, and a coral flower. She cherished a simple crocheted button from a church widow every bit as much as she enjoyed the jet button her grandmother had worn when she met Queen Victoria.

He knew she kept track of each button in a tiny, red leather book that had dainty, gold vines embossed down the cover. Her joy wasn't merely in having a collection of beautiful baubles; she used it as a means to remembering important events and cherished people in her past. Memory by memory, charm by charm, she'd recorded each addition to her button string.

Tad took a liking to the buttons because Charity made doing his sums and multiplication tables fun by concocting problems for him using her string. The kaleidoscopes, swirlbacks, paperweights, and charmglass buttons kept his attention long enough to cipher. When he was especially clever, Charity sometimes gave him another marble from the supply she bought back at Fort Laramie.

"Charity, I don't hold with paying my son to do essentials," Ethan said quietly after the kids were in bed one evening. He shook his head. "Kids must learn to do things just because they need to be done."

Charity's eyes darkened. "I'm sorry, Ethan. I mean no harm."

"You don't need to apologize, Gal. I just figured we'd best talk this over since Tad's marble bag seems to have developed a notable bulge."

"The only reason I have so many kaleidoscopes on my button string is because my teacher loved them and gave them to us as awards." She dipped her head. "I treasured them, and I simply wanted Tad to have good memories about learning."

He winced. "I didn't mean to hurt your feelings."

"He's your son, Ethan. As a father, it's your duty to step in when I've done something wrong."

He stayed silent for a moment. "You didn't do anything wrong, Charity. As a matter of fact, I recollect earning a few prizes for spelling bees and the like. I reckon it won't hurt to have the boy develop a fondness for studying.

I want him to learn and to help others because it is good and right—not so he can be rewarded."

"Your goal is noble, Ethan. I know God loves cheerful givers—and the giving isn't supposed to just be money in an offering plate. Tad sees how often you lend a hand to others. I hold no doubt he'll grow up to emulate the servant's heart you demonstrate. If you'll excuse me, I need to fetch my shawl."

She slipped away, and Ethan shook his head in disbelief. She thought *he* had a servant's heart? Those first days, he'd worried she was too dainty, frail—even prissy—to tend to matters. She'd proven him wrong. Little Charity Davis pitched right in. Just yesterday, he'd told Banner, "The word 'idle' isn't in Charity's vocabulary."

As a matter of fact, Charity's attitude made their wagon a pleasant place. She was a cheerful riser and always saw to it that everyone had a good, hot breakfast to start off the day. She corrected the children with a fair balance of firmness and humor. No task was too dirty, too small, or too tough. She was never too tired to help with one more thing or to see if someone else could use a bit of assistance. Who would ever guess this fine lady would walk long, dry, dusty miles each day and collect buffalo chips to fuel her cook fire?

With her acceptance of the hardships, those around her realized they had no more call to complain than did she. . .yet she sat there, complimenting him simply for doing a man's work to provide for his own and assure the wagon train kept moving.

Lord, what am I to do with this longing in my heart? Your Word teaches we set our affections. I'm doing my dead level best not to set my heart on that gal, but I'm failing at it. We're both believers, but other than that, we'd be unequally yoked. I'd never be the fancy kind of man she deserves, and I'd never be able to provide the kind of life she's accustomed to. Give me strength, I pray. . . .

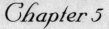

Chapter 5

The sun beat down unmercifully, and Charity wished for nothing more than a sip of cool lemonade and a chance to soak her feet. She'd already walked nine miles today, and from the looks of it, they'd cover another five or six before Jason called a halt. Cricket didn't want to ride in the bumpy wagon, but her legs were too tired for her to walk any longer. She lifted her arms high and pled, "Up."

"All right, Sweet Pea." All of the muscles in Charity's shoulders and back protested this new load, and she finally admitted to herself she couldn't manage this much longer. *Just a few more days,* she told herself, *but how can I last in this terrible heat without water?*

Patterson pushed them hard for the next three days. Now, as they used Sublette's Cutoff, they had no source of water whatsoever. Banner convinced Charity to stop wearing all three petticoats.

She wore two.

Instead of having one wet cloth to comfort them through the day, Charity started making two. She even caved in and started leaving the uppermost button of her dresses and shirtwaists unfastened. Patterson was firm about everyone keeping on a hat or sunbonnet. The storekeeper at Fort Kearny had flavoring bottles, and she'd bought a few. She took to placing a dab of spearmint or vanilla on the stones they sucked on to keep their mouths moist.

Even with it as hot as it was, Tad seemed almost immune to the heat. Cricket seemed more affected, and Charity finally took to dressing her in just her frock and drawers, leaving off the slip entirely. When Myrtle confessed she was doing the same with little Emily, Charity let out a small sigh of relief. Minding children demanded making hundreds of tiny decisions on a daily basis.

At noon, Cricket scooted into the wagon for a nap. Ethan silently saddled Charity's mare. "Charity, the oxen are straining in the heat. We'll reach water in two days, but you'll never survive the heat if you don't ride."

"But Queenie must be feeling the heat," she protested.

"Your mare's a fine animal," he said quietly. "But if it comes down to you or her, there's no choice to be made."

She blushed vividly. "Still, I cannot ride."

"Why not?"

Charity stared at the horse. "We don't have a lady's saddle."

He cupped his hands around her waist and squeezed in gentle reassurance. "Your gown's full, Charity. You can ride quite modestly. It's actually far more stable, and I'd not have you ride sidesaddle. Simply put, your safety is too important. Other women are riding western style, so you needn't fret."

Western style. He'd chosen his words carefully in order to avoid crassly mentioning she'd be astride. Before she could agree or disagree, he murmured, "Here you go, Gal," and lifted her into Queenie's saddle. Silently, he tugged her hem down to cover her, handed her the reins, and walked off.

She carried Cricket in front of herself for the next day and a half. Small as she was, the little girl still radiated heat like an oven. The hours in the saddle caused pains to shoot through Charity's lower limbs and back, but she knew it was the only way she'd manage to assure little Cricket and she would both survive until they reached water.

"Happy birthday, Charity!" Banner called over in the morning.

"Thank you! How did you know it was my birthday?"

Banner grinned. "Your ma mentioned you'd be having your birthday on the trail. I remembered because it's my anniversary."

"Felicitations, Banner! God surely blessed you with a fine man." Charity lifted the lid on the Dutch oven to check on her biscuits. "I brought along a bit of cocoa. I could bake a cake for us to share at supper."

"I thought you said you were just about out of eggs."

Charity shrugged. "I am, but my recipe only uses one." Folks stored eggs in the flour barrels to keep them from breaking. Several families had a few chickens in cages strapped to the sides of their wagons, but jostled around as they were, the hens didn't lay well.

It took a bit of ingenuity, but Charity's cake turned out fairly well. One corner got a bit crisp, but they'd all learned to eat singed food while on the trail. Food couldn't be wasted. They gathered about the campfire that night, and

Banner slipped something to Charity in a knotted hanky.

Charity gave her a questioning look.

"Go ahead. Open it."

Charity carefully unknotted the cloth and found three buttons inside. "The pewter one, that's from me. The other two, I swiped them from your mama's chest. She had them tied together with that there pretty little bow, so I reckoned she planned on giving them to you today."

Charity fingered them all. Her eyes filled with tears until she couldn't even see the buttons clearly anymore. "Thank you, Banner. You don't know how precious these are to me."

"Let's string them on now. You don't know how much I've worried about losing them!"

Within minutes, Hyacinth, Myrtle, Abby, Gracie, and Leticia all gathered about. Soon, more of the ladies from the train joined the circle around Charity. Each gave Charity a button as a birthday gift. While Charity visited, Banner carefully added each of the birthday buttons to the collection. The strand of thick thread was almost filled.

"Not many more, and you'll have that string done," Harriet decided. "We'll all keep an eye out for that thousandth button. When you get it from your beau, we'll all know your heart's taken."

After all of the women left, Charity banked the fire and turned toward the wagon. Ethan blocked her way. He pressed something into her hand. "I didn't want you to go to sleep without this. Happy birthday."

Charity turned so the moon would cast a beam on the button. Though just an inch across, the wood had been whittled into a bow with flowing ties. A tiny heart nestled in the center point. "Oh, Ethan, it's exquisite! Did you do this yourself?"

"It's nothing," he said modestly.

"I disagree! You astound me. Why, it even matches the ribbon carved on my highboy and headboard! Thank you. Thank you so very much. You're such a talented man. I'll treasure this."

"You can slip it on your string tomorrow. It's been a long day. You'd best turn in." He lifted her into the wagon and softly said, "Good night and pleasant dreams."

The next morning, Charity added Ethan's bow button to her string. Tad started playing with the opposite end and singsong counted along the strand. At one point, he frowned. "Miss Davis, I never noticed this wasn't just one button. Look."

She leaned over. "Yes. Those were from the Shay twins. See? One bell is silver; the other is gold." Charity secured Ethan's lovely bow to her string and tied the end.

"Can I ride in the wagon and look at your buttons this morning?"

"It'll be bumpy."

Tad hitched a shoulder. "I don't care."

A long while later, Tad jumped out of the wagon and ran to her. He grabbed her hand and paid no attention to the fact that several women and children were within earshot. "Miss Davis!"

"What is it?"

"Your button string. I counted it three times to be sure. You finished it. You don't need any more. . .and the button Pa gave you is the thousandth!"

Chapter 6

"Mr. Cole, I need a moment of your time." Charity clutched the button in her hand. She cast a quick look at the others. They milled about within hearing distance instead of tending to their nooning chores, so she tacked on shakily, "In private."

Never, in all of her years, had she felt so self-conscious or nervous. Not once in all of her lessons regarding etiquette and comportment had she been taught how to handle such an embarrassing catastrophe. Everything inside her quivered. She knew from the virulent heat of her cheeks that she had to be utterly, completely, unmistakable scarlet.

How could I have let this happen?

Ethan's forehead furrowed, and he studied her for a moment. "If you can wait just a jiffy, I'll see to the kids."

"I–I've already asked Banner to keep them for nooning."

His brow rose in surprise. "Very well, *Miss Davis*. What can I do for you?"

She hastily looked around and knew every eye was on her. On *them*. She pulled in a choppy breath and couldn't seem to find her voice. *Why can't I just keep it? Why can't he love me? I'd be a good wife to him. I already love his children, too. Too? Oh, mercy in heaven—I love him! What should I do?*

"Perhaps you'd like to sit down," Ethan said. His hand cupped her elbow.

He's such a gentleman. So polite, so concerned. This is dreadful. He'll probably do the honorable thing and ask me to marry him just to spare me the embarrassment.

"It's not like you to be this rattled. Are you feeling poorly? You're flushed." He seated her on a rock and pressed the back of his fingers to her cheek. "Perhaps I should get Banner or Myrtle for you."

"No!" The concern in his eyes shifted to surprise when she blurted out that one word. She heaved a very unlady-like sigh and cast away every hope or dream she might have entertained about having a happy future. She wanted this man. No other. No other man could ever make her as happy. *Then why am I going to let go of this opportunity? Because it's honorable. I never knew being honorable could hurt so badly. Dear Jesus, give me strength.*

Charity turned her hand over and very slowly uncurled her fingers. The lovely button lay cradled in her hand. She wet her lips and whispered, "I've inadvertently placed you in an untenable position. I'm so sorry, Mr. Cole."

"I'm afraid I don't understand. I thought you liked it." What could very well pass for hurt flickered in his eyes.

"Oh, I do!" Charity paused, then said somberly, "But I cannot accept it. Banner—she was helping me pack. I didn't realize. . . That is, I don't mean to hold her to blame, because I alone am responsible. . . ."

"Charity, what are you trying to tell me?"

"I lost count. She saved a few buttons off of Mama's clothes the night we were packing, and when I slipped them on the string, I lost count." Every word ached with the misery she felt as she whispered, "I take full responsibility, Mr. Cole. I wanted to give this back to you privately. Please understand, it was a lovely gift. I've never seen anything so wonderful, and no one ever troubled himself to make something by his own hands just for me; but I cannot keep it under these circumstances, and I hope you forgive me."

"What are you saying, Charity?"

She carefully transferred the button from her hand to his. His hand was large, rough, and callused. In his palm, the button looked minuscule. How had he managed to create anything so dainty? Charity stayed silent for a moment, then realized he still didn't comprehend what she was doing. "Mr. Cole, I was mistaken about how many buttons decorated my string. This," she swallowed and whispered thickly, "would be the thousandth."

"The thousandth." He repeated the word in a husky tone.

She wanted to run away. She wanted to hide from all of the prying eyes turned their way. She wanted to burst into tears. Most of all, she wanted him to slip that marvelous button back into her hand and ask her to be his beloved wife.

Instead, she tried to give him a smile. From the reflection in his eyes, Charity knew she'd failed miserably. "Certainly, I have no expectations. Had I been more careful, you'd not be in this awkward position. If you'd like, I'll be happy to sew it on the yoke of Cricket's new frock."

"I see." He stared down at the dinky ribbon. He'd spent

the last week making it. Twice, he'd broken it and had to start afresh. Charity deserved something wonderful, but this was all he had to give. The whole time he'd carved it, he'd thought of the elegant, fancy, and expensive gifts she'd undoubtedly received all of her life. This cost nothing but spare time, yet she acted like she appreciated it. That was another mark of her fine manners. She could make a pauper feel like a prince. Nonetheless, he was a pauper. He had no right to hope this princess would ever set her heart on him.

She blinked back the tears in her eyes. "I'm afraid Tad counted them and wasn't discreet in breaking the news to me. Though I know you might have wished otherwise, others already know. Truly, Mr. Cole, I never meant for this to happen. Please forgive me for my carelessness. I'll take responsibility. I'll be sure folks understand."

The temptation to take advantage of the situation nearly overpowered him. It would be so easy to simply insist she wed him. She'd accepted the button and added it to her string. He'd have her for his wife, and he'd cherish her every last day of their marriage; but would she resent him for taking advantage of this mistake, and could he maintain his self-respect for trapping her when she'd agreed to the union only to avoid social embarrassment?

Ethan cleared his throat. The words stuck. He wanted to drop onto his knee right there and pledge his heart, but the last thing he needed to do was humiliate them both by making a public spectacle of this mess so she'd feel even more obligated. It took every shred of self-discipline for him to tamp down his own wants and needs and put hers first. Finally, he rubbed his thumb across the loop of the bow. "What do you want to do about this, Charity?"

She pressed her fingers to her mouth to hold back a sob. Her shoulders shrugged in silent turmoil as a few tears slipped down her cheeks.

He tilted her face up to his. "Some things in life you don't rush. The decision to marry is definitely one of them. For the weeks we've been traveling together, we've prayed with the children. That was wise. I think it would be wise if we prayed separately and together about this. If we seek God's will, He'll honor our hearts and show us the way."

Charity nodded.

"Tell you what: Why don't you sew this button to the bonnet of our wagon? When we see it, it'll serve as a reminder to us to truly consider our paths and seek the Lord's intent."

"That would be best," she agreed in a strained voice.

"At any point in time—even now, if you know your heart and mine won't be a comfortable match, I want you to take it down and. . ." He searched his mind for what she could do with it. He'd never again want to set eyes on the piece. "Set it beneath a wheel so it is crushed and left behind in the dust so there will be no doubt and no keepsake to act as a thorn to our memories."

She simply looked at him. He knew she'd heard him, but she gave no response. "Charity, if you are mortified by even the possibility of being my wife, you can say so now. I'll still carry you and your things to Oregon. You know that, don't you?"

"We'll continue on and pray. I'll stitch it securely so it won't accidentally get jostled loose."

"Fine." He wanted to let out a shout. At least she hadn't rejected him outright. "I'm not letting you shoulder the explanation for this alone. Best we make a general announcement than let tongues wag."

He reached out his other hand. She took it, and he helped her rise. Their hands clasped for the first time as he bowed his head. "Father, Your Word instructs us to come to You for wisdom. Charity and I believe in You and want to live to please You. The union of two hearts is not a light matter. Please grant us strength to take time in considering this, and make Your plan for our lives clear. I want to thank You for the way You've allowed us to work together well thus far and ask that You would continue to bless us as we continue on, on the trail and in our lives. In Jesus' Name, Amen."

"Amen," she whispered.

Ethan didn't let go of her hand. He walked her to a small knot of folks who suddenly tried to appear occupied in anything other than observing them. Cricket skipped up. She wound her arms around his legs and looked up at him. "Pa, are you and Miz Davis gonna get married?"

"Sweet Pea, we haven't decided yet. It's in God's hands."

Chapter 7

A woman could hope. Charity threaded her strongest thread through the needle. With great care, she stitched the button to the wagon bonnet. Seven. Eight. Nine stitches to secure the shank to the fabric. No, ten. She couldn't resist putting that one last extra stitch in for good measure. She'd carefully chosen the place to sew the button so she'd see it first thing upon waking and last thing at night.

"Delight thyself in the Lord, and He will grant thee the desires of thy heart." She whispered that verse as she knotted the thread and cut it. *Heavenly Father, You know the desire of my heart. If it is not in accordance with Your wishes, please let me know right away.*

She gently, almost reverently, touched the piece, then turned to put away her sewing supplies. As much to avoid others as to get supper, Ethan suggested she drive the wagon in the afternoon while he went hunting. The time they had allowed others to gossip or speculate, so she and Ethan both hoped folks would be circumspect in the days and weeks ahead. Ethan had come back with a bighorn sheep, so as she sewed, he went to the edge of the campsite and dressed the meat.

Fresh meat was meant to be shared. When someone made a good-sized kill, he divided it up as he saw fit. Banner hadn't exaggerated that first night when she praised Ethan's prowess with a rifle. Most of the folks in the train had benefited from his hunting skills.

They'd seen another wagon train where folks strung strings across the wagon bows and hung thin strips of buffalo meat on them. Their guide, Mr. Patterson, spat in disgust over that practice. "Smells of blood. It invites wolves to close in. Indians, too. They depend on the buffalo for everything; white man wastes a good part of the beast. I know most of the other trains slaughter 'em, but I don't want anyone bothering buffalo unless there's no other meat to be shot."

By now, they were in the mountains. Obtaining water wasn't a problem any longer, but the terrain became much more difficult to cover, and the nights grew cold. Buffalo and their chips were mere memories. Other kinds of game abounded, but men still didn't hunt to their hearts' content because of the sheer work it took to get the wagons up and down the steep mountain grades.

"Charity?" Ethan's voice came through the wagon cover clearly. She closed her eyes for a moment and savored the sound of his voice. Like his velvety brown eyes, his voice held a depth that soothed and comforted.

"Yes?"

"I thought perhaps you'd like to decide how to divvy up the meat. I've already spitted half of this, so we'll eat freshly roasted meat tonight. If you don't mind my asking, I have a hankering for meat pie. I'll set off some of the smaller slivers and hunks of meat in the stew pot. Pies would make nooning easier tomorrow since it looks like it's going to be a grueling day."

"That does sound good." Thankful he'd given her a mundane conversation topic to ease their time together, she went to the end of the wagon and allowed him to lift her out. Was it her imagination, or did his hands give her a tiny squeeze a split second before he let go?

"Clara needs to build up her blood after the birthing. Do you mind if we give them the liver?"

He smiled. "No. I'll take it over."

"Oh, I'll fix it for her! She shouldn't be getting up yet."

"I'd like to give the Legacy wagons a hind quarter to share if that's all right with you. Abigail and her mama are both feeling poorly. I'm sure Hyacinth can cook for all of their family, and they can use the excess for tomorrow's meals, too."

Charity nodded. She nervously pleated her skirt and asked, "Would you mind if we asked the Laswells to join us for a roast? I want to be sure Banner knows I hold no hard feelings and don't feel she's to blame. Besides, the meat will spoil before we use it all ourselves, and they've got eight mouths to feed."

"You may as well ask Myrtle and her brood, too. She's looking fretful as a ready-to-foal mare. Best we calm everyone else down right away. We'll have enough meat for that, and all of you women can make meat pies with the leftovers afterward."

Lard buckets hung from the wagons. While the women cooked, Tad and Banner's two sons went from wagon to wagon and painted the axles to keep the wheels spinning easily and reduce the chance of the axles splitting. The boys saw to the milking and several other chores each day. After eating, they went off to the side and shot marbles. Charity mopped Cricket's grimy hands and face and tucked her into bed. After a prayer and a kiss, Charity touched the button and whispered a quick prayer before going back to her tasks.

A man could hope. Ethan rose earlier than usual the next morning. He'd stayed up late, praying. Just as he finished his devotional time, he'd seen Mrs. Jason scurrying toward the Legacy wagon. She carried her small box filled with glass bottles of medicinals. That fact let him know things had worsened.

Rob Laswell had quietly roused him this morning. He rose with a heart heavy. The task ahead was not an easy one. Jed Turvey joined them, and they headed off to a place beside the path. Silently, they dug three graves.

All yesterday, Ethan had hoped a miracle would happen and Charity would consent to be his bride. Today, his thoughts traveled a different path. He hoped they'd all survive. So far, he'd tried to ignore the deaths. Last night, their guide, Patterson, grimly stated the toll thus far: Five women, three men, four children, and two babes. . .but Abby, her mother, and Hyacinth's father all succumbed to a wretched fever. Seven, four, four, and two. . .seventeen dead. That kind of ciphering put the fear of God into a man. *God, I beg of You, wrap Your mantle of health and protection around Cricket and Tad and Charity.*

Travel that day was quiet out of respect for the grieving family. Men chopped down small pine trees and leashed them to the rear axles of wagons to help slow their descent down a steep road. Even with that precaution, the Adamses' wagon careened out of control and crashed.

A burst flour barrel left an explosion of white, and splinters of wood affirmed that the wagon and what little furniture in it were beyond repair. A trunk, shattered bits of china, and a dented washtub bore testimony to the devastation. Gracie sagged to the ground and melted into a puddle of tears. Steven knelt beside her, gathered her in his arms, and Charity heard him say in a hoarse voice, "Darlin', we're all fine. You and the kids—you're what matters."

A small group took sticks and beat about the rocks and shrubs to scare away any snakes, then set about trying to salvage what they could for the Adamses. Ethan took one of the shattered wheels and walked off a few paces. Soon thereafter, he took out some of his tools and started to tinker around. Charity and Leticia kept all of the children off to the side.

Soon, other women made nooning meals for their families. The day had already proved disastrous. Funerals and a decimated wagon left them all apprehensive, and sticking to a routine helped keep a sense of purpose. Though the train was full of believers, the midday prayers grew more ardent than usual.

Charity gave Ethan one of the meat pies. He mumbled a hasty thank-you, gobbled it down, and barely paused from his work. She handed him a second, and he twitched her a grateful smile. Even after he'd finished eating, she watched a few more minutes as he fastened the altered hub between a few square pieces of wood with a big bolt. He nodded to himself, then paced off toward Jason with the odd-looking device in his hands.

As block and tackles went, it was crude as could be. Still, Ethan felt certain it would be of assistance if they'd secure it around a tree and the men would thread the rope through it and lower the wagons in a more controlled fashion. "I grant you, it's not much to look at; but I'm certain it'll serve its purpose, and it could spare us another disaster."

Jason grimaced. "Are you willing to try it out on your own rig?"

"Yes."

It took more time than using the tree-drag method, but Ethan's contrivance worked. They lowered four more wagons, but six still remained at the top of the incline as dusk approached. Tonight, there'd be two camps and two sets of guards.

Charity tucked the kids into bed, then Ethan drew her off to the side. "Before we pray, I'd like you to see if you could spare a bit of lye soap. The two Legacy wagons are going to combine as we did. They've offered their other to the Adamses, but we're worried since the folks in that wagon perished from fever. Mrs. Jason thinks if they empty it out, air it overnight, and scrub it with lye soap, it'll be all right to use."

"Lye soap?"

"She read something by Dr. Semmelweis about hand-washing and soap stopping childbed fever. She vows washing seems to stop many fevers from spreading. I'm not sure I put any store by it, but Gracie is already so upset, if it makes her feel better. . ." He shrugged.

Charity opened the dish box hanging from the rear of their wagon and pulled out a cake of soap. Since Ethan used lye soap for everything and she'd brought along glycerin soap for bathing, they had a bit extra. "I'll take it to them."

Ethan curled his hand around her wrist. "No, Charity. I don't want you to be exposed. I'll take care of delivering the soap. Since we have two camps, I'll pull duty the first half of the night. Could I trouble you to put on some more coffee?"

"It's no trouble."

Ethan paced away with the soap.

When he returned, he sat on a felled log and patted the spot next to himself. "Prayer time."

Charity sat down, leaving discreet space between them. Unsure of what to do, she busied her hands by pulling her shawl more closely about her shoulders.

Ethan frowned. "Are you cold?"

"Not particularly. It will get much colder tonight. You'll need another quilt for your bedroll when you turn in."

"I'll be fine, Charity. Keep the quilt and share it with the kids."

His protective ways and concern for her warmed Charity's heart. *Lord, I know I'm supposed to be taking this time to seek Your will. It's so hard, Father, because my heart is already set. Please, give us Your blessing. I've already lost Mama and Daddy. I couldn't bear to be parted from Ethan and his children.*

Ethan reached out. "While we speak to the Father about our future, I'd like us to join hands." As soon as she placed her hand is his large, callused palm, his long fingers curled around to engulf hers. His strength and warmth made her heart beat faster. He gently squeezed and asked, "Are you ready to pray?"

"I already was," she blurted out. Charity felt her face go warm.

A rich chuckle rumbled out of him. "Oh, Gal, you

weren't alone. Heaven's gate must be atilt from all of the supplications I've been stacking up against it!"

Since Gracie needed to scrub and pack the wagon they'd been given and the Legacys needed to combine, the wagon council decided to take the next morning as a "rest and catch-up time." By afternoon, the men would lower the last wagons down the incline. The scout reported there was a good spot less than two miles ahead for stopping.

The sky hadn't even gotten a touch of gold to it when Charity rose. She made triple portions for breakfast and went over to the spot where the Adamses spent the night. "Gracie, bring your family to eat. I'll watch the children while you tend to matters." Gracie's eyes filled with tears, and Charity felt her own well up. She gave her friend a quick hug and a wobbly smile. "I know what a help that was when you minded the children the morning Ethan and I packed our wagon."

Ethan used the morning hours to inspect the Adamses' broken items. Without a blacksmith to forge new bands or straighten out bent hoops, it made no sense to try to repair barrels. He salvaged parts of two chairs and said he'd be able to construct one from them. A bit of clever patching fixed one trunk, and new leather "hinges" and a strap closed another. A few nails, and two crates came up to snuff.

By late afternoon, they'd gotten all of the wagons down and traveled to their evening campsite. A meandering creek outlined one side of the place. The scout insisted the water be used only for livestock and washing. "It's too slow-moving. Folks get sick when the water isn't white or tumbling over rocks."

"I'm afraid Cricket will take a sip if I bathe her."

Rob Washington rested his hands on his hips. "What say we string laundry lines betwixt trees and a wagon to make up a bathhouse? The water's chilly, so we could collect enough dead wood to make a fire and heat it a bit."

"Women ought to go first," Rick proposed. "I figgur they'll want to wash their hair, and if they wait till later, they'll catch a chill."

Myrtle giggled. "Are the menfolk offering to bathe the children?"

"Sure are," Ethan said as he hoisted Cricket into his arms.

Cricket squirmed and shook her head. "Wanna be with Miss Davis. She gots pretty flower soap, Pa. Makes me smell good."

"Don't be stubborn, Cricket. We're trying to do something nice and spoil the womenfolk."

"I'm a womenfolk, Pa. I even gots ninety-'leven buttons on my string!"

Charity laughed. "I'll take her, Ethan. It's no trouble."

"You deserve to be spoiled," he said under his breath. The look in his eye and the tone of his voice warmed her more than the hot water in the bath she took a short while later.

Breakfast, nooning, and supper, they said grace before their meals. Now, Ethan and Charity snatched a bit of time out each evening to set their future before God. She noticed he'd sometimes touch the spot on the bonnet where the button was sewn when he passed it outside. Once, he gave her a scampish wink when he knew she'd seen him do it.

Nothing momentous happened to give them a sense of direction. "Waiting on the Lord isn't an easy task for me," Ethan confessed one night.

"I'm not a very patient person, either."

Ethan looked at her and shook his head. "Gal, I can't believe you said that. You're more long-suffering than a saint. I can't imagine for the life of me how you've listened to Tad's endless soliloquies about wanting a jackknife, carried Cricket when her little legs got too tired to walk, and settled their squabbles. You've put up with me when I've been grumpy after a long day, too."

Charity looked at him at length. "Ethan, I grew up as an only child. You simply cannot know how much I relish spending time with the children. To my way of thinking, a man who misses half a night's sleep and drives a team of oxen all day is entitled to being a shade moody. I tried to drive for just a few days, and I was a weeping mess."

"You'd just lost your pa and ma, Charity. You've gone through terrible hardships on this trip."

"I won't pretend it's been easy," she averted her face. "But my trust lies in the Lord."

Ethan cupped her cheek and gently coaxed her to look at him. "Do you think you could learn to trust me, too?"

"I already do." Her lashes lowered. The intensity of his gaze made her heart beat far too fast.

"You must know you have my complete trust. I've put my children in your care. A man cannot show his confidence in a woman more plainly. I believe it's my turn to pray tonight.

"Our Praised Heavenly Father, we give You our gratitude for seeing us through another day safely. Each night, Lord, we've come to ask for wisdom in the matter of our hearts. You abide in each of us, but we still wait for the assurance of Your blessing or the clear sign that You do not will the union of marriage betwixt us. Grant us courage and composure as we endure. Prepare our hearts so we can carry on Your will. We pray in Jesus' precious name, Amen."

He lifted her into the wagon for the night. Charity curled around Cricket with his prayer still threading through her mind. As far as she was concerned, marriage to Ethan was the only way God could make her happy. How was Ethan able to lay the matter before the Lord day after day so impartially? Though he spoke well of her and to her, could it be he fostered no deep, heartfelt affection for her? She buried her face in the pillow and wept over that notion.

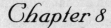

Chapter 8

In the middle of the night, Charity knew something was amiss. She lay still and tried to decide what woke her. Tad mumbled something and thrashed. She smiled. He was a restless sleeper. Ethan had made a bundling board to divide the bed to protect Cricket since Tad never stayed stationary. Charity started to caress Cricket's hair but stilled at once. She was burning hot!

Charity whisked on her wrapper. She felt for a lamp and hastily lit it as she called out, "Ethan! Ethan! Wake up! Cricket's sick." Her voice broke. "It's a fever."

They quickly established Tad was well, so Ethan moved him under the wagon. Charity hastily stripped Cricket out of her nightgown and sponged her off. She glanced up at Ethan. "She's so hot! Oh, Ethan, she's so hot."

"Willow bark," he decided. "Willow bark tea works fine on her. We'll give that a try. I brought a bit." He brewed the tea, but Cricket barely roused enough to take a few scant sips.

By morning, Mrs. Jason paid them a brief visit. "She doesn't have a rash, and she doesn't have dysentery. There's nothing to be done but to give her plenty to drink, sponge her off, and try to knock that fever down."

Charity and Ethan exchanged anguished looks. They'd spent the whole night doing precisely that—to no avail.

Mr. Jason wore an apologetic look. "The whole train can't afford to stay put here when only one child is ailing. If we don't push ahead, we'll be stranded in the mountains in the winter instead of reaching Oregon. At least with two hale adults, one of you can tend the lass while the other keeps the wagon in formation."

Charity spent the whole day sponging Cricket and drizzling little bits of broth and willow bark tea into her. Wagons had no springs—something she'd learned her very first day on the trail. Instead of the buffered ride of a springed carriage, wagons jolted and bumped dreadfully. Every yard they covered felt like a mile.

By midday, Cricket started coughing. Charity held her upright so she'd breathe a bit easier. Ethan took a turn while Charity took an essential moment at that stop, and Mary Pitts brought over bacon and fry bread for their noon meal. "How's the little one?"

Ethan gave no reply. He looked down at his daughter. Every shred of his love and concern showed on his grim face.

Charity dunked the washrag in a water bucket and sponged Cricket as she whispered, "She needs prayer." After Mary left, Charity fretted, "Her cough is worsening. I have an elixir in the bottom drawer."

Ethan somberly handed his daughter over and moved his heavy toolbox so the drawer could slip open a bit of the way. "I don't see any medicinals in here."

"I'm sure they're there." She pressed the damp cloth to Cricket's fever-cracked lips. "Oh. You're looking for glass bottles. Daddy said the glass would likely break. He had the apothecary pack all of the tinctures, concoctions, and elixirs into metal containers. There's a small book with them that holds the labels and notes from the doctor."

Ethan tilted the kit and yanked it free. As he did, the false bottom of the drawer slid aside, revealing a wealth of twenty-dollar gold coins. He ignored them and reached for the half-inch-thick book wedged alongside another box. He pulled the book free and set it on the bed. A small velvet bag enveloped each container. Frustration flooded him. He needed to access the medication quickly. Charity had opened the book and told him, "We need flask number eight."

Desperate, Ethan dumped the whole kit and started to rifle through the bags.

"Oh! They were in order in the satchel!"

Her cry came too late. At least each bottle was etched with a number. Together, they exposed each flask until his fingers closed around the right one. "Number Eight! How much do we give her?"

"The book says half a teaspoon, accompanied by a mustard and onion poultice."

His worry for his daughter erupted into unreasonable anger. "Mustard and onion? Just how am I supposed to get those out here?" He waved at the flasks with disgust. "Silver and gold don't take care of all of life's problems."

Charity gave no reply. Ethan stared at her and saw the hurt in her eyes. She dipped her head, and her lashes lowered. Her cheek pressed lightly against Cricket's. In a thick, hushed voice, she directed, "My measuring spoons are in the top drawer."

His anger fled, only to be replaced with remorse. *A*

soft answer turneth away wrath. The verse ran through his mind as he poured the cherry elixir into the spoon and gave it to his daughter. "Charity—"

"If you hold her," Charity interrupted, "I'll make the poultice." She didn't look at him. Instead, she shifted Cricket.

Ethan accepted his daughter's limp form and wondered afresh how dainty little Charity had managed to prop her up these past hours. "Charity—"

She shook her head. "I need to think. Please don't distract me." Her voice was thick with tears. She said nothing more. Neither did he. The drawer holding spices had a tin of mustard. The drawer with dehydrated fruits and vegetables scraped open. Most folk hadn't been able to afford much of them, but the Davis family brought along a wide variety. To keep the flavors from mingling, they were stored in decorated tins.

Less than ten minutes later, Charity pressed the compress to Cricket's chest. She'd torn her own flannel nightgown to use for the fabric, and since no fire had been struck for nooning, she'd melted the lard in a pie tin over the kerosene lantern, then added in the onions and mustard. With the plaster made and in place, Charity said in a tight voice, "The wagons are starting to pull out. Do you want to hold her while I drive?"

"The terrain is rough. I'd better drive." Charity sat on the edge of the feather bed, and Ethan carefully transferred his daughter's weight into her arms. "Get better," he murmured to Cricket, then gave her a kiss on her cheek. His head lifted a bit. He cradled Charity's jaw. "Gal, now's not the time, but we need to talk. I'm sorry—"

"Now isn't the time," she cut in. She pulled away, but

not before he saw tears sparkling in her eyes.

Ethan let out a groan of remorse and climbed onto the seat. He let out the brake, took up the reins, and set them into motion. "Holler if you need my help," he called to her. It was a useless thing to say. He couldn't make a difference. Almost as bad, he'd just crushed Charity's tender heart, so turning to him was probably the last thing she'd want to do.

By nightfall, Cricket's cough was still bad, but Charity managed to care for her as well as could be expected with the plaster and elixir. Sucking on the lemon drops seemed to help Cricket's throat feel better. The fever concerned them most. Cricket stayed hot as a pistol. Common sense dictated they each take a shift during the night with her so they'd both be able to function the next day. Neither slept much at all—worry interfered. Mrs. Jason warned them against using the quinine for the fever because her medical book said it wasn't to be given to young children.

By the third evening, Ethan knew his little daughter couldn't weather another night of the fever. Out of desperation, he looked at Charity and said, "We have to give her the quinine. Look it up in that book. Whatever the lowest dose is, we'll give her half of what they recommend."

Charity fumbled with the book and found the correct pages. The label stripped from the original glass bottle warned not to administer quinine to small children. In a neat hand, the pharmacist had added several comments and admonishments.

Ethan put a few drops of the bitter medicine in a small cup and added a bit of water. He stared at it. "God, I'm fresh out of prayers. My little girl's in Your hands. Please," he let out a mix between a sigh and a groan, "please. . . ."

"Amen," Charity breathed. She gently stroked Cricket's throat to make her swallow.

Ethan watched tears pencil down Charity's wan cheeks. She was hollow-eyed and pasty. *Oh, not you, too.* He touched her forehead, but she drew back. "You're exhausted. Go lie down."

She shook her head. "I can't leave my little girl." She dipped the cloth and wiped Cricket's tiny body by rote, yet every move was done with loving tenderness.

Ethan stilled her hand. "Just curl up on Tad's side of the bed, Charity. I'll see to her awhile, then you can take the rest of the night."

Charity barely laid her head down before she fell asleep. Ethan leaned his head against a wagon bow as he rolled up his sleeves. It took a long while until he was sure: Cricket's fever was waning. He coaxed a bit of cider and more cough elixir into her, and she fell into a peaceful slumber.

Ethan looked at the button on the canvas and knew he had one last thing to do.

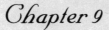

Chapter 9

How could a woman go from the heights of elation to the depths of despair in a single heartbeat? Charity was thrilled beyond words to wake and find Cricket felt better. Then, she saw the bare spot where the button belonged. She scrambled out of the wagon with more haste than manners, but she didn't care. She sat at the edge of camp, out of sight, her spine pressed to the trunk of a tree. All she wanted was to be alone.

Alone.

Yes, she was by herself. She folded her knees up, wound her arms around them, and buried her face in her skirt. She wept half an ocean. From how he'd acted, she'd suspected Ethan had made his decision. After his comment about silver and gold, she'd cut him off before he could tell her then. She'd hoped maybe, after the strain of Cricket's illness waned, he'd reconsider. He hadn't. The missing button said it all. Though she'd suspected it, it still crushed her to know the man she loved chose to reject her.

"Pa?"

"Yes, Tad?" Ethan looked over the tailgate of the wagon and smiled at his son.

"Sissy didn't die and go to the Hereafter?"

"No." He grinned. "God was good. Sissy's much better."

"Great!" Tad's features twisted into confusion. "Then why did Miss Davis go tearing through camp, weeping?"

Charity heard the crunch of boots and tried to stop crying. "Aww, Honey-gal," a velvety voice crooned before she had a chance to wipe away the tears.

Ethan! I can't bear to have him see me like this. She needed time to regain a semblance of composure. How could she do it? She was committed to helping him with the children for the rest of the trip, but knowing he didn't want her or love her was too painful. Another sob welled up.

He knelt beside her and made a soft hushing sound as he pulled her into his arms. For an instant, everything within her rebelled. Charity tried to push him back and scramble away, but he held her fast. "I'm not letting go of you, Honey-gal. Not now. Not ever."

She couldn't believe he'd said that. Charity rested her forehead on his shoulder and still cried. He pressed his lips to her hair and stroked her arm and back.

"I've been a fool, Charity. I've let my pride and your possessions come between us instead of seeking the truth. The truth is, you are one of the sweetest gifts God ever gave me. I got to thinking last night. If God sees the sparrow fall and can count the hairs on my head, He certainly counted the buttons on your string. He knew I was carving that button. He knew the desire of my heart, too. I'd been fighting it for weeks—wanting you as my wife, but I kept telling myself and anyone else who asked that I wasn't worthy of you. You're a wealthy woman—"

She looked up at him with aching eyes. "You're the rich one, Ethan. All of the silver and gold in the world wouldn't ever buy me a f—family." Her voice cracked. "I—I have nothing."

"Sweetheart, that's where you're wrong. Last night, you called Cricket your little girl." She gave him a blank look, so he nodded to punctuate his words. "Yes, you did. You said, 'I can't leave my little girl.' That said it all, Charity. In our hearts, we've blended until we're already a family. The only thing missing is a ring on your finger to make it official."

He'd brought her shawl. He reached to the side and unfolded it to reveal her button string. "I'm no good at stitching." He chuckled. "You knew that, seeing the sorry way I'd tried to mend my own clothes before you came along. I couldn't wait, though. Last night, I took that button off of the wagon bonnet and secured it to your string. It's the thousandth, Charity Davis. I know it full well, and I'm staking my claim. I'd best warn you I knotted this button on so tight, it would take a twenty-mule team to pull it off. I'm giving you my heart with that button, and you'd better know it's given with all the love God put in my heart for you."

He pressed his lips to her temple.

"I love you, Honey. I need your sweetness and comfort. I want to be your strength and protection. Maybe things haven't started out like a storybook, but that doesn't mean they haven't been arranged for us by the hand of the Almighty. I love you. Don't you love me?"

"Oh, Ethan, I was so scared. I never wanted to give the button back in the first place! That night, I realized I'd lost my heart to you."

He slipped her button string around her neck. "Then Miss Charity Davis, will you do me the honor of becoming my wife?"

"Ethan Cole, I love you. Nothing would make me happier."

He dipped his head. "Let's seal it with a kiss and a prayer."

With the resiliency of youth, Cricket recovered quickly. After Charity was sure all was well, she dug to the very bottom of her trunk and brought out the white satin Mama had brought along. Ethan would have been satisfied for the wagon train captain to wed them straight away, but he said she deserved the wedding of her dreams. According to their scout, they had ten days until they made it through The Dalles and reached the Willamette Valley. There was a church at the end of the trail, and Charity was determined to have a bridal gown done by then.

"Ethan, you may as well go on over and share the fire with Rob," Banner said. "We ladies are fixin' to help Charity with her finery. Everyone knows a man's not allowed to see it till the wedding day, so you can just resign yourself to being kicked out of the way for the next week or so."

Charity giggled as he winked and paced off. Soon Banner, Myrtle, Mary, and Gracie helped her spread the bonnet she'd saved from her wagon on the ground to protect her satin. When they unrolled the bolt, Charity gasped. Mama hadn't just packed the satin—she'd included elegant lace and packets of seed pearls and minute, crystal beads.

Myrtle oohed and aahed. Banner's brows knit for a moment. "I can't imagine why she didn't just bring her gown for you. Certainly, you were both of a size that would have made it possible."

Charity smiled. "Mama was the middle of three daughters. Though she wore the gown, according to family tradition, it belonged to the firstborn daughter."

Gracie said, "Then it's time to start a gown for a new family. Ladies, it's time to gild our lily. Let's get busy." They measured, talked, snipped, and pinned. True friends that they were, they worked afternoon and evening with her until the last stitch was done.

The gown featured a tightly fitted bodice that ended in a downward point. Fabric swagged from side seam to side seam in order to form horizontal scallops down to the floor, and the back draped over a bustle. Closely fitted sleeves hugged her arms and came to a traditional medieval point to call attention to her slender finger where Ethan would place the wedding ring. Lace and seed pearls adorned the entire bodice, then edged the hem and sleeves.

"Your mama's veil is your something old, and this gown is your something new," Banner said as she and Charity hid the completed gown away from Ethan's sight. "I made a garter for your something blue. Have you borrowed anything yet?"

Charity smiled. "I'm borrowing Ethan's children, but I'm not giving them back. I'm keeping them as my own, forever."

At the end of the trail, everyone camped for the night. The next day, after folks had a chance to do laundry and visit the bathhouse, they all met at the church. Cricket, dressed in a pretty little sky blue frock Charity made for her, skipped down the aisle, carrying Charity's beloved Bible. She took her place beside her daddy.

Ethan forgot to breathe when he saw Tad escort Charity down the aisle. Her gown sparkled, shimmered, and flowed like a dream. Through her mama's veil, he could see her smile. As she drew closer, his smile broadened. Instead of ribbons, her beloved button string draped around and hung from the bouquet.

Epilogue

M a, you'd best better get in here," Tad hollered. "Cricket's getting into your fancy talcum powder and making a mess!"

"Cricket!" Charity's feet pattered on the hardwood floor of the beautiful home Ethan had built for them. "Mama didn't want you to get messy! We're supposed to surprise your papa with the anniversary cake as soon as he gets home!"

Ethan stood behind his children. He rested a hand on each of them. Tad hadn't lied one bit. Cricket had gotten into the violet talcum he'd gotten Charity for Christmas. The whole bedroom smelled like a flower garden. Hopefully, his wife would be so taken with this next gift, she'd ignore that misbehavior.

The crystal doorknob turned, and they all held their breath. Charity entered the room and stopped cold. "Ethan! When did you get home?"

"While Tad had you out in the garden."

"Can we say it now?" Cricket whispered loudly.

"Yes."

"Surprise!" Ethan, Tad, and Cricket exclaimed in

unison. They moved to the side, revealing the wedding chest he'd been making in secret. The look on Charity's face made all of his work worthwhile.

"Oh, Ethan! It's lovely! Oh, it matches!"

He rocked back on his heels and proudly gazed down at the front panel of the piece. He'd sent back East just to get walnut for it. He'd used the last of his own money to do it, too. "Yup. I traced the highboy and headboard to be sure the ribbon was just right."

She wound her arms around him. "I was thinking this matched the button you gave me. It's beautiful, Ethan. Thank you."

She kissed him, and Tad groaned. "Can we please have the cake now?"

"Go ahead and cut it." Charity held Ethan back while the kids dashed to the kitchen.

"You can keep your wedding gown inside, Honey-gal. I lined it all with cedar. Look." He opened the lid. Charity's laughter pleased him. Inside the lid, he'd wood-burned a design of a string of buttons. "It took me a while, but this is my groom's gift to you."

"I have a surprise for you, too." She took his hand and placed it on her tummy. "How about if the chest becomes a family heirloom?"

A Letter from the Bride

To my dear daughters, granddaughters, and all future brides,

I thought it would be a wonderful tradition for each bride to write a little note and leave a legacy for those who come after her. How I wish my own mother had lived to see my wedding day and been present to share her wisdom!

I make no pretense at being wise, but God is. The Bible says we can ask for wisdom, and God will honor our request. As you consider marriage, first seek God's will and ask Him to direct your heart. Do not hasten to take your vows. Pause and reflect before you take such a momentous step, and be sure your mate honors God. A marriage is not just between a man and a woman—it is a holy union which must include the Lord to flourish.

Ethan was God's gift to me. His patience, strength, and companionship were like a balm to my grief. We learned to work together and rely on one another until respect and affection sparked. Love came softly and grew in our hearts. How I thank God for bringing us together and blessing our union!

Though hardships test us and extraordinary things thrill us, life is made up of mundane days. Love each other in the little, commonplace matters of life to strengthen your marriage, or it will wither from neglect. Appreciate what you have, and forgive as freely as you laugh.

My darlings, my prayer is for you to make wise decisions of the heart—first in devoting your spirit to the Lord, then in giving your hand to a man. May each of you be blessed with a godly mate and know the joy of growing close together and growing old with him.

With love, hope, and prayers,
Charity Davis Cole

CATHY MARIE HAKE

Cathy Marie is a Southern California native who loves her work as a nurse and Lamaze teacher. She and her husband have a daughter, a son, and a dog, so life is never dull or quiet. Cathy considers herself a sentimental packrat, collecting antiques and Hummel figurines. She otherwise keeps busy with reading, writing, baking, and being a prayer warrior. "I am easily distracted during prayer, so I devote certain tasks and chores to specific requests or persons so I can keep faithful in my prayer life." Cathy Marie's first book was published by **Heartsong Presents** in 2000 and earned her a spot as one of the readers' favorite new authors.

THE
WEDDING
QUILT BRIDE

by Colleen Coble

Chapter 1

Only a full partnership in your business would tempt me to marry your daughter, Sir. She has nothing to recommend her beyond an alliance with your family." Adam Richter's deep voice held a trace of contempt. "I confess I'm shocked you would offer so little."

Her hand on the library door, Faith Cole listened to the hurtful words. She swallowed the lump in her throat and let her hand drop from the door handle. Backing away, she almost stumbled as her shorter leg caught in the carpet runner. She wheeled to flee but stopped at her father's outraged voice.

"My daughter is better unmarried than to be yoked with the likes of you. You have deceived me and my daughter. I thought you truly cared for her."

So had Faith. Blinking back the tears of humiliation, she gathered her composure. Though hampered by her pronounced limp, she hurried away before the men could catch her eavesdropping. That would be the final humiliation.

She scurried up the staircase to the sanctuary of her room. She should have known better than to dream of finding a man who would love her for herself. What man would want a cripple? If she possessed great beauty, perhaps no one would notice she'd been born with one leg shorter than the other, but her colorless appearance made no man's heart beat faster.

With a sigh of relief, she shut her bedroom door behind her and sat in the rocking chair by the window. She had to get her emotions under control before Papa called her down to the library. How would he justify denying Adam's suit? She knew her father well enough to know he would be as gentle as possible. If she hadn't overheard the conversation, it was unlikely she would ever have known the full truth.

Faith glanced around her room for something to occupy her hands. Filled with examples of her quilting expertise, the gaily patterned quilts, bears, and wall hangings made her itch to take her needle and stitch her sorrow away. Her bureau was filled with blue ribbons from the county and state fairs for her quilts, but they meant nothing to Faith. She'd seen the sympathy in too many judges' eyes to believe she'd won them on her merits alone.

Her mother always said Faith could make her needle talk, but Faith felt it listened more than it talked. With her needle she could pour out her pain, humiliation, longings, and dreams. She sighed. From now on, no more listening to men sweet-talk her because they wanted a connection with her family. Her father had built a successful carpentry business that had expanded into a furniture-making enterprise that employed two hundred men. They were one of the most prominent families in town.

A man wasn't capable of truly loving her for herself alone; she'd bought that dream far too long. She would be content with her lot of helping her mother manage the household and corralling her three younger sisters. Once her older siblings, Tad and Cricket, had married and moved away, her mother depended on her more and more. She pushed away the tears. She wanted no one's pity.

She straightened her room and then read for awhile. Echoes of life downstairs drifted under her door: the mail-man ringing the bell, the housekeeper scolding the new maid, and the cracking of ball against mallet as her sisters played croquet in the backyard. Her stomach growled at the aroma of lunch cooking. Bread pudding, it smelled like. She would be rousted from her sanctuary soon.

"Faith!" Her father bellowed her name from the bottom of the steps.

"Coming," she called. Hastily scrubbing the last of her tears from her cheeks, she paused to glance in the mirror on her dressing table. Though pale and wan, she thought her father would detect nothing wrong. Not a stray blond hair escaped the confines of its decorous bun, and her gray gown appeared sedate and proper. Her hazel eyes were somber, but that was usual. She pinched a bit of color into her cheeks and opened the door.

Her father's scowl lightened when he saw her coming down the stairs. "There you are. I have some important news for you," he said gruffly. "Come into the library." He courteously held the door open for her.

She was surprised to find her mother waiting with tea and cookies. Her mother, Charity, smiled at her, but

Faith wasn't fooled. She could see Mama's anger and a hint of sorrow in her eyes. She sat beside her mother on the horsehair sofa and accepted the cup of tea her mother handed her.

Her father went straight to the point, as was his way. "You're twenty-seven years old, Faith. Much as we love having you around, your mother and I have been concerned that we've sheltered you too much. How would you like to see something of the country?"

Her head snapped up, and she stared at him in disbelief. "What about Adam?" The words escaped before she could stop them. Heat crept up her neck, and she dropped her gaze.

"He is not worthy of you," her mother snapped. Lips tight, she reached over and touched Faith's hand. "You can do better than a man like him."

She smiled at her mama lovingly. "I'm happy with you and Papa." Faith put her cup on the table beside her and folded her hands in her lap. She was surprised to find the words were true. Her parents loved her fiercely. How could she *not* be happy?

"You've never met my family in Pennsylvania," Charity began. She held a letter in her hand and waved it in the air. "I received a letter from my grandmother today, and she's asking for you to come for a visit. Your father and I have decided to allow you to go." She choked a bit at the last sentence and dabbed tears from the corner of her eye with her lace handkerchief.

"Great-grandmother Preston wants me to come to. . . to Pennsylvania?" Wide-eyed, Faith stared at her mother. Excitement thrummed along her veins. "Will you be coming for a visit with me?"

Her father, Ethan, cleared his throat. "No, Faith, you will be traveling alone. If the timing were different, your mother would have accompanied you, but she will be a bit under the weather for the next few months."

The import of his words took a few moments to sink in. Faith stared at her mother and saw the faint pink stain her cheeks.

Her mother nodded at the question in her eyes. "There will be a blessed event in about five months." The flush on her cheeks deepened.

A new baby! "Then you will need me, Mama." The wild rush of excitement faded. She couldn't leave her mother to cope alone with a new baby on the way.

But her mother shook her head firmly. "We shall manage splendidly, Faith. It's time for you to spread your wings. Besides, your great-grandmother needs a bit of help. She's nearly ninety, though still spry. If you don't go soon, you will be too late to get to know her." Her mother continued to talk and make plans. Ethan would buy the ticket that very afternoon, and Faith would be on her way to Johnstown, Pennsylvania, within two days.

Her head in a whirl, Faith was dispatched to her room to pack her trunk. Even her limp didn't slow her down as she flew around her room, deciding what to take with her. Her youngest sister, ten-year-old Callie, tried to help but was more hindrance than help, and Faith soon sent her to the kitchen to help Milly, the cook.

Two days later, the entire family stood at the train siding. Faith tried to tell herself it was the acrid sting of the cinders that brought the tears to her eyes, but she knew better. She'd never been away from her family, and the thought of not seeing her mother's smile over breakfast made her ache with loneliness already. How would the twins get their lessons without the prodding of their older sister? Who would listen to Margaret's youthful dreams of romance? She pushed the misgivings away and forced a smile. It was too late to back out now.

The whistle blew, but still Mama clutched her hand. The twins, Callie and Constance, fidgeted excitedly while fifteen-year-old Margaret stared at her with wistful eyes. She'd begged to go, too, but Papa had insisted this trip was special for Faith alone.

"I've instructed the conductor to keep an eye out for you," Ethan said. "Don't talk to strangers, and don't wander from the station at stops."

"Yes, Papa," Faith said obediently.

"Here's a basket of food." Her mother's voice was low, and tears swam in her eyes.

Faith took it and hugged everyone. Fighting the tears, she stood on the first step of the railcar and waved, then took a deep breath and stepped inside. This was a new adventure, and she meant to savor every moment.

Several days later she wasn't so optimistic. Her leg ached from sitting in the seat for long periods, and though her father had purchased a sleeping compartment, the laughter of several men playing cards into the wee hours had kept her awake nearly every night. She would be glad to get off the train in Johnstown. Would Grandmother Preston like her? She'd heard her mother talk about growing up in Johnstown with its steel mills and fast-growing industry. Traveling through America's great desert, she already missed the soft green of Oregon. What would Pennsylvania be like?

She spent the trip watching people and imagining

stories about them. Were the young couple two rows ahead of her on their honeymoon? The soft looks and laughing whispers showed their love, so Faith was fairly certain she was right about them. A gruff older man with a quiet young woman of about Faith's age intrigued her. Was she his wife or his daughter? Faith couldn't decide.

A harried young man with windblown black hair and a rumpled suit got on at Chicago. Slim of build, he was nearly six feet tall. Sitting in the seat across the aisle from Faith, he kept digging in a leather bag at his feet. She caught glimpses of some kind of tools, but she couldn't decide what his profession was. One piercing glance from his blue eyes told her she was staring, and she averted her eyes hastily.

He intrigued her, though. The next two days, she studied him surreptitiously from under the sweep of her lashes. The only time he noticed her was when she limped down the aisle to the rest room, and then, the only expression he displayed was pity. Not many people noticed anything but her limp. In her plain-colored gown, tightly wound hair, and nondescript features, she faded into the background. It was just as well. None of the single men on board had bothered with her. They all chased the lovely little brunette six rows back. Not that Faith minded. She didn't know how she could have handled any attention by herself.

"Next stop, Johnstown, Pennsylvania." The conductor's bored tones penetrated Faith's perusal of the man across the aisle. She flushed to realize she'd been staring again. Her heart pounded with excitement as she looked around to make sure all her belongings were back in her basket.

The man across the aisle began to collect his belongings as well. He must be getting off, too. Not that it mattered to her. She didn't even know his name. She resolutely turned and stared out the soot-covered window at the town nestled in the valley. Hopefully, Grandmother would have sent someone to meet her. Papa had promised to send a telegram with her arrival time.

Gathering her things, she stood and moved into the aisle behind the young man. The train lurched, and she jostled him with her basket. "Sorry," she murmured.

He shrugged and muttered something that sounded like "Cats right."

"Excuse me?" she said. He turned and smiled. That full force of those blue eyes nearly took her breath away.

He tilted his head. "I said, that's all right. You staying in Johnstown?"

Lost in those blue eyes, she suddenly realized he was waiting for an answer. "All summer," she said. She wasn't supposed to talk to strangers, but he seemed harmless. At least physically. She offered him a tentative smile. "How about you?"

He shrugged again. "Until my job is done."

She started to ask him what he did, but the engineer applied the brakes, and the squeal of the rails drowned out further conversation. He turned to face forward again, and she felt a stab of disappointment. He seemed so pleasant, in spite of his distracted air.

The conductor opened the doors. "Johnstown, Pennsylvania," he announced.

Faith followed the man as he stepped down onto the siding. Maneuvering her basket and valise, her foot searched for the next step but failed to find it. Flailing wildly, she tried to catch herself, but her shorter leg made her balance even trickier. She gave a slight scream and pitched toward the landing. The man wheeled at her sound. Dropping his leather bag, he caught her before she landed on the ground.

Except for her father, Faith had never been so close to a man before. His broad chest was hard with muscle, and the scent of his hair tonic was pleasing. Transfixed by his blue gaze, she didn't move for a long moment, then she saw the amusement in his eyes. Laughing at the poor cripple; but why should she be surprised? She'd been dealing with that all her life. She would just get out of his way as quickly as possible.

Pulling away stiffly, she straightened her hat. "Thank you kindly, Sir." She looked around for her valise and basket and limped over to retrieve them.

"You're welcome," he said.

She could feel his gaze boring into her back. He was probably snickering under his breath at her infirmity. Her shoulders stiffened, and she held her head high.

"I'm Daniel Nelson." He came up behind her and picked up her basket. Holding it a bit longer than necessary, he made her look at him.

She tilted her chin up. "Thank you again, Mr. Nelson." Her pronounced limp made it difficult to exit gracefully, but she held her head high anyway and marched off to find her great-grandmother.

Chapter 2

Daniel followed the prim young woman through the crowd. My, she was prickly! He wasn't sure why he felt a need to make sure she was met by someone. One glance from those cold hazel eyes had been quite enough to put him off. With her blond hair scraped back into a bun and not a tendril of hair to soften its severity, she attracted no attention from the steelworkers hurrying home from work. He felt he'd handled the entire incident badly. He could tell she'd thought he was laughing at her clumsiness. In truth, he'd been amused at the thought of catching a young woman like a football.

Black cinders from the steel smelters coated the streets, and the odor of hot metal stung his throat and left a bitter taste on his tongue. Johnstown crouched in a valley in the Allegheny Mountains. To the northwest of the Pennsylvania Railroad station, he could see the brick buildings that housed the Cambria Iron Works. Smokestacks, over sixteen feet in diameter and seventy-five feet high, towered above the dirty buildings. It was too late to go there today, but he would check in with his employer tomorrow.

Gawking, he almost missed seeing the young woman climbing into a carriage. The fine black conveyance had the letter P emblazoned on the door. Strange. She hadn't appeared to be wealthy. Upper middle class, yes, but not wealthy enough for a coachman and fancy carriage. Frowning, he stopped in the middle of the street and stared after the departing vehicle. Someone was taking care of her; that was all that mattered. He shrugged and hailed a hansom cab to take him to the Hulbert House Hotel.

He peered out the window as the hansom rattled over the paved streets. Johnstown was an impressive city with fire hydrants and electric lights. The carriage rattled past the park, lush with azaleas and other colorful spring flowers, a new hospital, mansions, and opera houses. Too bad he wouldn't be staying long. He could get to like this city.

The opulent entry of the Hulbert House promised a comfortable stay, but Daniel was pleasantly surprised by his room and the bath with indoor plumbing. Indoor plumbing was not a common convenience, and after the long, dirty train ride, he was glad to take a bath and feel human again. Eating supper at The Picket Fence restaurant down the way from the hotel, he found himself looking for the young woman from the train. How ridiculous. She was well cared for, and even if she wasn't, it was no business of his. Still, he wished he'd gotten her name.

The next morning he found his way down Washington Street and out to the general offices of Cambria Iron Works.

Nathan Greene came around his desk when the

secretary announced Daniel. "Daniel, my boy! I've been wondering when you would show up." He shook Daniel's hand vigorously. "Have a seat." He indicated a chair. "Have you been to the site yet?"

"Not yet. I thought you might want to take me there." Nathan looked much the same as the last time Daniel had seen him. A bit grayer, maybe, but his brown eyes were just as keen as they'd ever been, even at sixty.

"Oh, I'd rather you went incognito." Nathan frowned and shook his head. "We're in for trouble, Daniel, I can sense it."

Daniel nodded. "Can you tell me a bit more about what's happening?"

Nathan sighed. "I want you to look at it from a fresh point of view and give me your honest opinion. If you think I'm being an old fool, tell me so. But I don't think I am, Daniel, I really don't think so. You're one of the best civil engineers I know, and I want your honest opinion about that dam."

Daniel stared at him uneasily. If Nathan Greene thought there was a serious problem with the dam, there was likely something to worry about. His father and Nathan had been best friends for thirty years, and Nathan wasn't someone who cried wolf. He nodded slowly. "Give me directions, and I'll head out there now."

Nathan wrote down the directions, and Daniel took the train to the South Fork depot. Several men and women, their stylish clothing and jewelry proclaiming their wealth, disembarked at the depot with him. They were met by carriages to be taken to the South Fork Fishing and Hunting Club. In the press of people, Daniel slipped away to begin his study of the dam.

He walked along the crest of the dam and saw the face of the massive dam drop into the valley. A blue expanse of clear mountain water, dotted with sailboats, canoes, and yachts, looked inviting, but Daniel's eyes were on the dam. The dam had obviously been repaired by someone inexperienced in engineering. The sluice pipes were closed, and a breach in the dam had been filled with all kinds of material.

Daniel shook his head. This didn't look good. The club had built two trestle bridges across the spillway which obstructed the free spillage of water. They'd also placed fish guards of heavy screen wire between the supports of one of the bridges which was clogged with debris.

He fought a sense of rage and impotence. This bordered on criminal. What happened if there was an unusually heavy rainfall? Did the club management care so little about the safety of the towns below? He shook his head. Rounding a corner, he almost knocked down a young woman, a parasol over her head, strolling along the lake shore.

He stared into the startled hazel eyes of the young woman from the train. Bowing slightly, he reached out a hand to steady her as she rocked on her heels.

"You!" She bit her lip at her admission of recognition. Her eyes filled with tears, and she jerked her arm out of his grip. "I'm not a cripple," she snapped. "I know that's what you think." She drew herself up to her full height of five feet three inches or so. "What are you doing here? This is private property."

He scowled at her and stepped back. Her tears moved him more than he wanted to admit. "I didn't realize that. I'd heard how beautiful the lake was and wanted to see it.

I'm glad to see you again." He was surprised to find he meant it. Her plight had worried him.

"Why?" Her anger seemed temporarily forgotten.

He shrugged. "You disappeared before I was sure you'd found the person you came to meet. Could I take you to tea?" He pushed away the shaft of guilt that smote him. He needed to get inside and find out more about the dam and what the club intended to do about it. He hated to use her, but it was for a good cause.

She glanced back at a swan serenely gliding along the lake's surface. The soothing sound of the wind soughing through the treetops added to the perfect setting. Azaleas bloomed with profuse color along the lake path. The security of the place seemed to calm her. "I suppose you could join my great-grandmother and me for tea. It should be just about ready."

"May I ask your name? I can't very well call you 'the lady from the train.' Mine is Daniel Nelson, in case you've forgotten."

"I haven't forgotten, Mr. Nelson," she said.

Daniel suppressed a grin at the way she bit her lip again. She hadn't wanted to admit she remembered his name. "Your name?" he pressed.

"Faith. Faith Cole." She turned and started back toward the clubhouse. "Come along. Great-grandmother hates to be kept waiting for tea."

He offered Faith his arm, and after a moment's hesitation, she took it. She limped along the path, and he matched his stride to her steps. She was obviously self-conscious about her limp, for her color was high and she bit her lip several times when she stumbled and had to clutch his arm for support.

The clubhouse boasted a wide front porch that looked out over the lake. Several young men lounged about on the porch furniture and railing. One of them watched them come up the boardwalk and turned to his companions with a whispered comment. All three of them laughed, and Daniel saw the contempt in their grins when they turned and watched Faith lead the way to her great-grandmother's Queen Anne cottage farther along the wooden walkway. Daniel had only a moment to admire the fish-scale shingles on the peak and the rounded turret. He helped Faith up the steps and tried to ignore the laughter of the men across the path.

Daniel had to admire the way Faith handled the derision. Her head held regally high, she mounted the porch steps on his arm and swept into the front hall. The men's derisive laughter floated after them. Was that a shimmer of tears on her lashes, or was she used to such treatment? He wished he could make a comment about their manners but knew it would make it worse if she knew he'd noticed.

She dropped her hand from his arm. "Wait here a moment while I find my great-grandmother." She went to the parlor doors and slid open the pocket doors. Closing them behind her, she left him alone in the hall.

Glancing around, he saw a sweeping staircase to the second floor. A plush burgundy flowered runner ran the length of the hall while another ran up the stairs. A magnificently carved hall butler stood beside the door with umbrellas, cloaks, and hats neatly arranged on it. The home whispered money and privilege. Several comfortable chairs were arranged around a table along one wall, and he headed for the closest one.

Before he could be seated, Faith opened the door to the parlor and beckoned for him to follow her. Daniel squared his shoulders and followed her into an elegantly appointed parlor. Plush, overstuffed horsehair furniture, a magnificent grand piano draped with a fringed scarf, and numerous tables and shelving filled with memorabilia and statuary welcomed him.

The woman seated on the sofa glanced up at him through keen blue eyes. Though her face was softly wrinkled, she had obviously been a beauty in her day. Her white hair was braided and coiled around her head in a way that was no longer fashionable, but it suited her. The smile curving her lips was genuine, and Daniel felt his spirits lift. Perhaps she would listen after all. She looked much more approachable than her great-granddaughter.

"Grandmother, this is Mr. Daniel Nelson. I met him on the train," Faith said. "Mr. Nelson, this is my great-grandmother, Lady Nell Preston."

"Have a seat, Mr. Nelson," Lady Preston said in a husky, musical voice. "Meg should be bringing tea in shortly. You'll join us, won't you?"

He sat in a high-backed chair with a tapestry seat and an ornately carved back. "Thank you, Ma'am. I should like that."

Her gentle smile warmed him and made him feel he was the one person she'd been waiting to see. He knew a man would never have had a chance to resist her when she was a young woman. Too bad her great-granddaughter hadn't inherited her charm. Daniel slanted a glance at Faith. Her hands folded in her lap, she sat beside her great-grandmother and avoided his gaze. But in spite of her infirmity and severe appearance, there was something that drew him. He liked spirit in a woman, and he suspected she had some lurking beneath her controlled façade. But he couldn't let pity for her dissuade him from his purpose.

Chapter 3

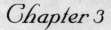

Faith allowed none of her inner turmoil to show on her expression. She sat with her hands folded in her lap and listened to Daniel speak with her great-grandmother. The sight of his untidy black hair and tall figure as she rounded the corner had driven all coherent thought from her. Why did he have to be around every time she was humiliated? She wanted to weep at the memory of the laughing men at the clubhouse, but she stiffened her shoulders and tilted her chin into the air. They would never know how much they had hurt her. Though she should be used to it, she realized now just how much her parents had sheltered her from the ridicule. The buffer of their love had cushioned the blows.

The maid brought in a tray laden with dainty pastries, a teapot, and teacups. She set it on the table in front of Faith. "Would you like me to pour, Ma'am?"

Lady Preston shook her head and motioned her out of the room. She played idly with the gold chain around her wrinkled neck. "What are you doing in the area, Mr. Nelson? Are you relocating?" She motioned for Faith to pour the tea.

Daniel's intense blue gaze fastened on her, and Faith felt the warm flush creep up her cheeks. She wanted to sink into the sofa and escape the pity she saw in his gaze. She didn't want pity, she wanted admiration. She realized now she'd never seen admiration in any man's gaze except for her father's. Tears pricked the backs of her eyes, and she blinked rapidly and leaned forward to pour the tea.

"I'm visiting a friend of the family for a few weeks. My father's best friend works for Cambria Iron Works and has been trying to persuade me to come to work for them."

Lady Preston frowned. "You would do well to stay away from that company," she said firmly. "We have had all manner of problems with them. They've had the audacity to accuse us of running an unsafe dam and have stirred up the town with their hysteria. We have a competent man in charge of the dam, but they refuse to accept his opinion." She shook her head. "What do you do, Mr. Nelson?"

Daniel hesitated. "I'm an engineer," he said.

She nodded. "They hire many engineers and pay them well, I have heard. Still, an ambitious young man like yourself would likely find greater opportunity in a larger city. Are you married?" She cast a sideways glance at her great-granddaughter.

Faith's face burned. She could tell where her great-grandmother's thoughts were headed, and she was painfully sure Daniel could tell as well. Why couldn't her family give up the useless quest to get her married? She was perfectly happy just as she was.

"No, Ma'am."

"Engaged?"

He grinned, and Faith's heart flipped. She'd never seen him smile, and his wide grin relaxed the worried air he seemed to carry with him. He ran a hand through his untidy mop of black hair and shook his head. She wanted to rush from the room, board the train, and go back to the safety of her parents' home. But instead she tilted her chin in the air and met his amused glance with dignity. The tension eased out of her shoulders at the warm understanding she found in his gaze.

"How long will you be in Johnstown?" she asked. She had to get her great-grandmother off the subject of Daniel's marital status.

"Probably until after Memorial Day. I'm going to work with Nathan a bit and see if the job suits or not."

"I noticed you brought a case of tools with you." Too late she realized her comment betrayed an immodest interest in him.

Her great-grandmother's eyes gleamed at the comment, but before she could resume her inquisition, Daniel stood. "Thank you for the tea. I fear I must get back to Johnstown now. Nathan will wonder what has become of me." He thrust his hands into his pockets and bowed slightly to Lady Preston and Faith. "I should like to call again, if I may."

Faith's eyes widened. Could he possibly be interested in her? She refused to even entertain the thought. Down that road lay heartbreak. She searched for a way to decline his request gracefully, but Lady Preston answered before she could muster her thoughts.

"We should like that, Mr. Nelson. In fact, we're hosting a ball tomorrow night. Would you care to attend?"

He hesitated, and his gaze shot to Faith. Her throat

swelled with pain when she saw the pity there again. Her eyes pleaded with him to decline, but he nodded instead.

"I would be delighted, Lady Preston."

"Seven o'clock sharp," Lady Preston said. "I can't abide tardiness, Mr. Nelson."

"Nor can I," he said. "I won't be late."

"Faith, walk him out, please." Lady Preston's tone brooked no argument.

Faith stood, and he offered her his arm. Her fingers closed around his arm, and she could feel the muscles under his coat. Unshed tears burned the back of her throat, but she walked to the door with him. Once he was gone, she would have a heart-to-heart talk with her great-grandmother. She had to cease her matchmaking.

She tried to minimize her limp but only succeeded in stumbling more than usual. In Daniel's company she felt more clumsy than usual, and for a moment she hated him for it. She clung to her favorite verse: 2 Corinthians 12:9. *My grace is sufficient for thee: for my strength is made perfect in weakness.*

At the door, he placed his other hand over hers and stared down at her with those intense blue eyes. "I'll see you tomorrow. Thank you again for the tea."

She dropped her hand. "You're welcome." She wanted to apologize for Lady Preston's matchmaking, but the words stuck in her throat. She didn't think she could bear to see the pity in his gaze again. She closed the door firmly behind him and went to find her great-grandmother.

Lady Preston smiled at Faith when she came back into the parlor. "Such a nice young man, Faith," she said approvingly. "You would do well to cultivate a friendship with him."

"He pities me, Grandmother," she said. "I would rather you not encourage him to come here. Men aren't interested in me."

"Nonsense, Faith. We shall show Daniel just what type of woman you are, come tomorrow." Her blue eyes were gleeful. "He'll be astounded when he sees you at the ball."

"What do you mean?" Faith had a sinking feeling there was no stopping her great-grandmother. In just twenty-four hours she'd discovered Lady Preston could be implacable.

"I have the perfect dress; it just wants a bit of fitting. My personal maid will do your hair. You wear it much too severely, Faith. It's no wonder men are put off."

"Men are put off, as you call it, by my infirmity."

"Nonsense. You make too much of it. Show a man your inner strength and beauty, and he'll never notice that slight limp you have." She stood. "Now come with me, Dear, and we'll get started."

"Grandmother, please, I have no interest in pursuing Mr. Nelson."

"I think you protest too much, Faith. I could tell young Daniel had caught your eye. And I intend to see you have a chance with him. Now follow me."

She took Faith's hand in a surprisingly strong grip and tugged. Faith sighed and followed her. She would have to find some way to dissuade her from her quest. Maybe she would get a chance to talk to Daniel tomorrow night and ask him to refuse future invitations. She would make it clear she had no interest in him.

Lady Preston opened a trunk and the aroma of cedar wafted into the room. The dress she pulled out took Faith's breath away. It was a confection of pink ruffles and white lace that wouldn't have been out of place in a Cinderella play. Lady Preston called her personal maid, Molly, to assist Faith in disrobing.

"I wore this dress the day I met your great-grandfather," she reminisced. "It was the only thing my grandmother would give me. She had it made by the premier dressmaker in town and said she'd done her part to get me a husband. I went to the ball, and your great-grandfather came as a guest of my cousin's. He was keeping company with a young woman of great fortune, but he took one look at me and forgot all about her, though I brought no dowry. We were married three months later." Her eyes moistened, and she gave a heavy sigh. She made an obvious attempt to push the memories away and turned her bright eyes back to her great-granddaughter.

The silk rustled over Faith's head and settled around her feet. Molly exclaimed over the dress as she fastened up the back and drew the sash around the waist. Faith felt like a princess in it. Seed pearls glittered on the skirt and bodice.

"It just needs a tuck or two," Lady Preston said, tilting her head and inspecting her. "You'll be the belle of the ball, Faith, just as I was."

Faith submitted to Lady Preston's insistence and allowed Molly to measure and tuck. When the next day came, the dress, newly cleaned, pressed, and altered, hung in her wardrobe. When Molly appeared to arrange her hair, she felt like a Christian being fed to the lions. Why couldn't her great-grandmother realize she would never appeal to any man? Dread congealed her stomach. The men would laugh again, and this night would end in tears.

Molly had her sit on a stool, and she began to arrange Faith's hair. "Cor, Miss Faith, but your hair is like spun gold. You shouldn't wear it drawn so tight. Surely it makes your head ache."

Faith smiled feebly but said nothing. Molly was being polite. The brush rippling through her hair was soothing, and she closed her eyes while the maid's nimble fingers curled and tucked, twisted and looped. With her eyes closed, she imagined what it must be like to walk into a room and have everyone turn to look because she was beautiful, not because she was crippled. She sighed, a faint whisper of defeat.

"There. Now let's put a bit of color in your cheeks and lips."

Before Faith could protest, Molly whipped out a pot of rouge and a tin of powder. Faith sneezed as the powder went up her nose, then Molly applied a touch of rouge to her cheeks and lips.

"You look smashing, Miss Faith." Molly stepped back and looked at her handiwork approvingly. "Now we'll pop you into your dress, and you can go along to Lady Preston's chambers. She wanted to see you when we was done."

Faith stood, and Molly slipped the dress over her head. When she was buttoned in, she turned to go to her great-grandmother's room.

"Aren't you going to look at yourself, Miss Faith?" Molly's voice rose with astonishment.

"It doesn't matter, Molly. I'm sure you did the best you could." Faith was afraid to look. She knew she would look like a common straw hat decked out in lilies. She would have to be strong to face the ridicule and derision tonight. She wished she could stay in her room and plead a headache, but her great-grandmother would see right through that ruse.

She squared her shoulders and went down the hall. Pecking on the door, she stepped inside at Lady Preston's command. Her great-grandmother was seated on the edge of the bed. Her diminutive figure was swathed in blue lawn, and she turned to smile at Faith. Her mouth dropped open in a decidedly unladylike manner.

"Faith, my dear girl, you look lovely." She stood and approached Faith. "Turn around, let me see the back of you."

Faith twirled around, enjoying the feel of the silk swishing around her legs.

"Are you happy with your appearance?"

"I haven't looked," Faith admitted. She felt a shaft of curiosity. Did she really look all that different?

Lady Preston indicated the full-length mirror. "You must look, dear child."

Faith approached the mirror cautiously. The girl staring back at her didn't look anything like her. This young woman's golden hair gleamed in the late afternoon sun shafting through the window. Pulled loosely back from her face, the waves gave an added softness to the curve of her cheeks and lips. Curls hung down her back and over one shoulder in a most becoming way. The pink gown deepened the color in her cheeks and enhanced her slim figure.

She stared in awe at her image. But when she turned to go, she still limped, and a lump grew in her throat. No matter how different she looked, she still had an infirmity that would bring her ridicule tonight. Why had her great-grandmother bothered? It would be better to be her usual wallflower and not bring attention to herself. Nothing had changed. Nothing at all.

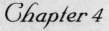

Chapter 4

Daniel pulled at the tight shirt collar with its bats wing tie squeezing his neck and mopped his brow with a handkerchief from his pocket. Why had he ever agreed to this party? He felt a stab of guilt over the way he'd neglected to tell Faith and Lady Preston the real reason for his interest in the club, but he didn't feel he had a choice.

The house hunkered on its site like a grand dame on her throne. The new electric lights crowned the look of opulence. Daniel approached the wide steps feeling like a worm wriggling on a hook. He was trapped and would simply have to endure the evening in the company of people who put money before the safety of the town, people who didn't care what their pleasures cost the working man below them. The thought was as uncomfortable as his evening dress clothes.

He followed a man and woman up the steps to the door. A butler greeted them and pointed them to the drawing room. He would have been able to find it himself by following the sound of the small orchestra. Daniel gazed around trying to see Faith or her great-grandmother but saw only strangers sipping punch and nibbling on dainty sandwiches. Serving maids dressed in white scurried among the guests, and he found a corner out of the way of the crush of people.

A flutter of pink caught his eye as a young woman entered the room. She limped, and his mouth dropped. Was that Faith? She turned toward him, and he saw the sweet curve of her cheek and the spill of golden hair. What had happened to the prim young woman with the hair scraped back into a tight bun? She was lovely. Another stab of guilt smote him, but he forced it away and went toward her.

"Miss Cole, how lovely you look," he said formally.

Her hazel eyes widened in astonishment, and a becoming pink rushed into her cheeks. She glanced away and studied the tips of his boots. "Thank you," she said nearly inaudibly.

Had she never received a compliment before? Daniel stared at her averted face and shrugged. Probably not. Remembering her plain gowns and hairstyle from their previous meetings, he realized why he'd never noticed how lovely she was. It was likely no one else had, either. Was her slight limp the reason she hid her true beauty that way?

"Mr. Nelson, how good of you to come." Lady Preston swept through the door behind her great-granddaughter. Dressed in black bombazine with a lace collar, she looked every inch the matriarch.

The music swung into a cotillion, and Daniel bowed. "May I have this dance, Lady Preston?"

She laughed and waved her white lace handkerchief at him. "I allow you asked merely for propriety's sake,

Mr. Nelson. Ask my great-granddaughter. She would enjoy it more than I."

Faith's color deepened, and she took a step back. "I. . . I don't dance, Mr. Nelson. My. . .my infirmity prevents a graceful pose." Though she stammered, she raised her eyes and met his gaze defiantly. "You go ahead and find another partner, though. I enjoy watching." Her eyes dared him to doubt her words.

In spite of her words, he saw the longing in her eyes and wondered if anyone had ever asked her to dance before. "Lady Preston has already denied me, and I love a cotillion," Daniel said. He took her elbow and led her firmly to the polished dance floor in the center of the room where other couples were forming sets of four people. "No one will notice your limp unless you let them," he whispered. "You're the most beautiful woman here." He smiled at her encouragingly. "Follow my lead."

She stiffened and pulled away a bit. Her hazel eyes flashed, and he knew his reference to her limp had annoyed her. He started to apologize but knew he would just embarrass her further.

The couples bowed to one another and the dance began. As they moved around the dance floor, Faith's cheeks flushed even more, but she followed him well. And Daniel ceased to notice her limp in the enjoyment of watching the wonder on her face.

"Might I get us some punch?" he asked when the dance was over and a waltz had begun.

"Yes, please."

He hid a grin at Faith's breathless voice. This had turned out to be more fun than he'd expected. He pushed his way through the crowd and snatched two glasses of punch from a maid carrying a heavily laden tray. Turning to make his way back to Faith, he overheard a conversation that caused him to stop and dawdle.

"I'm sick and tired of Cambria interfering in our business." The speaker, a heavyset man with florid cheeks and a drooping jowl, clenched his fist for emphasis. "They had the nerve to hire an engineer when we began work and even offered to pay to repair it their own way. We told them what they could do with their interference."

"And time has proven us right." A slender man with hair as thin as his frame rubbed his bulbous nose, then continued. "We've had severe floods the last two years, and the dam has held fine."

The third man snorted. His shock of white hair bristled with outrage as he shook his finger at the other two men. "Mark my words, gentlemen, we will live to rue the day this hunting club ever repaired that dam. And the sorry thing is that we in the valley below will have to pay the piper, not the club. They'll sit up here on the mountain all safe and secure while our homes are carried off by the flood waters."

"Lamont, there's no reasoning with you," the first man said. Shaking his head in disgust, he started to edge away. "You see trouble behind every bush. Why can't you just move on to a new topic of doom? The club has been a good thing for our businesses. Why, sales at my millinery shop have doubled in the past nine years, and it's all due to the club."

"Tell me that again after the water washes your goods away," the man they'd called Lamont muttered darkly. He stalked away and disappeared into the crowd.

The thin man chuckled nervously. "He sure seems convinced."

"He was convinced too many photographs with the Kodak snapshot camera would make you sick, too," the other man chortled. "He hates progress, that's all it is."

"Absolutely. There's no question the dam is safe."

Their voices faded as they moved away. Thoughtfully, Daniel carried the punch to Faith. He needed to check the water levels of the past two years' floods and see just where they stood.

Faith pleated the skirt of her dress with trembling fingers. When she'd first seen Daniel, she'd been nearly speechless with admiration. He looked very handsome in his black claw-hammer coat. The white shirt and black coat made his hair appear as dark and glossy as a bear's pelt. It was even neatly combed today. And had that really been admiration in his blue eyes? She didn't trust her own views about such things anymore. What if he was just after her great-grandmother's money? She resolved to guard her heart. She couldn't take another rejection like Adam's.

Daniel handed her a glass of punch. "Sorry I was so long." He offered no reason for his tardiness, and she didn't ask. They stood in silence a moment watching the dancers waltz around the floor.

Faith glanced at him from beneath her lashes. He seemed preoccupied now. What had happened to distract him? Her face flamed at the thought that maybe he had heard snickering about her limp. Maybe he was embarrassed to be with her. She hadn't heard any so far, but with her head in the clouds, she might not have noticed any tittle-tattle.

"Would we be allowed to go on a boat ride on the lake?" Daniel's face creased with a frown, and his gaze was far away.

"Certainly. My great-grandmother owns a very nice sailboat and said I could use it any time. I know nothing about sailing, though." Why didn't he ask her if she'd like to go? Faith was a bit piqued that he seemed to take her acceptance for granted. But could she blame him? He didn't see any other suitors knocking on her door. If he was even a suitor himself, and she wasn't at all convinced of that yet.

"I love sailing. I have a small boat myself on Lake Michigan." His gaze sharpened, and he finally stared directly at her. "Might you do me the honor of accompanying me on a boating trip, Miss Cole? You can choose the day."

The intensity of his gaze discomfited her for a moment. His blue eyes burned with purpose, and her mouth went dry. Why did it matter so much to him? She should refuse him, but the temptation to find out more about him was too great. "I. . .I should like that," she stammered.

The tension went out of his shoulders, and he nodded. The look of satisfaction that spread over his face puzzled her, but she was too happy at the thought of spending the day in his company to think much about it. Luckily, they would be in full view of the clubhouse at all times, so she thought she could talk her great-grandmother out of requiring a chaperone.

"Might I call on you tomorrow and discuss it?" he asked.

He caught her off guard, but she gathered her composure hastily. "If you come around eleven, we can have lunch with Grandmother before we go."

He nodded. "I should enjoy that. I like Lady Preston. She says what she thinks, which is a refreshing change."

What did he think of her? Was she too prickly, or did he like the way she spoke her mind, too?

He touched her hand and answered her unspoken question. "Her great-granddaughter takes after her."

Faith cut her gaze away before he read how much his words had touched her. Why did she feel this connection with him? She wasn't sure she liked it. The thought of being hurt again made her shudder inside. Adam's derisive words were burned into her memory. But this man drew her in ways she had never felt before. She had to step out and risk something, or she would never be able to live with herself.

Lady Preston approached. "Well, Mr. Nelson, I see you've been taking good care of Faith. I might allow you to squire me to supper. Joseph McCarty has requested Faith's presence beside him."

Faith gulped and stared at her great-grandmother. Joseph McCarty? He was old and married. His wife had just had a baby, so he'd come alone. She narrowed her eyes and stared at her great-grandmother.

Daniel frowned but offered his arm to Lady Preston. "I should be delighted," he said.

As she strolled away on Daniel's arm, her great-grandmother gave her a conspiratorial wink, and Faith understood what she was doing. She was trying to make Daniel jealous! She knew her great-grandmother meant well, but when was the last time she'd looked at Faith realistically?

Men didn't play such games for the likes of a crippled woman, and while her great-grandmother's schemes were a compliment, they were also an embarrassment.

Chagrined, Faith shook her head and scowled at Lady Preston, but her great-grandmother ignored her and went with Daniel to the dining room. How could she stop this before it went any farther? Normally she could hold her own with anyone, but Lady Preston was intimidating and used to having her own way. Events had gone too far already.

Joseph McCarty approached while she stewed over what to do. "I'd been wanting to chat with you about making a quilt for the new baby," he said. "Lady Preston told me you've won state awards for your quilts." He escorted her to the dining room and seated her at the table, then slid into the chair next to her.

The dining table easily held thirty people, and Daniel and her great-grandmother were at the other end of the table and on the same side, so Faith's view was obscured by other diners. She sighed and turned her attention to Mr. McCarty. "I enjoy quilting," she said politely.

"I should like to commission you to make something really unique and outstanding for my new daughter. Would you have time?"

Though she should be flattered, Faith found it hard to keep her attention on the man's request. "I should love to," she said distractedly. She heard Daniel laugh and leaned forward to peek down the table. Mary Carter was seated on his other side, and it was obvious he was enjoying her flirtations. So much for Grandmother's grand plans. Jealousy told Faith that while her heart was guarded, it was not completely shut away, in spite of all her attempts to do just that. Would Daniel even want to take her on the lake tomorrow?

A great sadness swept over her. She was here in borrowed plumage. Daniel knew what she was really like. Why would he be interested in a cripple like her when he could attract a beauty like Mary? She wanted to flee to her room like the little maid Cinderella in the fairy tale. If she left a glass slipper behind, would Daniel care enough to try to find her? Faith didn't think so. She could vanish like the mist, and no one would notice. Especially not Daniel.

Chapter 5

Faith pressed cold fingers against her cheeks and stared at her reflection in the mirror. Her stomach fluttered at the thought of spending the day with Daniel. It had been nearly two weeks since he'd first appeared at the path by Lake Conemaugh, and she still couldn't believe he'd shown up every day since then. She'd sent off a letter to her parents this morning but had refrained from any mention of her new acquaintance. She wished she could be sure Grandmother had been so circumspect in the letter she'd mailed off. She could just imagine the stories Grandmother had told Mama. She'd probably told them an eligible young man had come to see their daughter every day for the past two weeks. And today the weather promised to be fine enough to take a promised jaunt on the lake.

Poking at the wavy tendrils framing her face, she bit her lip and began to run a comb through her unmanageable tresses. She stared at her reflection then sighed and began to scrape the recalcitrant curls away from her face. She pinned the heavy hair securely in place. Her dove gray skirt with a white blouse completed the picture of a polished and demure young woman. Faith pushed away the stab of regret at the plain appearance she saw in the mirror. She was tempted to soften her hair just a bit, but then pressed her lips firmly together and turned away. A meek and quiet spirit was more important than mere outward beauty.

Holding her head high, she descended the staircase. The sound of Daniel's deep voice echoed from the parlor. She smiled and pushed open the pocket doors to the parlor. Her great-grandmother's face fell when she saw Faith's subdued appearance, but she merely nodded and didn't reproach her, and for that, Faith was relieved. One thing she found hard to adjust to was Grandmother's blunt speech.

Daniel stood, and his smile brightened when his gaze met hers. "Good. You've dressed casually."

"I asked Meg to pack you a lunch," Lady Preston said. "It's a lovely day, and you might as well spend it on the lake instead of around the dining table with an old woman."

"You're not old," Faith protested. "I love being with you." She tried not to stare at Daniel. He looked more the man she'd met on the train. His black hair was unruly, and he wore the casual clothes that seemed to fit his personality so well.

The pink in her great-grandmother's cheeks deepened at Faith's words. "That's lovely, dear girl. But you two young ones go along now and have fun. Don't forget your basket of food."

"You're welcome to come with us, Lady Preston," Daniel said. "Wouldn't you enjoy sailing around the lake?"

"I'm a bit tired," her great-grandmother said. "I think I'll have a nap after lunch. Will we see you for supper?"

Daniel hesitated a moment, and his gaze sought Faith's. She gave him no encouragement, but he nodded anyway. "I would be delighted to join you."

Faith didn't know if she was glad or sad. She didn't know how to read him. What did he want with her? Was he interested in her or her family? She gave a tiny sigh. Only time would tell.

She kissed her great-grandmother good-bye, then took Daniel's proffered arm and walked with him to the hall. Meg met them with a wicker basket which Daniel took in his other hand. The bright sunshine smote her in the eyes as they stepped out from under the protective overhang of the porch, and she stumbled. He steadied her, and the heat rose in her face. Her clumsiness always bubbled to the surface around him, and she inwardly vowed to be more careful. Surely she was capable of more grace if she slowed down and concentrated.

There had been an uncommon amount of rain so far this spring, and drops of moisture hung from the trees and dripped on their heads as they walked through the pines and massive trees. Faith pointed out the boathouse, but the sailboat already gleamed in the sunshine. Lady Preston had ordered the craft to be readied. It rocked in the gentle swells in its mooring at the dock.

Daniel helped her into the boat then handed her the basket. Untying the rope, he tossed it into the boat and hopped aboard himself. A wide grin stretched across his face, and he lifted his chin to catch the slight breeze. "I love the water," he told her. "Someday I want to own a house along one of the Great Lakes where I can look out on the waves from my parlor."

"So you don't intend to settle here?" Had she misunderstood him? She thought he was considering a move here.

He bit his lip and cast a sidelong glance at her. "I guess it wouldn't have to be a Great Lake," he said. "Any large lake, or even the ocean, would be fine."

He hadn't really answered the question. Faith frowned a bit and looked away uneasily. Lake Conemaugh glistened like a pearl in the sunshine. She could see Daniel's fascination with it.

Daniel fiddled with the oars then handed her one and showed her how to steer. The boat picked up speed, its bow cutting through the glassy lake surface like a shark fin through the sea. Faith leaned over the side a bit and let her hand trail in the lake. She was conscious of his gaze but avoided his eyes. She just wished she knew why he was seeking out her company.

Their path seemed to be a strange one, or so it seemed to Faith. Daniel had her guide the boat close to the shoreline instead of heading to the middle of the lake. His blue eyes scanned the shore, and he stopped the boat at the dam and stared at the top of the abutment for nearly fifteen minutes.

"What are you looking for?" Faith tried to see what he was looking at. His mouth was tight and pinched with his nostrils flared, but nothing seemed off kilter to her.

He took a deep breath and smiled, but it seemed forced to Faith. "I'm interested in dams," he said. "It's always been that way. My father built dams, and we looked at construction techniques every time we went anywhere. It's a habit. Sorry. I'll try to be better company."

His blue eyes begged for forgiveness, and she smiled.

"Do you suppose there are any fishing poles on board?"

He widened his eyes. "You fish?"

"I don't know how, but it can't be too hard." She had to bite the inside of her mouth to keep from laughing at his hopeful expression.

"I can teach you. Have you noticed the fish teeming under the water? Maybe we can talk Meg into fixing some for us." He lowered the sails, and the boat glided to a stop near some lily pads.

"You're assuming we'll catch some." She smiled cheekily.

He chuckled then rummaged in the bottom of the boat. "I'll have you know, I've won several bass fishing championships. It's not a question of catching 'some' but of how many." He found the tackle and poles under a tarp. "Here we are. But what can we use for bait?"

Faith looked around. "I'll check in the lunch basket." She flipped up the wicker lid and rummaged through the contents. "Would bread work?"

"Sure." He held out his hand, and she tore off a chunk of bread and passed it to him. He expertly baited the hooks then showed her how to toss her line into the water.

The breeze teased tendrils of curls from her neat bun, and she blew one out of her eyes.

"You look pretty with your hair looser," he remarked.

Faith felt the scarlet color run up her neck. She didn't know what to say. Men usually didn't compliment her. "Th—thank you," she stammered, feeling happier than she had in a long time. They fished for awhile in companionable silence, then she felt a tug on her line. Her red and white bobber dipped below the water, and she stared at it.

"Hey, you have a fish." Daniel moved closer. "Let me show you how to land him."

"I can do it." She stood and jerked up on the pole.

"Careful!"

Before Daniel had gotten the warning out of his mouth, she lost her balance and swayed in the boat. The fish came sailing out of the water straight for her head. She screamed and flinched back. The boat rocked with her sudden movement, and her arms flailed out but to no avail. The boat tipped over and flipped her and Daniel both into the water.

Faith came up sputtering and thrashing in the gentle swells. "Daniel!" What if he'd drowned because of her stupidity? She gazed around wildly. Her skirts, heavy with water, dragged at her, and sputtering, she went under again. When she came back up, Daniel was there supporting her.

"It's okay, I've got you." He guided her toward the boat and had her cling to the side while they righted the boat. "Let's get you into the boat," he told her.

She was very conscious of his nearness as he gripped her around the waist and helped her climb into the boat. She flopped onto the floor and lay gasping on the bottom of the boat like a fish. Daniel clambered over the side moments later. Sitting on the boat seat, he leaned forward and took slow, deep breaths. Faith's clothing clung to her in a sodden embrace, and she knew she must look terrible. So much for grace.

"Are you all right?" His blue eyes concerned, Daniel touched her shoulder.

"Only my pride is hurt," she admitted.

He stared at her a moment then burst into laughter.

"The look on your face as that fish came at you was priceless," he chuckled. "Did you think it would bite?"

It wasn't funny, but the corners of her mouth quirked. "It's really too bad of you to laugh," she said severely. She glanced away from his dancing eyes and saw her fishing pole floating forlornly in the lake. Her mouth quirked again, and she lost her fight for solemnity. Peals of laughter burst out, and she bent forward, holding her sides. "You have a lily pad in your hair," she chortled.

"You have leeches on your neck," he grinned.

"What?" She half stood and ran a hand over her neck.

He grabbed her arm and forced her back onto her seat. "I was just kidding!"

"That was cruel. Just for that, you get no lunch."

"I think you already took care of our lunch," Daniel said dryly. He pointed to the picnic basket floating half-submerged about eight feet from the boat. The lid had opened, and the contents floated nearby.

Faith covered her mouth to keep back the snicker. Where had her prim, ladylike manner gone? Her great-grandmother would be horrified to see the way she had behaved.

"I can see the laugh waiting to come out," Daniel said. "You might as well let it. No matter how proper you look the rest of our acquaintance, I'll always remember you with wet hair and lily pads. My water sprite."

"A gentleman wouldn't remind me," she said primly, but her mouth quirked again.

"I'm an engineer," he grinned. "Engineers have never been accused of being gentlemen."

She laughed and shook her head. "I'm not sure how to

act with you now that we've faced death together."

"Just be yourself," he said. "I much prefer the real Faith to the one with the prickly exterior who was afraid to have fun." He saw her shiver. "I should get you home to dry clothes."

Was that regret in his eyes? Faith didn't want to go in herself. What if the next time they met, their relationship was back to the strained way it had been? "We could always go for another swim first," she said.

Daniel gave a bark of laughter. "Your great-grandma would have me run out of town on a rail if I let you get sick."

"I'm not an invalid. A little dunking won't hurt me." As if to belie her words, she sneezed.

"See, you're getting sick already. We'd better go in."

"I suppose," she said glumly. "What about you? You're soaked, too."

"I have a feeling Lady Preston will find me some dry clothes if I ask her nicely." He raised the sails and pointed the boat toward the dock.

Faith's heart sank as she saw the shore approach. Out here on the water, she had been someone else. Now she would have to be Faith Cole, crippled spinster again. She much preferred water sprite.

Chapter 6

The fireplace warmed the last traces of the shivers away. Daniel glanced to Faith and was relieved to see she seemed no worse for her dunking. Her sense of humor and care for others drew him irresistibly. Most women he knew would have had hysterics at a dunking like that and drowned them both. When he swam to her, she had surrendered herself into his keeping without a murmur. The thought of her trust warmed him as much as the fire did.

Lady Preston bustled into the parlor. "Supper will be ready in a few minutes. Faith, is your hair dry?"

"Yes, Grandmother. I'm fine." She sneezed, a sound that resembled a soft exclamation rather than a sneeze.

Daniel found it hard to keep his gaze from her. Golden curls fell in riotous profusion down her back, and he found himself longing to plunge his fingers into those strands of gold. He felt they'd broken through into a new level of their relationship, but Faith seemed to avoid his gaze.

Lady Preston clicked her tongue. "You shall have a cold come morning, Faith. I had so hoped to introduce you to my friends at church tomorrow." She turned to

Daniel. "Would you care to attend worship with me tomorrow, Mr. Nelson?"

Daniel smiled. "I would be honored, Lady Preston." He hoped Faith was well enough to attend, too. He needed to see where she stood with the Lord. Just why that was so, he wasn't ready to investigate. He told himself it was only that she intrigued him with her proper exterior and prickly manner that melted away like snow in sunshine and revealed her true gentleness and good humor. There was something in her eyes that spoke to his soul, something he wasn't ready to name yet.

"I won't miss worship, Grandmother," Faith said firmly.

Daniel breathed a sigh a relief. She was a Christian, too. "Where do you attend, Lady Preston?"

"The Franklin Street Methodist church," she said. "I'll have my driver stop and pick you up on the way to church if you tell me where you are staying."

"Don't bother. It's only a couple of blocks from Hulbert House Hotel. I'll enjoy the walk."

"As you wish." She inclined her head. "Now I have a proposition to put to you, Mr. Nelson. You say you are an engineer. Do you suppose you would know enough about dams to inspect ours? There are yokels in the valley who have been stirring up dissension about the safety of our dam. I would like to put those outcries to rest once and for all. If I can have an expert report on the dam's safety, we might be able to do just that."

Daniel choked back his answer. How much of his knowledge did he dare disclose? Nathan had forbidden him to reveal his true purpose, but he was growing more and more uneasy with that order, especially after what he'd seen on the lake today. "What if I find the dam is unsafe?" he asked.

Lady Preston frowned, and she tilted her chin up. "You will find it perfectly safe," she declared.

Daniel thought few people contradicted that fierce blue gaze. If she ever found out his true mission, she would forbid him to see Faith. That thought distressed him for some reason. He pushed the uneasiness away. "I would be glad to look at the dam, Lady Preston, but I must tell you that if I think the dam unsafe, I will have no choice but to go to the town with my report. If you want someone who will simply be your mouthpiece, you've got the wrong man."

For a moment he thought he had pushed her too far. Her lips tightened, and her glare intensified. Then she looked to Faith and back to Daniel then relaxed her shoulders and nodded slowly.

"That integrity will make you more believable when you tell them the dam is safe," she said.

"Is there any chance of the dam being unsafe?" Faith asked. "And even if it was, the town is a long way away. Surely, the danger wouldn't be that great."

Her great-grandmother gave an exasperated sigh. "To hear the town people talk, it would be a flood of biblical proportions that would sweep the town away and kill hundreds, if not thousands."

"They're right." Daniel couldn't resist telling them the truth, and he saw Faith's eyes widen in horror.

"But there are women and children in the valley. How quickly would it come? Could they get to safety?" Faith sneezed again, but leaned forward and stared at Daniel.

"It would be much too fast for most people to get to

safety," Daniel said. Her interest gave him hope. If her great-grandmother wouldn't listen, maybe Faith would.

Lady Preston waved an imperious hand. "The dam is perfectly safe, and we will set this gossip to rest once and for all. Can you start investigating it tomorrow? I shall pay you well."

He pushed away the shaft of guilt at her offer. "I don't want any money. I have no duties at the iron works so I'm free to look around. I'll start on Monday." He could sense Faith's eyes on him. Turning, he smiled at her. "Maybe we could actually eat our lunch on the lake instead of feeding it to the fish," he told her.

Her cheeks bloomed color, but she didn't drop her gaze. "I promise to remain seated this time," she said. "In fact, maybe it would be best if I don't try to fish at all."

He grinned. "Or you could wear a bathing costume in preparation for the dunking."

She sneezed then smiled. "I think I will forgo the dunking."

"Coward," he said under his breath. The impish smile she sent told him she'd heard the comment. He was glad Lady Preston was hard of hearing.

The next morning Daniel dressed in his good suit and set out for the church. The quiet streets soothed him, and he loitered, gazing in the store windows as he passed. Other families strolled along on their way to church and greeted him as they passed. The height of fashion these days was to go walking on Sunday to show off the ladies' gowns. He wondered if Faith would enjoy doing that then remembered her limp. Did it pain her? If he found the right opportunity, he resolved to ask her. She was a plucky little thing. In spite of the ridicule she sometimes received, she held her head up high and went on with her life. He had to admire that.

The Methodist church, constructed of stone and the largest in town, was already filling up with worshipers. Daniel gazed around the packed pews until he saw Faith and Lady Preston. Faith saw him and lifted one gloved hand in recognition. He smiled and made his way toward her. Their pew was three rows from the front, and he had to dodge a woman with an eighteen-inch hat and a man gripping two toddlers by the hands.

Faith scooted over and let him sit nearest the aisle. "I was beginning to wonder if you were coming," she said softly.

"It was a lovely day for a walk. On the way here, I noticed there's a comedy playing at the Opera House called *A Night Off*. Would you like to go one evening?" As soon as he issued the invitation, he could have bit his tongue. He needed to begin to pull away, not continue to find ways to spend time with her. Once she found out his real mission, she would likely think he'd used her. Pursuing this relationship would only bring both of them pain.

"Grandmother might like to go, too," Faith said. "She loves to get out and be seen."

A smile tugged at her lips, and he grinned with her. Lady Preston was a force to be reckoned with. The service started, and they both settled in to listen to Reverend Chapman. Daniel kept glancing at Faith and was warmed by her obvious attention to the message. She nodded several times, once when the minister asked whether there was any interest in starting a soup kitchen for indigents.

When the service was over, Lady Preston invited him back for dinner, but he had already decided to decline if asked. He needed to see Nathan, and he didn't want to get any closer to Faith than he already had. The full story would have to be told very soon.

He tipped his hat to the ladies and made his way down Main Street. He stopped at the hotel long enough to eat then strolled down the street to Nathan's imposing brick home. White pillars flanked the wide steps like sentinels standing at attention. The butler answered his rap, took his coat and hat, and showed him to the parlor.

Nathan was seated on the sofa, with his wife seated across the table from him in a chair. They were engrossed in a game of cribbage, but Nathan looked up with a smile when Daniel came in. "Daniel, my dear boy, you are here just in time to save me. Alice was winning."

"I'm still winning. Daniel has only postponed your demise." His wife, her soft gray hair coiffed in a loose, becoming twist, stood and hugged Daniel. "Daniel, you look more and more like your father! How good to see you. I'll let you gentlemen talk while I see about some tea." She patted his cheek then hurried from the room.

Nathan indicated the chair his wife had just vacated. "Tell me what you've found out, my boy. I can see from your grim expression the news isn't good."

Daniel sighed. "No, Sir. First off, there is no discharge pipe so there's no way to lower the water level to repair the other problems I found."

Nathan shook his head. "John Fulton said the same thing nearly nine years ago, but the club wouldn't listen to him. What else?"

"The height of the dam has been lowered to provide room for a road and that has reduced the capacity of the spillway. I saw some evidence that they may have screened the spillway, I assume to prevent fish from escaping. I plan to go out again tomorrow to see just what they've done. I've also noticed there seems to be a sag in the middle. I was too far away to tell for sure, but that would be most serious if true."

Nathan leaned forward, his brown gaze intent. "You must get close enough to tell for sure. I don't know how you can do that without their cooperation."

"I have their cooperation." Daniel told him of Lady Preston's request and how he had met her great-granddaughter at the train station.

Nathan's approving smile did nothing to ease Daniel's feelings of guilt. "I intend to tell them the truth once I discover the true state of the dam," Daniel said. He stared into Nathan's eyes to let him know he would not be dissuaded, but his employer didn't argue.

"Fine, my boy. Whatever you say."

The words made Daniel feel worse not better. He did not want to see Faith's hazel eyes fill with the pain of betrayal. He suspected other men had hurt her, and that had been the reason for her initial prickliness. He resolved to try to explain the situation fully. Maybe she would even help once she knew the full story.

Chapter 7

Dress warmly, Dear," Lady Preston advised. "It may feel warm here in the shelter of the trees, but that wind cuts right through a body."

Faith had already laid out her wool cloak, but she nodded. Her great-grandmother didn't seem to realize she was a grown woman. She turned away and folded up the baby quilt she was working on. With her back to her great-grandmother, she checked the time on the little watch pendant around her neck. Eleven o'clock. Daniel should be there any time. Her heart sped up at the thought. Why was he seeking her out like this? She was beginning to believe he was attracted to her. It seemed an incredible thought to Faith, but there was no other reason for his attention. He didn't have to keep coming up the mountain. There were plenty of women in the Conemaugh valley. The last few weeks had been the most wonderful of her life.

"You're doing a marvelous job with your quilting, Faith." Lady Preston ran a wrinkled hand over the quilt top. "When your mother bragged of your ability, I thought she was exaggerating. Truly, I've never seen finer stitchery. Have you made one for your wedding chest?"

"I've never wasted the time, Grandmother. I'll never marry." She walked away and placed the baby quilt in her sewing basket. She didn't want her great-grandmother to see the hope in her eyes.

But her great-grandmother didn't argue with her. "Would you make me a wedding ring quilt? I love the design. I believe you could do it to my satisfaction."

"I'd be happy to. I should finish this small quilt within the week." She jumped at the rap on the door, and her breath caught in her throat. That must be Daniel. The butler answered the door, and Faith composed her expression into one of aloof welcome. He must never know the way he affected her. If he didn't feel the same, she couldn't face the humiliation.

The butler showed Daniel to the parlor. He wore a pair of dungarees and a warm flannel shirt. His shock of black hair had been ruffled by the wind and stood up in a shaggy thatch. He carried his black bag of tools in one hand and a basket in the other. "I brought lunch today," he said. "I had the cook pack it in waterproof containers."

Faith's lips quirked. "Are you saying you don't trust me?"

"I pointed no fingers," he said with a sly grin. "Maybe I'll tip the boat this time."

"Do try to stay dry today," Lady Preston admonished.

"We'll do our best," Daniel said, his grin widening. "You ready, Faith?"

Her name on his lips gave Faith a warm glow. He'd never spoken her Christian name before, and the way he said it was so casual, as though they'd been friends forever. She nodded and picked up her cloak. Kissing her great-grandmother's cheek, she followed Daniel out the door.

Their steps stirred the pine needles on the path, and

the pine scent mingled with the sweet fragrance of lilacs blooming in the thickets beside the path. The blue sky overhead promised a lovely day, and Faith felt her spirits lift. Daniel helped her into the boat then climbed in after her and untied the sailboat from its mooring. The breeze caught the sails, and he expertly guided the boat toward the dam. Faith caught herself admiring the way his muscles flexed under his shirt and turned her gaze away in embarrassment. What would he think if he saw her staring? The hot blood burned in her cheeks, and she avoided gazing in his direction and forced herself to examine the face of the dam.

Daniel trimmed the sails and dropped anchor. He sat in the stern and stared at the spillway.

It looked perfectly fine to her. She sighed in relief. The thought of the ravage all that water could rain on the valley below had given her nightmares last night. She sneaked a glance at Daniel. A muscle in his jaw twitched, and his eyes narrowed as his gaze traveled the span at the top of the spillway. Three carriages rattled along the top on the road and two of them passed near the center. Daniel's lips tightened, and he shook his head. He took a tool from his bag and sighted the top of the dam along it, then muttered.

"What did you say?"

He cleared his throat. "I was questioning the sanity of the person who lowered the dam enough to build that road. There's a definite dip in the center, too. Can you see it?"

Faith studied the lines of the dam and shook her head. "No, it looks level to me."

"It's hard to tell without the sextant, but believe me,

it's there." He sighed and straightened his back. "The dam is not safe, Faith. The entire valley below is in dreadful danger. If we get a heavy rain and the water begins to spill over the dam, it will erode right in the center where the dip is. If that happens, it's only a matter of hours before the entire dam simply gives way. Millions of tons of water will come surging into the valley. Thousands will die if that happens."

She shook her head more in denial of the picture of destruction he painted than a real disagreement with his pronouncement.

"It's true, Faith." He sighed. "Lady Preston may not believe it, either."

"It's not that I don't believe you. It's just that I find it hard to imagine that much destruction happening from such a beautiful lake. How likely is it that we would ever have a rain like you describe?" She wanted him to give her hope.

"Maybe not this year or next, but certainly sometime. It's no longer a question of if but of when. If we had several days of rain and the dam filled up and then just a few hours of really hard rain, the valley would be in big trouble."

"We must tell Grandmother. She'll make the men listen." Their lunch forgotten, Faith just wanted to get back to the cottage and tell Lady Preston. What if it began to rain? As if in answer to her unspoken question, the sun dimmed behind a heavy cloud, and she looked up. Storm clouds were building to the east, black and ominous. She caught her breath. They couldn't live with this constant fear of danger. Grandmother's friends, her cousins, they all lived in the valley. A sense of urgency made her restless.

Daniel nodded and raised the sails again. "We need

to hurry anyway, or we'll get wet after all. Your great-grandmother may never let you go out with me again."

In spite of her anxiety, his words warmed her. He acted as though it was a foregone conclusion that they would continue to see each other. She glanced at his face turned up into the wind. The gale had ruffled his hair even more and brought the color into his cheeks. He saw her gaze and smiled. She smiled back, at peace with their relationship for the first time. She would fight at his side for the town. Together they would convince Grandmother.

He tossed the rope to the attendant at the dock and jumped onto the planking, then helped Faith out of the boat. Tucking her hand into the crook of his arm, he matched his stride to hers, and they hurried up the path to the house. Nearing the porch, Faith suddenly realized she hadn't thought about her limp all day. Daniel never made her feel self-conscious about her infirmity. In his presence she felt whole and strong. She liked the feeling.

They found Lady Preston taking tea in the parlor with two gentlemen from the club. Roger Wilson and Alex Porter were both shareholders. Good. They would all hear the news together.

"You're back earlier than I expected," her great-grandmother said. Her gaze traveled over Faith's face.

"We must speak with you, Grandmother," Faith said, stopping to catch her breath.

"In private?" Lady Preston's stare traveled from Faith to Daniel and back again.

She smiled, and Faith suddenly realized her great-grandmother thought she was about to announce her engagement. She didn't know how she knew that, but she was certain of it. Alarmed, Faith glanced to Daniel and saw he had no inkling of Lady Preston's thoughts. "You might as well all hear what Daniel has to say."

Lady Preston's imperious stare searched Daniel's eyes. "Very well. Proceed, Mr. Nelson."

Daniel took a deep breath. "I have carefully examined the dam, Lady Preston, and I must tell you that it is not safe. My instruments show a dip in the center of the dam that will give way if water begins to spill over the dam. The spillway is clogged, intentionally, it appears, leaving no way to relieve the pressure when the dam reaches full capacity."

Roger Wilson snorted. "You go out for an idle sail and come back an hour later with the decision that it's not safe. Forgive me if I fail to see how you can make such a pronouncement." He turned to Lady Preston. "Where did you find this so-called expert, Ma'am?"

"I had examined it before today, Sir. Today was merely verification." Daniel took a step closer to the three older people.

Faith stared at Daniel. When had he examined the dam? And why? He saw her searching gaze and turned to face her. Taking a deep breath, he shattered the budding hope she'd nursed the past few days.

"I was hired by Cambria Iron Works to determine the safety of the dam. I'm sorry I deceived you, but it was vital that I find out the danger involved with this lake. I had hoped to find it safe, but the possibility of grave consequences is very real." He reached out a hand to touch her arm, but she flinched away.

The words were a death knell to her dreams. He was just like every other man she'd met. His attention was a screen he'd used to shutter his true purpose. She swallowed hard and took a step back. He mustn't know how close she'd come to loving him. Tears blurred her vision, and she blinked them away fiercely. She tilted her chin up and stared at him with contempt. "You used your friendship with the family to gain access to the dam, is that what you're saying?"

He ran a hand through his hair in that way she'd found so endearing mere hours before. "Yes. No. I mean, at the beginning that was true, but I soon found myself caring for you, Faith. For your courage and gentleness." He held out a placating hand. "Can't you see this issue is bigger than our courtship? The lives of thousands of people are at stake."

"This is balderdash, Lady Preston," Alex Porter sputtered. "We've employed a true expert to oversee all repairs. The dam is perfectly safe. Clearly this man is only trying to impress your great-granddaughter."

Daniel gave Faith a beseeching gaze and turned back to face the other three. "You want to believe that because to believe anything else would show you how you let money and profits come before people. Get an opinion from another civil engineer. You'll find I'm right." He held up a hand when Roger Wilson would have interrupted. "The worst thing about this dam, gentlemen, is that there is no way to fix the problem. The lack of foresight in closing up the drain holes is near criminal. The lake cannot be drained to make repairs. If we get a heavy rain and the water begins to spill over the top, the communities in the Conemaugh valley are doomed. Take a look around you. The rivers are already running high. We've had nearly one hundred days of rain already this year!"

Roger Wilson sputtered again and hefted his considerable bulk to his feet. "This is ridiculous!" He pointed a pudgy finger at Daniel. "I shall call security and have you thrown off the property. If I find you here again, you will be arrested for trespassing."

Daniel gave a desperate glance toward Faith, but she bit her lip and turned away. If he thought she would help him after his deception, he was mistaken. It was all she could do to hold on to her composure enough to keep from rushing to her room and weeping.

"I'll go," Daniel said slowly. "But I have to report this to Cambria Iron Works. I'm sure they will tell the town. This is too important to hide."

"If you get the town riled, we shall have to sue you for slander," Wilson retorted. "You'll run us out of business."

"That's the problem. You see only dollars, not lives." Daniel stalked to the door. "I pray to God the dam doesn't break until we can find a way to fix it. Otherwise, death and destruction will be on your greedy hands."

Faith watched him go with a broken heart. It felt like the image in her mind of the dam breaking. Just a crack at first, but widening until the pain came crushing down and destroyed her. She kept a tight rein on her emotions until she heard the front door slam then whirled and raced up the steps to her room. She needed to lay it before the Lord. Her great-grandmother called her name, but the tears wouldn't be held at bay any longer.

Chapter 8

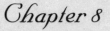

T he betrayal in Faith's once trusting gaze haunted Daniel. He squeezed his eyes shut, willing the vision away, but it stayed with him. She'd struggled valiantly against the tears, but he'd still seen the shimmer of moisture in her eyes. He hadn't meant to hurt her. She had become important to him. Too important. He needed to keep his focus on his job, his goals for his life. He wasn't ready for a wife yet. *A wife.* Where had that thought come from? His eyes widened with the realization that the thought of Faith as his wife had been at the back of his mind.

The cold, hard rain began again as the train pulled into the station. Daniel bounded down the steps and made his way to the Cambria Iron Works office. As he strode past the front desk, the secretary tried to stop him from entering Nathan's office, but Daniel brushed past her and threw open the office door.

Nathan looked up from his conference with another man. An expression of irritation crossed his face until he saw who it was. "Daniel, my boy, I was just talking with Joshua, one of my foremen, about your investigation."

He eyed Daniel's thunderous countenance. "Do you have bad news?"

"The worst kind," Daniel said. He crossed the room and dropped into the worn leather chair beside Nathan. "The dam is totally unsafe. It's already near capacity. If we get a real downpour, it will begin to run over the top. There is a depression in the center. It's only a matter of time before the whole dam gives way. We have to come up with a way to drain the lake and repair it. With no drainage holes, it will be difficult."

Nathan rubbed the side of his nose and stared at Daniel. "How much time do we have?"

Daniel shrugged. "It could fail tomorrow or five years from now. But sooner or later, it *will* fail." At least Nathan was taking the danger very seriously.

The other man, about forty with a thatch of red hair, finally spoke. "We need to get the town on our side. With enough public outcry, the club will have no choice but to repair the dam. We will renew our offer of financial assistance, won't we?"

"Of course," Nathan said. "Tomorrow is Memorial Day so we won't get anything done until after the holiday. I'll contact George Swank. As editor of the paper, he has an obligation to the people, even if he disagrees with our findings."

Daniel sighed, and the tension eased out of his shoulders. It felt good to turn the problem over to someone who could do something about it.

Nathan rose and clapped him on the shoulder. "Thank you, my boy. You've done a fine job. I'd like to have you stay on with Cambria Iron. I have a position in mind for you."

"I've already accepted another position in Chicago,

but thanks just the same." Daniel wanted to be as far away as possible. Maybe if he didn't see Faith's honest hazel gaze, he would be able to forget her. And he had to forget her. She would never forgive this betrayal. He'd seen that in her eyes. Why had it taken him this long to realize he cared for her?

"If you change your mind, there's always a spot here for you," Nathan said.

Daniel thanked him again and went past the secretary who glared at him in reproach as he stepped out into the driving rain. This was the twelfth day of rain so far this month. While he didn't see an imminent danger, it would surely come if this rain continued. Hurrying toward the Hulbert House, he skirted mud puddles and carts splashing dirty water. The doorman opened the front doors, and Daniel knocked the moisture off his hat then took the elevator to his room. He would get out his Bible and turn this problem over to God. It was well beyond his own abilities to fix.

People crowded Main Street, and Faith stood on tiptoe to see past the sea of hats and coats. The parade to the cemetery should be starting anytime. She found herself looking for Daniel's familiar black hair and forced her gaze back to the street. She didn't want to admit, even to herself, that Daniel was the real reason she'd been eager to attend the Memorial Day celebrations.

The city was in its merriest mood. Flags flew from porches and yards, banners waved in the breeze, and the spring flowers added even more color and cheer to the holiday gaieties.

"The parade is late, as usual," Lady Preston remarked. She held Faith's arm for support in a surprisingly firm grip. "I've never seen the streets so full. It must be that Ancient Order of Hibernians' annual convention."

Her faded blue eyes scanned the melee, and Faith wondered if she was looking for Daniel, too. She'd voiced her disappointment with him many times in the past twenty-four hours. The band started playing about two-thirty, and the parade headed out. Women waved hand-kerchiefs, and men cheered as the veterans marched by. Some of the Grand Army men looked as though the hike was a bit more than they were up to as they came huffing by with red faces.

The crowd followed the parade to the cemetery, but Faith made sure her great-grandmother was safely en-sconced at the café with a cup of tea before she left for the rest of the parade. Moving with the crowd, Faith thought she saw Daniel's familiar dark head once, but it may have been wishful thinking, and she soon lost him in the crush of people.

On the way back, around four o'clock, a light rain, almost more a mist than even sprinkles, began to fall. Faith huddled inside her cloak as the cold dampness pen-etrated her bones. She would be thankful to get home to the steam heat. The disappointment at not seeing Daniel was as piercing as the cold. But why should she be disap-pointed? He had betrayed her like every other man in her life except her father. He'd had a hidden agenda and had used her to get close enough to the dam to promote his own views. She wished she could forget him as easily as she had every other man who had betrayed her.

Glancing around at the people, Faith trembled with

an awful premonition. Could the dam be as dangerous as he said? She didn't want to believe anything he said, but the weaknesses he'd pointed out made sense. Shrugging the thought away, she refused to think about him any more. She would get her great-grandmother and go to their warm home and forget all about Daniel Nelson.

By the time they got back to the house, the rain had stopped, but the road from the train was muddy. Several times the mud mired the carriage and the coachman had to get down and shove it with his shoulder to get it unstuck. The scent of mud and wet vegetation hung on the porch, and Faith was glad to step into the brightly lit hall. The butler took their dripping cloaks, and Faith insisted Lady Preston settle into the comfortable leather chair by the fire.

The rain began again around nine. Several times during the night Faith awoke to the heavy drum of rain on the roof. She thought about getting up to check the level of the lake but knew such a thought was foolish. She wouldn't be able to see anything in this black night without going outside. At one point the house rattled as if a train were racing by right beside the house. Faith huddled in her bed and prayed for morning to come. The strange foreboding she'd felt since the rain began wouldn't go away, and she needed to see what was happening outside.

She finally got up about seven-thirty. No one else in the house was up yet so she decided to go to the clubhouse for breakfast and to see if there was any news. She pulled on gum boots and her cloak and managed to make it down the path. The rain had stopped, but a heavy mist hung in the air like a milky veil of wet fog. There was water everywhere. What had been a creek beside her great-grandmother's house was a raging torrent.

Even at this early hour, the dining room was full of people, mostly men. Her heart rushed to her throat at their grim expressions. "What is it? Has the dam failed?"

John Parke, the clean-shaven young engineer, stared into his coffee cup. "Not yet," he said.

A band tightened around Faith's chest at the hopelessness in his voice. "It's about to?"

"Unless we can find some way to release the water, it will begin to run over the top of the dam in a matter of hours." He took a gulp of coffee and got to his feet. "I need some volunteers."

"What about the valley?" Faith's heart hammered in her chest. Daniel was in the valley.

"We'll send word if the situation worsens." Several men followed him to the door.

Faith couldn't sit inside. She had to see for herself. She traipsed behind them to the porch and down into the mud. When they got to the dam, she saw men and boys trying to throw up a small ridge of earth along the top of the dam to raise the height. They weren't having much success with the hard-packed dirt in spite of their picks and shovels. Faith gasped as she neared the dam. The water level was only two feet from the top.

At the west end of the dam, another ten or twelve men tried desperately to cut a new spillway, but their meager ditch would not be done soon enough to help. Faith knew she couldn't do much, but she could help by supplying hot coffee and food. She whirled and dashed back to the clubhouse. The next several hours were a blur of carrying pots of coffee and trays of food.

Ready to drop with fatigue, her leg aching abominably, she stopped short at a familiar head of black hair. Her mouth dry, all she could do was stare.

"The only thing that could save us now is to tear out the iron fish screens in the main spillway," Daniel said. He gestured with an emphatic hand. "It would increase the capacity of the spillway."

"That will ruin the dam," Colonel Unger objected. As president and overall manager, his word was law.

Daniel clenched his fists and took a step nearer. "The club's shortsighted profit-taking is what got us into this mess! You have the chance to save lives here. Do it before it's too late."

"Several others have suggested that, but I fail to see how that could help."

"Do it!" Daniel roared. He strode to the dam and began tearing at the debris with his bare hands.

Colonel Unger watched a moment then motioned for some of his men to assist Daniel. But it was no use. The pressure of the debris jammed the screens against the dam. Daniel sighed and turned slowly. His eyes met Faith's, and the emotion that jumped into his eyes made her heart pound.

He came slowly toward her. "It's happening, Faith. Will you help me? The town is already flooded. We need to warn them and begin evacuation."

"I'll make that decision," Colonel Unger snapped.

"I'm making it for you." Daniel took Faith's arm and led her toward the clubhouse. The warm press of his fingers bolstered her flagging strength.

"Why did you come?" she asked softly.

He was silent a long moment. "I had to find out if the

dam was holding, but more importantly, I had to see that you were all right." He stopped in the track and pulled her closer.

Staring into his blue eyes, hope fluttered in Faith's breast. Was that concern, or maybe even love, in his gaze? He ran his fingers along her jaw, and Faith felt the tenderness in his touch. Tenderness from a man other than her father was a new experience, one she wanted to savor.

"I love you, Faith. I tried to fight it, but I couldn't. I want to marry you when this is all over."

Faith began to tremble. "Ma—marriage? Are you sure, Daniel?"

"Very sure." He tucked her hand into the crook of his arm and led her toward the carriage. "Now let's get to town and see about saving some lives."

Her heart soared into the clouds pressing down on the mountain. He loved her! She would have an opportunity to wear Mama's wedding gown after all. If the dam didn't sweep them all away before the night was over.

Chapter 9

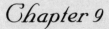

Every stream, every creek was a raging torrent. Faith stared out the train window at the wet world outside. As the train stopped at the South Fork station, she saw John Parke go racing by on a horse. Colonel Unger had evidently decided to warn the valley. Faith shared a relieved glance with Daniel. She clung to his hand; the comforting warmth and pressure reassured her.

At the Johnstown station, Daniel helped her down the train steps, and they stared in dismay at the town. Water from two to ten feet deep covered the streets of the town.

An old man in a shapeless gray hat shook his head. "It's higher than it was in eighty-seven. I ain't never seen the town flooded like this. Good thing the dam held."

"It won't for much longer," Daniel said.

The old guy shrugged. "That's what they say every year. I don't reckon there's any reason to think this year is any different." He didn't wait for a reply but splashed off toward Main Street.

Daniel shook his head. "I shouldn't have brought you

here, Faith. It's much worse than I expected."

"I wanted to be where you are. At least John Parke has warned them by now, and we can help with the evacuation." She smiled and squeezed his arm.

"Let's find where they are putting the people. You can help there while I see if I can find a boat and bring people to the shelter." Daniel looked down at the muddy water then back at Faith. With a grin, he swung her into his arms. "Maybe I should be thanking God for this opportunity," he whispered.

Sheltered in his arms, Faith clung to his shoulders. The muscles rippled under his shirt, and his breath came hard as he labored through the water and mud. Knowing he loved her gave her the freedom to loosen the rein she'd held on her emotions. Love for him tightened her throat and released a joy that blossomed inside her soul like a sunflower reaching for the bright rays of morning. Her fear of rejection was gone as completely as though it had never existed. God had truly blessed her in this one shining moment.

Pandemonium reigned in town. There was no real shelter set up. Most families had gone to family or friends. Daniel stared around the ravaged town then pointed to a warehouse on the hillside. "That would likely be high enough to be spared when the dam gives way. Let's set up a shelter there." He carried Faith to the steps leading up the hill and set her feet on the stony path.

"You go help the men," she said, touching his cheek. "I'll organize the shelter."

He hesitated as though unsure of leaving her then nodded. "I'll be back as soon as I can with a load of people." He turned and slogged through the knee-deep water.

At the Hulbert House he turned and lifted his hand then rounded the corner and disappeared from Faith's view.

She whispered a prayer for his safety and made her way up the path to the warehouse. Other people had already found their way inside. Frightened faces turned toward her when she pushed the door open. Smiling reassuringly, she instructed some of the men to clear the aisles and make room for the people. The thought of Daniel's trust in her to help filled her with fresh courage and determination to make a difference here.

By four o'clock nearly two dozen people had found their way to the shelter. Faith's leg ached, but it was a pleasant sort of pain. One of accomplishment and purpose. The people sat in their spaces with what few belongings they'd managed to save and talked in subdued voices. She organized men to go after food and had them put it on her great-grandmother's bill.

A little after four she stepped outside for a moment of fresh air. The torrent of rain had lessened to a drizzle, and she leaned against the rough siding and stared down at Johnstown. The flood waters had risen, and the roofs of nearly submerged houses poked through the expanse of water like the backs of some strange kind of turtle. A strange rumble and vibration shook the building against her shoulder.

Then a train whistle blared out. It didn't stop but kept blowing a frantic warning that brought her heart to her mouth. The rumble grew to a roar, an avalanche of sound that nearly deafened her. She knew instantly what had happened. "The dam!" she screamed. She raced along the top of the hill and searched for Daniel's familiar thatch of black hair. Praying frantically, she missed the onslaught of the huge wave until the roar became a shriek of destruction.

Barreling down the mountain, the black wave, churning with trees, bits of houses, animals, and other debris, towered nearly forty feet. A black mist that looked like smoke preceded the wave like an advance guard of destruction. Faith's blood roared in her ears nearly as loudly as the crash of buildings going down and glass shattering. She looked on in dumb horror as the water swept toward the area of town just below where she stood.

Houses blew apart, and people clung to bits of wreckage as they swept past her perch. She leaned out to try to catch the hand of a man clinging to a barrel of pickles, but though her hand brushed his, the force of the water flung him past her. Then she thought she heard someone call her name. Scanning the boiling mass of debris, her heart stopped at Daniel's face, black with mud and red with blood from a cut on his head. He clung to the shattered remains of a roof.

He shouted as the wave bore him past, but the roar was too loud to make out the words. She reached out trembling hands toward him, but he was too far away to touch. The expression in his eyes told her good-bye, then the roaring wave bore him past her beseeching gaze in a moment. The strength ran out of her legs, and she sank to the ground as Daniel disappeared on the crest of the wave. Too stunned to cry at first, she lay there in the mud as the awful truth penetrated her numbed mind.

Gone. Daniel was gone. There was no way he could have survived that churning mass of destruction. The horror of that knowledge finally worked its way past the cocoon of disbelief, and weak tears leaked from her eyes.

She was tempted to fling herself into the water and join him. But he wouldn't want that. He'd put her here to keep her safe. But how did she deal with this despair? She moved her lips in a silent plea to God. Gripping, wrenching pain assaulted her soul then calmed. Daniel was in God's presence. She would see him again someday. The thought brought a small breath of comfort.

She lost track of time and had no idea how long she lay prostrate in the mud with the rain falling on her back. The shattering of her hopes left her feeling as though she walked in a dream. Finally, the screams in the town turned to shouts of purpose as men began to search for survivors. She slowly got to her feet. Daniel was gone, but he would expect her to carry on and help those who were lucky enough to survive. When this was over, she would go home to Oregon and seek the comfort of her parents' arms.

"God is our refuge and strength, a very present help in trouble. Therefore will not we fear, though the earth be removed, and though the mountains be carried into the midst of the sea." The familiar verses of Psalm 46 gave her strength through the long night. She would see Daniel again someday in heaven. His eyes had promised that as the wave carried him past. The thought brought a modicum of comfort to her aching heart.

Chapter 10

The black wave carried Daniel along like the roller coaster he'd ridden in Chicago. The memory of the white oval of Faith's face sustained him in the face of certain death. He prayed for her safety, not his own, as the flood waters barreled down Main Street.

All around him he saw people clinging to bits of wreckage. One roof that floated past held nearly thirty people. A man and a little girl on a mattress went shooting past his perch at one point. He prayed for them, too. His arms grew numb from the strain of hanging on, and he knew he would have to let go soon. Oddly enough, he felt no fear at the thought of death. The thought of seeing the face of his Savior gladdened his heart though he sorrowed for the pain his death would bring Faith and his parents.

Just when he thought he couldn't hold on another minute, the roof he clung to shuddered and caught on a tree that was still partially embedded on dry land. Two fingernails tore loose, but Daniel managed to hang on. When the pitching of the roof stopped, he managed to get to his knees and look around. For the first time, he thought he might survive this. If he was careful, he might be able to crawl along the tree trunk to safety.

His breath whistled through his teeth with the strain of trying to maintain his balance. The rough bark cut into his knees and the palms of his hands, but he scarcely noticed. Inching his way along, he managed to get to where the tree branched into two trunks, neither of which looked substantial enough to hold him. He took a deep breath and prayed for guidance, then chose the one with the fewest twigs sticking up.

The branch shuddered with his weight but held as he made his way toward shore. Just as he put a hand into the mud of solid ground, he felt the tree shift. Throwing his body forward, he gripped the ragged remains of a telegraph pole in time to prevent being swept back into the maelstrom.

His strength spent, he dropped his head into the mud and whispered a prayer of thanks for his deliverance. Before the darkness claimed him, he asked God to keep Faith safe until he could find her again.

When Daniel awoke, light streaked the eastern sky. He tried to move, then groaned with the pain of his torn body. He managed to sit up and looked out on the devastating scene that had once been a prosperous city. He saw mostly huge piles of rubbish and vast, vacant tracts of mud. A few buildings had survived: the Methodist Church, Alma Hall, and Union Street School. But for every building that had survived, dozens more were totally swept away. His hotel, the Hulbert House, was totally gone.

Gritting his teeth against the pain, he managed to get to his feet. He lurched down the street toward where he'd last seen Faith. He had to find her. Though an inner desperation drove him, he couldn't ignore the cries for help. By midday he still had gone no farther than Jackson Street. Daniel dragged people from the mud and dug through debris for hours though his body protested. He was in much better shape than some of the others, a fact for which he thanked God.

It was nearly sunset when he finally managed to begin the climb to the warehouse where he'd last seen Faith. Though exhausted, his steps were lightened with the knowledge that he would soon gaze into her face again. He pushed open the door and gazed around the cavernous room that held moaning people to its full capacity. His heart sank when he didn't see her blond head. Fear gripped him. Could she have fallen into the flood as it passed? He'd seen her in the first stages of the water's rampage.

Then he saw a familiar set of slender shoulders and realized why he hadn't noticed her at first. Her shining blond hair was matted with mud and hung like a filthy black veil down her back. Weariness and numb despair had etched grim lines in her face. She walked the floor with a crying baby in her arms and murmured words of consolation.

Daniel stood for several long moments and drank in the sight of her. Though she'd been through the fire, she had found the courage to help those around her. Pride welled up as he watched her gently lay the sleeping child beside his mother. She turned and pushed a lock of lank hair out of her face.

Her eyes widened when her gaze caught his. A whisper of breath escaped her lips, and her face whitened. She reached out a trembling hand, but she was still too far away to touch him. "Daniel?" The words were tentative as though she feared he was a mirage born of fatigue.

In three quick strides he reached her side and took her in his arms. She reached up her hands and placed them on the sides of his face. "I was sure you were dead," she whispered. She wiped a streak of mud from his cheek.

"I promised to marry you," he said with a grin. "I'm a man who keeps his promises."

Tears shimmered in her hazel eyes, the only clear spot on her dirty face. "I'll never doubt that again," she whispered before his lips came down to meet hers.

Epilogue

Faith put the last stitch in the wedding ring quilt for her great-grandmother then stood and stretched the crick out of her back. The past few months had been a flurry of activity as they'd helped the people in the valley and made plans for the future. Over two thousand people had died in what the papers were calling the worst natural disaster in modern times. The devastation had brought help from all over the world, but nothing could bring back those poor souls who had perished. Entire families had been wiped out in seconds.

Slowly, so slowly, the town was rebuilding, and her wedding was nearly here. But Faith had been determined to finish the quilt for Lady Preston before the wedding. Grandmother had let her choose fabrics from the attic, and it was a real heirloom of her mother's family. She wanted to give it to her great-grandmother before she and Daniel left for Michigan.

Carrying it to the parlor, she gave it a snap and spread it out for her great-grandmother to admire. "It's finally finished, Grandmother. And not a minute too soon. Mama has been hounding me to go through the chest."

"I have not been hounding you," Charity said, getting to her feet. "Faith, it's exquisite! Your best work ever."

Her great-grandmother merely stared at the quilt, then Faith saw tears begin to fall down her wrinkled cheeks. "Don't you like it, Grandmother?"

"It's lovely, dear child." She took a deep breath and touched the quilt with a wrinkled hand. "It's also my wedding gift to you and Daniel."

Faith's jaw dropped. "I did it for you," she protested.

"It's a bit of family you can take with you to your new home. You said you'd never made a quilt for yourself. Now you'll have something to put in that beautiful chest your father made." Lady Preston patted Faith's hand. "Why don't you put it away now?"

The lump in her throat threatened to choke Faith, but she nodded and carried the quilt to her room. She knelt beside the chest, and the sounds of her mother's soft voice downstairs as she gave the cook directions for the wedding dinner faded away. Lifting the lid, she held her breath and drew out the silken folds of the creamy white wedding dress. Beneath it was a matching garter, a string of pearls, and tarnished silver candlesticks. Cricket had gone to Canada and married a man there, so the items had never been used since her parents' own wedding.

Touching items gently, she took them from the chest as well. She would use them all at her wedding. The last item was a folded piece of paper. She took it and opened it up. Tears flooded her eyes as she read the tender words her mother had written. Fishing for her handkerchief, she sat in her rocking chair and took some paper from her writing box. She would write her own note as well.

To the loved ones who come after me,
As I write these words, the town of Johnstown
is rebuilding from a terrible disaster. In the midst of
it all, my Daniel and I prepare to begin our new life
together out of the ruins of this catastrophe. But the
one thing I've learned through all this, my darlings,
is that God goes with us even through the hard times.
We can trust Him when the very heavens roar and
the foundations of the earth seem to shake. There is
no trial too great for our Lord, no circumstance so
black that He is not to be found. When all seems lost,
simply trust Him. He will guide your path and bring
you safely home. This is the legacy I leave you.
Faith Cole Nelson

Her mother tapped on the door. "Enough of this," Charity said. "Your father is pacing and tugging at his tie, and Daniel will be here any minute. We must get you into your dress. I'll press it now."

The door opened. Margaret, Callie, and Constance were already dressed in their new finery, identical gowns of sea foam green, and they filed into Faith's room. Margaret carried baby Thomas, who slept through the frantic preparations with his thumb corked in his mouth. The girls watched with awed faces as Charity slipped the lace gown over Faith's head. The identical sighs from her three sisters encouraged her. Though she knew Daniel loved her for who she really was, it was good to know she wouldn't disgrace him this day.

Her mother arranged Faith's curls on her shoulders, and they were ready. The girls went down first, then Charity gave her a final kiss. "Your Daniel is a fine man," she said softly. "May you have as many years full of love and laughter as your father and I have had."

Faith swallowed the tears burning in the back of her throat. "Thank you, Mama." It was all she could say.

Her mother squeezed her hand again then slipped out the door. Faith followed her moments later. Standing at the top of the steps, she saw Daniel turn and stare at her. His eyes widened, and he held out his hand to her. The love in his eyes drew her forward, and she stepped down the stairs to meet her future. She was accepted and beloved, by both her Lord and her man.

COLLEEN COBLE

Colleen and her husband, David, raised two great kids, David Jr. and Kara, and they are now knee deep in paint and wallpaper chips as they restore a Victorian home. Colleen became a Christian after a bad car accident in 1980 when all her grandmother's prayers finally took root. She is very active at her church where she sings and helps her husband with a young marrieds Sunday school class. She enjoys the various activities with the class, including horseback riding (she needs a stool to mount) and canoeing (she tips the canoe every time). She writes inspirational romance because she believes that the only happily-ever-after is with God at the center. She now works as a church secretary but would like to eventually pursue her writing full time.

BAYSIDE BRIDE

by Kristin Billerbeck

Dedication

To my grandpa Arnold Bechtel,
my first knight in shining armor,
who taught me what it was to be spoiled!
And to the Highway Community and its members
for keeping me grounded
and for always pursuing God's Truth in
a place where it's often hard to find.
And finally, to Colleen Coble
for being my "adult conversation" each day
and helping me hone the writing craft.

Prologue

December 1928

Josephine Mayer looked to her younger sister, afraid that her teary eyes gave the news without words. "It's done. Father has married her." Jo tossed the letter aside and hugged her sister.

Claire sniffled on her shoulder. "She stole everything we have, Jo. She took Mother's wedding gown, the family chest, and now our father."

"It's all possessions, Claire, nothing more. Father is not gone; he will return to us." Jo tried to be stoic for her sister's sake, but she understood the enormity of their father's actions. It meant nothing would ever be the same. Adulthood would come much earlier than they had planned.

Claire couldn't hold her emotions as easily. "Father will be back, but it will never be the same. Marian should have been married in Mother's gown. Instead she married in gray wool while that *creature* took the gown. It was our gown," Claire wailed. "Generations of brides, our legacy, gone. Does that woman have no heart at all?"

"I'm sure she was only doing what she thought would please Father." Josephine looked to the floor, afraid that her eyes would give away her own struggling emotions. "We just have to remember to keep it to ourselves and not let Grandma Faith know. Her health is far more important than a box with some keepsakes in it."

"The dress probably hung well above Agnes's ankles, she is so unbearably tall." Claire clicked her tongue distastefully, pulling away. "I can only hope Dad remembered the beautiful vision Mother was in that gown." Claire picked up a silver-framed photo of their mother in younger, healthier years. "I'll have this waiting just in case he's forgotten." She placed the photo on the cherry hutch near the front door. The reminder wouldn't be missed by Agnes; nothing ever was.

Josephine garnered contempt for her new stepmother, but she held her tongue for Claire's sake. Harmful words served no purpose now. "Mother would have gladly let her heirlooms go, if it made Father happy."

"Father will never be happy with *her*, Jo. How can you even think such a thing? He only married her to give me a mother while he's working on the rail. A railroad man with children needs a wife, I suppose." Claire, although only thirteen, was an astute child. Sometimes too intelligent for her own good. "I suppose it's all my fault. Father couldn't possibly love Agnes."

"Practicality often makes up for a lack of love, Claire." Jo knew better than to condescend to her little sister, but Claire needed a legal guardian. At seventeen, Jo wasn't quite old enough. The irony of her age only fueled her annoyance.

Claire stamped her foot childishly. "Father gave away Mother's only legacy because Agnes is an old maid! No dressmaker would fit her with such a fine gown of white lace without laughing hysterically. Seed pearls indeed, on a woman her age! She probably looked like a man in Mother's beautiful dress."

"Now, Claire, we mustn't be disrespectful. This is our new stepmother, whether we like it or not. Father provided for us the way he saw fit." Jo tried to be the voice of reason, though it pained her. "We shall welcome her into the house just like the day Father brought her home as the hired help." Jo squared her shoulders, determined to make the best of the situation. Their father's job as a railroad man took him away from them most of the time. He didn't have time to provide food *and* his presence. Unfortunately, he also hadn't the time to see Agnes for who she really was—a selfish, vindictive woman with her own agenda.

Jo would make the best of it, if only for Claire's sake. Jo would take the rail pass her father's job provided and pave a way for them. Their new stepmother certainly wouldn't take responsibility. Agnes would continue on as before, acting the proper mother for Father's eyes, and turning into a raving madwoman when he left. A virtual battleground awaited, unless Jo did something to change it.

Jo would find refuge with their sister Marian in California. She hated leaving Claire alone, but the quicker Jo earned her own money, the quicker Claire would be free of Agnes. Any other alternative was only temporary.

Once Claire was settled, Jo would send for the wedding chest. Certainly, their father wouldn't deny them their heritage, the last vestige of their mother. Agnes would be powerless if their father took charge.

Claire's head snapped up. "This means you're leaving, Jo, doesn't it?"

"It's the only way, Claire. I'll go west and send for you as soon as I'm able. It's time. One less daughter in the house will make things easier for Agnes. Perhaps she won't have as much to be bitter about."

"I can only hope," Claire answered.

Jo swallowed hard. They could *both* only hope.

Chapter 1

February 1929
San Francisco, California

Jo fell onto the ragged davenport. "Nothing. There's no work out there, Marian. Everyone wants me to be older, widowed, or the mother of six to qualify for work. What am I going to do? Every day I'm out here, Claire is on her own with Agnes. Maybe I should just go back on bended knee and finish school."

Marian folded the tiny cloth diapers and placed them neatly on the shelf. "Times are tough, Jo, and if I'm to believe my husband, they are only going to get worse. There are lots of men out of work, and certainly they take precedence over a single woman. Some of them are veterans of the Great War. Would you rather have families go without?"

Jo looked at her squalling nephew and cringed. "No, of course not."

"Then be thankful for what you have." Marian, although only twenty-four, seemed so much older and wiser.

In Michigan, Marian had been full of energy and excitement, but here she was simply focused on her next task. Aged already with flecks of gray in her brown hair and just trying to make ends meet. Jo wondered if that's what lay in wait for her, as well—a hard life etched out in laundry and keeping house for a humble man and his baby.

Jo scanned the one-room flat she shared with Marian, Mitch, and Davy. She was thankful. She just planned things differently. She expected immediate work, to bring Claire out within a month or so, and to have a flat of her own. Instead, reality was a far cry from expectation. As it turned out, she was lucky to have a spot on this rickety davenport in her sister's one-room apartment.

"Oh, Marian, of course I'm thankful." Jo picked up Davy. The baby gurgled in delight. She snuggled her face into his sweet-smelling head, tickling him into an unrelenting giggle.

Marian smiled. "Must you do that? You'll get him too excited for his nap. Besides, you have work to find. You can't give up now; we need the money with an extra mouth to feed."

Jo grimaced in guilt. "Oh, Marian, I know, and I'm so sorry. I won't be a liability much longer. I'll find something soon, I promise. I want Claire out here and away from Agnes more than you know. Mitch works hard enough for his family; I don't want to burden you anymore."

Marian shrugged. "God's timing, Jo. Not yours. Times are tough, and Mitch doesn't mind. We like the extra set of hands for Davy, and we're not suffering any more than the next man. At least we're happy. By the way, set an extra place. Glen is coming for dinner."

"Glen?"

"He's our upstairs bachelor, a carpenter's apprentice, and he just loves to play with Davy. He lives with his sister and her husband, but they don't have children yet. Glen comes down every once in a while to give them some privacy and keep that little man busy." She smiled at Davy, and he cooed lovingly at his mother.

"And I don't suppose this has anything to do with me, your unmarried sister?" Jo prodded. She lifted the baby, and once again, Davy squealed happily.

"Glen's not in a position to marry, Jo. He makes three dollars a day as a carpenter's apprentice. He's only in step two of the four-step process. He doesn't even come home until the last streetcar passes. He's coming to spend time with Davy. That's all. If I was trying to arrange a marriage, I'd let you know first."

Suddenly Jo's eyes sparkled, and a smile flickered. *Marriage.* It hadn't occurred to her before, but perhaps that was the way out of this hopeless mess. San Francisco was a city full of wealthy bachelors from families who had made their money long ago and new entrepreneurs. The city was teeming with money. Jo just needed to find where it was hidden. *It is just as easy to fall in love with a rich man, isn't it?* She'd just find one who went to church and shared her values. It was the perfect, and probably the quickest, solution. A new resolve hidden in her heart, Jo went about setting the table with a happy whistle.

The doorbell rang promptly at six. Jo went to the door, rolling her eyes at the thought of a dinner guest. Mitch worked hard enough each day, but now he was expected to feed the neighbors, too? Her emotions wrestled themselves when she got a glimpse of the simple carpenter from upstairs. Glen Bechtel smiled, and Jo felt her world shift. The full array of his perfect white teeth shone.

Glen displayed the physique of a man who did physical labor for a living: broad shoulders, strong, long legs, and an expansive chest, tightly surrounded by a clean work shirt. His appearance was hard to ignore, especially when combined with clipped, blond Nordic locks, and a carved jawline. All in all, Jo would have to say he was the most perfect-looking specimen of a man she'd ever seen. *Too bad he is so poor*, Jo thought wistfully. Maybe it wasn't quite as easy to fall in love with a rich man. Rich men usually didn't develop the picture-perfect physique of a man who did strenuous labor. Jo chastised herself for thinking such ludicrous thoughts.

"You must be Jo," Glen said, placing a work-roughened hand in hers. "You're as pretty as your sister." His eyes went past her and rested on the baby as he walked knowingly into the flat. "But not quite as sweet as my boy, here." Glen scooped Davy up into his arms, and the child wiggled his chubby little hands in euphoria. "Davy, what has my boy been up to all day?" Glen put the baby on the floor and settled himself next to him, playing a silent game of patty-cake. "Smells great in here, Marian."

"Thanks, Glen; it's almost ready. Mitch will be home soon."

"No hurry. Davy and I have some catching up to do, don't we, Peewee?"

Jo remained at the front door, her gaze lost in the confusion of the situation. Jo had never seen a man take such an interest in a baby. *It's unnatural,* she mused. Crossing her arms and finally shutting the door, she watched the two together as Davy giggled constantly.

"Ahem," Jo abruptly coughed. While no raving beauty,

she wasn't used to being ignored. And she didn't like it one bit. "Mr. Bechtel, my sister tells me you're a carpenter's apprentice."

"That's right," he answered without looking up. "I'm working up at the Linton estate on Nob Hill. Doing a little add-on and finishing work for the family."

"Estate?" Jo asked as casually as possible. "Is there a *Mrs.* Linton?" Jo caught Marian's glance at her, as though her older sister knew exactly what she was thinking. *Am I that transparent?*

"Oh, that's right, you were looking for work, weren't you?" Finally, Glen looked up from the baby and focused his gray-blue eyes on her. She forgot what she asked momentarily, and couldn't possibly think of an answer to his long-forgotten question.

"Are you still looking for work, Jo?" Glen repeated.

"Work," she felt her head nod. "Yes, I'm still looking for work."

"Why don't you take the streetcar with me tomorrow? I'll introduce you to the housekeeper, and you can see if they're in need of a new girl. They seem to go through house girls pretty regularly. The Lintons are very private folks. Can't say I ever see much of them, but their son is around quite a bit."

"Their son? Does he have a nanny? Where are his parents most of the time?"

"Their son is about twenty-five, Miss Jo." Glen laughed. "He hangs around the estate quite a bit. He's a nice chap, too, a regular joe, very interested in the building going on at the house."

Jo's ears perked. "A son. Of course, they'd have a son. About twenty-five, you say? Yes, Glen, I'd love to go to the estate tomorrow. What time should I be ready?"

"I leave about six in the morning to catch the streetcar."

"Perfect." And it was, too. Young Mr. Linton was the perfect age and had all the qualifications she required. He was rich, unattached, and about to meet his match.

Chapter 2

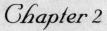

Six A.M. was an ugly hour. She emerged from her flat, bleary-eyed and grumpy, only to be met with the Nordic's big, expressive frown. Glen stared at his watch. "I said six."

"Close enough," she groaned.

"Not for the streetcar. Mussolini couldn't run a better system. Come on." He grasped her hand and bolted up the hilly San Francisco street, dragging her along behind him. By the time they reached the car, Jo needed to bend and catch her breath. But the crowded streetcar jolted, and Glen grabbed her to keep her from pitching off the side. He helped her into the last available seat, and they rode cattle-style up the long, arching hill. *Who would have thought all these people would be up at six in the morning?*

"Do you have a problem with mornings?" Glen asked, his burly arms crossed.

"Only that they start too early for my tastes." Jo's eyes fluttered shut. *Must he talk so much? It's far too early to be engaged in conversation.*

"I can't recommend you for any job with the Lintons if you have trouble with mornings. They'll need a good,

185

hardworking girl, not a spoiled princess. I daresay they've had enough of them. I'm not going to put my neck on the line for you. I've worked too long for this job. If I lose my apprenticeship, I lose my future. Here." He dropped a quarter in her hand. "You can catch the next streetcar back." The streetcar lurched to a stop, and she was thrown into him. He began helping her off the car before she realized what was happening.

"No!" She climbed clumsily back up into the cab. "No, I need this job! I'm sorry, I'm sorry I was late."

His jaw was set. His steely blue eyes unwavering. "It's not your tardiness that's the problem. It's your attitude. You've never worked a day in your life, have you?"

Jo thought back to all the chores Agnes forced on her after school. The soaps that dried out her hands, the iron that often burned her, and worst of all, the constant darning of the endless mountain of socks. *It had to be cheaper to buy more socks!* She knew what it was to work.

Jo put her hand on Glen's. His rough hand flinched under her touch, and she felt something she didn't care to examine further. A connection with the hard-hearted carpenter she felt to her very soul. She caught her breath, remembering her situation. "I'll work, Glen. I promise I won't let you down. I'll be on time, and I'll work harder than any girl they've ever had. Just please give me the chance to prove myself."

He stared again. With an icy look from his blue eyes, he warned, "I've only got one shot to be a carpenter. There are four stages, and I'm only in stage two. If I ruin my apprenticeship, I can kiss my trade good-bye. A man without a trade is destined to failure as times get tougher."

"I'm a hard worker, Glen. Grandmother Faith always commented on that. When my mother was ill, I took over many of the chores." Jo swallowed hard. "Even more of them when my stepmother came to live with us."

"Frankly, you haven't shown me you know how to work, Miss Mayer. Your sister Marian knows how to work, so I'm assuming you've seen it put into action at some point. But so far, I've only seen the spoiled princess in action." His eyes continued to assess her, and she unconsciously crossed her arms in front of her.

She couldn't help but wonder if he was right. Her mother had spoiled her, and when Agnes came, her own pride had intervened when she was asked to do something. Perhaps she was spoiled, but she hated the thought. A spoiled woman could never earn enough to care for herself and Claire. If she was indeed spoiled, things needed to change, and quickly.

"No, Glen! You've got the wrong girl. I'm a hard worker, or at least I can be. I came here from Michigan by myself so I could earn enough money to bring my sister Claire here. I want to learn how to earn my own living. If I've been spoiled, it's only because I didn't know any better. Please take me to the Lintons'! I won't let you down, I promise."

His expression was unwavering. His narrowed eyes scanned her, as if checking her for honesty. How could she make him understand how badly she needed this job? How badly she needed to bring Claire out and make a life for herself? Of course, she'd never let him know her true plans for meeting the young Mr. Linton, but she wouldn't let that stop her from working hard. She didn't examine why his opinion meant anything to her, but his negative assessment stung. She had no wish to ruin Glen's reputation or her own.

"I'll recommend you on one condition," he finally said.

"What's that? Anything, Glen, anything."

"If you get hired, you keep the job for an entire year, doing your best regardless of the circumstances. No matter what happens, do we have a deal?"

"A year?" she stammered. "Why would you care if I stayed a year or not?" His requirement simply didn't make sense. What would require such a promise? She was incredibly uncomfortable with the condition, but considering her remaining options, she didn't know if she had a right to protest.

"Because, Jo, in my estimation, a man, or a woman in this case, is only as good as his word. When you're hired for a job, you do it until completion. That's what the Bible preaches, and that's what I believe. If you're willing to make the commitment, so am I, otherwise. . . ," he trailed off, leaving her to decipher his final meaning.

"But what if—"

"A year, Josephine," he answered resolutely.

Jo thought about her options. They consisted of going back to Michigan a failure, continuing to take food from her nephew Davy's mouth, or taking this job for a year. A job, which may or may not exist when she reached the top of the hill. For now, that was only a possibility.

"A year," she relented, holding out her hand to shake on the deal.

The electric streetcar ambled up the last hill, chugging desperately to the city's highest point. She knew sweeping views of the sapphire blue San Francisco Bay were all around her, hidden behind the shroud of morning fog. Stepping off the car, Glen took her hand in his and helped her from the vehicle. He smiled at her, and for a moment she forgot there was any conflict between them at all. There were only his shining eyes, his gaze warmer now, and his masculine carriage.

His chivalry quickly disappeared, however. Carrying his metal lunch box in one hand and his toolbox in the other, he took off at an unnatural pace up the stifling grade. Jo scrambled to keep up.

The stately homes of Nob Hill reeked of money. Elaborate columns and Victorian details provided a sight unlike anything Jo had seen. If times were hard, it certainly wasn't apparent here. They stopped in front of a stylish three-story stone mansion.

"Now, Mrs. Houston will want to know you're coming. She doesn't like surprises. Wait out here," Glen said. "I'll check whether she's willing to see you this morning."

"Mrs. Houston? Who's Mrs. Houston?" Jo was looking forward to meeting Mrs. Linton, and hopefully being introduced to her son.

"She's the housekeeper, Jo. Rich people don't bother with the likes of us." Glen snorted.

"They don't?"

"Wait here, I'm going to be late otherwise." Glen disappeared behind the house, leaving Jo alone on the sidewalk. She looked up at the enormous house, removed her hat, and patted her carefully created bun. Reality struck with the thick, icy fog. She had about as much chance of marrying the wealthy, young Linton chap as she had of being struck by lightning in a city where it was rare.

"Are you waiting for someone, Miss?"

Jo was startled by the voice. She turned to see a dapper young gentleman sitting in a shiny Duesenberg with all the windows rolled down. The man maneuvered the auto against the curb, twisting the wheels until they ground themselves into the curb on the steep street to keep it from escaping. He emerged from the car dressed in a tuxedo, a camel's hair overcoat, and velvety black top hat. Tipping his hat elegantly, he spoke again, "Good morning. Mr. Winthrop Linton at your service." His voice was a low growl, as though tinged with intention.

Jo stood up straight, smoothing the folds of her thick, wool skirt. She had dressed in her finest that morning, but suddenly she felt as raggedy as a street urchin. Winthrop Linton's finely tailored clothing was just another reminder that he was well out of her reach. His charms were an eerie reminder that she wasn't versed in fine society. Her marital aspirations disappeared as quickly as they'd appeared.

"Miss Josephine Mayer," she stammered.

"What brings such a young beauty to my doorstep this fine Wednesday morning?" Under his top hat, Winthrop Linton boasted a mop of curiously sloppy brown hair. He had light brown eyes and nondescript facial features, including a complete lack of chin. Jo scrutinized his face again, but there was no shadow or clothing across his face; he simply lacked a chin. Although small in stature, his dress made him appear bigger and more important.

"I, um, I was waiting to speak with Mrs. Houston about a job," she blurted nervously.

"Well then, you must come in, she'll be waiting." Mr. Linton took her arm and began leading her up the front path. Jo now understood enough to know her presence would not be welcome in the front parlor at such an early hour.

She tried to pull herself from his gentle grasp. "No, Mrs. Houston doesn't know I'm coming. I mean, I haven't been invited in yet."

"Nonsense. I'm inviting you in. I think you're a ripe little beauty, and Mrs. Houston always hires such plain-Janes. It would be nice to have an ornament for a change. Come in." With one final tug, Jo was standing in the extravagant foyer. The marble entryway, covered by a domed, glass ceiling, was larger than Jo's entire flat—a family of three could have easily lived in the foyer.

"Glen Bechtel is asking—"

"Ah, so you're Glen's girl." Winthrop Linton clicked his tongue. "Well, I've had enough of my girlfriends wag their tongues over him; it's only fair he should end up with a beauty like you." He crossed his legs at the ankles and leaned against the great mahogany banister.

"I'm not Glen's girl, I'm just a friend," Jo said hastily. She didn't want him to think she was unavailable. "He lives in the flat upstairs."

"Winthrop, is that you?" an operatic voice called. A large, elegantly dressed woman who appeared to be about fifty years of age came down the stairs. Her deep violet clothing shuffled with the sound of expensive material and was clearly styled in the latest fashion.

"Yes, Mother. Come see who Mrs. Houston's hired." Winthrop Linton wore a devious grin as his mother lumbered down the great stairwell.

Mrs. Linton scrutinized Jo, then summarily ignored her presence. "Were you out all night again, Winthrop?"

"Oh, Mother, you know the parties hardly begin before

sunup. I had a marvelous time." He kissed his mother's cheek, and her expression immediately softened.

"When it's time for you to take over your father's business, you won't be able to keep such hours, Son."

"Nor will I, Mother. Mother, this is Miss Josephine Mayer. She is a friend of our own Glen Bechtel. The carpenter?"

"Well, Miss Mayer, I'm sorry Glen didn't explain certain things to you, but the hired help uses the rear door and stays out of sight of the family. Otherwise, well, otherwise we might not be the genteel sort of family we are. We'd be common, do you understand?"

"Yes, Mrs. Linton. I understand perfectly. I'm sorry to have bothered you this fine morning. If you'll just point me in the right direction, I'll be happy to find Mrs. Houston." Jo felt a shaft of irritation that Winthrop had placed her in such an awkward position, but if it helped her get the job, she was grateful.

"Nonsense, I'll take you. I'll meet you in the dining room, Mother." Winthrop once again took her arm chivalrously and led her to the back of the extensive house. "Sorry about Mum, Sweetheart. I'm afraid she's living in a very Victorian age. She hasn't quite realized we are all of equal stature here in the twentieth century."

When they reached the cavernous kitchen, Glen was waiting with a scowl. He stood beside a particular-looking, stout woman who simply appeared angry. "Mrs. Houston." Winthrop placed a kiss on her irate forehead. "I met this little woman on the sidewalk in front of our home. It appears she's looking for work. You'll take care of her, won't you?"

"Yes, Sir," Mrs. Houston replied curtly. Her eyes thinned at Jo. "I'll take care of her, indeed."

The disappointment in Glen's eyes could not have upset her more. He had placed his job on the line for her, and however misinterpreted, she had risked his apprenticeship with her folly. Why hadn't she told Winthrop she was walking to the streetcar or something else? Remembering the inane thoughts of marriage to a wealthy magnate that she'd entertained, she wondered if she hadn't done it on purpose. Perhaps her own foolishness had led her here. Another dead end for work, and now Glen, her only connection, was upset by her foolishness.

She reached for Glen's broad shoulder. "I'm sorry, Glen, I didn't—"

He flinched and pulled away. "I've got work to do. Here's a quarter for the streetcar." He tossed it at her, and his crystal, gray-blue eyes disappeared as he backed out the door.

"You haven't got the sense of a puppy if you don't know enough to use the service entrance," Mrs. Houston bellowed. "And I promise you no work. This is my house, and I run it accordingly. Mrs. Linton understands that. She trusts my worthy opinion."

"Yes, Ma'am. You're right, and I'm so sorry about my entrance. I wasn't thinking."

"Well, you'll have to learn to think if you plan to work here. Girls without a lick of sense mustn't work for me."

"Ma'am?" Jo questioned.

Mrs. Houston sighed. "It isn't every day we see the likes of a worker like Glen Bechtel. You're a bit too attractive for the job, but if Glen is your beau, I can't say you would be tempted by the likes of Winthrop. If Glen recommends you, I'm capable of forgiving one mistake, but let it be your last."

"Yes, my last mistake. Absolutely, Mrs. Houston." Jo knew better than to correct the housekeeper about Glen, but she'd also probably hear about it later.

"You'll begin today with dusting and bathroom shining. You'll receive two dollars a day, six days a week, with Sundays off." Jo nodded pleasantly, trying to keep her disappointment at the low salary from showing. "I'll get you a uniform immediately, and Miss Mayer. . ."

"Yes, Mrs. Houston."

"The Lintons are a very private family. You'll keep your presence out of theirs, do you understand? No more appearances in the family rooms when they are present unless you are called as a servant."

"Yes, Mrs. Houston." Jo's joy over employment was overshadowed by Glen's frustration with her. She fingered the shiny quarter in her hand, knowing the owner of it cared enough to get her back home, but that was probably all he cared. She'd make him understand her mistake. Certainly, he wasn't unreasonable.

Chapter 3

Every muscle in Jo's body ached. Darning socks was child's play next to scrubbing bathroom fixtures with a vengeance. Mrs. Houston was a stickler for the smallest details, and she noticed everything. If there was the slightest smudge, Jo was forced to scrub the fixture as though it hadn't been touched. She found herself cursing indoor plumbing by the time the day was up.

Glen met her at the back door. "How was your first day?" His voice was far too cheery, his muscular body unmatched by the day's work.

She nearly fell into his arms as an answer. Her weary body clamored for the sanctity of her bed, and the idea of the trip to the streetcar overwhelmed her. "Good," she replied feebly.

He laughed out loud. "You don't look all that good. Mrs. Houston has exacting rules, but she'll soften up. Once she knows you're capable."

Jo's legs buckled underneath her as she tried to walk down the steep hill toward the streetcar. Glen noticed her stumble and gave her a pitying glance. He tucked his metal lunch box under his arm—the same arm that held his heavy toolbox. Then he took her hand and held her up by just his presence.

"Is this why you said a year? Does anyone make it through the first week?"

He chuckled. "Oh, Jo, you're just not used to hard work. Give your body two weeks to adjust, and you won't even notice anymore. I think if you work for a year for Mrs. Houston, there won't be a challenge you can't meet."

"Will my arms look like yours?"

Glen had his work shirt folded above the elbows, and the material stretched precariously where it needed to hold his muscles. "I don't think so, Darlin'."

He helped her to the streetcar stop. Jo thought she'd cry at the sight of the full cabin; her body ached with desire to sit. Luckily, a gentleman gave up his seat, and Jo thanked him profusely.

"Seriously, Jo," Glen said, leaning over her, "I know the Lintons aren't an easy family to work for, but I think you'll find if you stick it out, it will be worth your while. They've been so good to my boss and me. They've kept us working for nearly two years now. Soon I'll have my carpentry apprenticeship finished, and I'll be able to go wherever I want. The union is paying about eight dollars a day now."

"Where is it you want to go?"

Glen shrugged. "Nowhere in particular. I'm happy with my life here. I'd like to move out of my sister's apartment, though. That flat can get awful cramped with three of us."

"Try it with four," Jo replied miserably.

"I doubt you'll care how crowded it is tonight."

"That's the truth. I'm exhausted."

"Tomorrow will be easier."

The streetcar rolled to a stop, and Glen hopped off, holding up his arm to help her down. As she stood, Jo found out just how sore she was and tumbled off the streetcar. She fell into Glen's arms, and his lunch box clattered onto the street. He pulled her to the safety of the sidewalk before returning for his dented lunch box. As he put the contents back into the box, Jo smelled the stench of strong drink. Prohibition made the alcohol scent even more obvious since it had been so long since she'd smelled it. She looked around her nervously to see if there were other witnesses, but only she seemed concerned.

Glen looked up with a guilty shrug. "You wouldn't believe me if I told you." He placed a broken bottle back into the lunch box.

Jo's strength returned. "I don't want to know anyway." She dusted herself off and walked resolutely toward their building.

"Wait, Jo. It's not what you think."

What else could it be? Jo had long since heard of men addicted to strong drink during Prohibition, but she'd never met one. "You're carrying liquor in your lunch box?" Jo's downcast head just shook. "I can't believe it, Glen. My sister trusts you."

"Please just let me explain. Winthrop—"

"You yourself told me the Lintons don't socialize with the likes of us, and now you're going to try to blame this on Winthrop?"

"No, I'm not blaming Winthrop. Just please let me finish."

"Never mind. The less said, the better. Just stay away from Davy, or I'll tell my sister you carry strong drink to work. I doubt she'd want a drunk near her child." Jo slammed the door to her apartment, scarcely hearing Glen's last protest. It was well known that men who drank must have frequented the illegal speakeasies, and flappers, or loose women, were known to be there as well. Jo was indignant. She knew speakeasy life was a form of rebellion that many young people had taken to, but she wouldn't have believed it of Glen. Not unless she'd seen it for herself.

"But it's not mine, Jo!" Glen called through the door.

"Not mine. As though someone would carry an illegal substance for someone else." She answered in a whisper, rolling her eyes. The recent Valentine's Day massacre in Chicago had shown Jo vividly that alcohol was nothing to play with. Just days ago, seven men, who thought they were undergoing a routine police inspection, were killed in cold blood by a rival bootlegger.

"How was your first day, Jo?" Marian's tired expression tried to muster up some enthusiasm.

"It was fine. I'm tired, but I'll survive."

"Where's Glen? He was coming for dinner." Marian shut the oven door, wiping her brow with a dish towel in her hand.

"You don't want him here, Marian. He's not the right sort to be around Davy. Debauchery is contagious, after all."

"Debauchery? Jo, I don't know what's gotten into you, but Glen is not capable of such a thing. Your hard day's work has gone to your head. Now go upstairs, apologize, and bring him back here for dinner. We're having pot roast. It's his favorite. Besides, his sister will be looking forward to the quiet night with her husband."

"I will not go, Marian. He's. . .he is simply not the man you think he is. Trust me. Just please trust me."

"Jo, you always were so dramatic. You'll be starring with Gary Cooper one of these days in those moving picture shows," Marian said through clenched teeth. "Go upstairs and bring Glen back down here. Mitch looks forward to their evenings and their card games." Marian wiped her hands on her apron, clearly frustrated with the conversation.

If only Jo could tell Marian what she knew. Glen got her the job, and she owed him her silence. If he wanted to ruin his future with strong drink, that was his business, but she wouldn't let him near Davy. But neither could she afford to lose this job by offending him. Not now. Claire could come out within six months if pennies were counted. Free rail fare would make only room and board necessary. Although the money would be tight, they'd manage.

"Jo, I mean it," Marian barked.

Jo let out a heaving sigh. "Does Mitch approve of alcohol?" she hissed.

"My husband has never taken a drink in his life, and neither has Glen. Go upstairs and get him."

Jo reluctantly climbed the concrete steps, only to find Glen sitting on the stair landing. He didn't even look up when she approached. "What are you doing out here?"

"My sister made a special dinner for her husband. I'm trying to give them some privacy." He looked up, his steely blue gaze meeting her own. "Why can't you just listen? I listened to you when you came through the front door with *Winthrop*." Glen dropped his head again. "You are so spoiled, and you're just determined to think the worst of people."

Jo, incensed by his accusation, railed at him. "I'm not spoiled. Cut that out! I worked hard today, and you know it! Don't try to turn this back around on me. Liquor, last time I checked, was illegal in this country. You are carrying it around in your lunch box like it was apple juice. What would my sister think if—"

"Your sister would think there was some misunderstanding, because your sister doesn't jump to ridiculous conclusions."

"Ridiculous? You still smell of it, how ridiculous is proof?" She sniffed again. "Ninety proof!"

"You know, I could jump to some conclusions of my own. Like how you managed to worm your way in the front door with Winthrop Linton easily enough. The servants' entrance wasn't good enough for you, was it? You know, Winthrop has a notorious reputation with the ladies."

"Funny, that's what he says about you."

Glen's crystal blue eyes thinned. He stood up, walking toward his apartment door. "Is it?"

"Where are you going? My sister wants you for dinner!"

"What do *you* want, Josephine?" He came close. Uncomfortably close. She felt herself gulp, and she made the motion to square her shoulders. Unfortunately, they didn't heed her call.

"I want to understand what people see in you. What do you do to fool them into thinking you're a decent guy? We both know better."

"I am a decent guy," he replied softly. He was still close. She trembled in his proximity but tried to hold her uncompromising stance. She couldn't let him know he affected her. Besides, what was it her sister said? He was a carpenter's apprentice, with three dollars a day to his name. She rolled her eyes.

"A decent guy who just happens to carry liquor in his lunch box?"

"Yes," he answered. "Now, what about you? You tell me you're not spoiled, where's my proof?"

"Your proof is that I'm here in California. I'm earning enough to bring my sister out here, and then I'll support her, too. Would a spoiled brat do that?"

"Depends," he answered, crossing his arms, "on why you want your sister out here. What are you three running from? All three sisters come to California with times as tough as they are?" he asked treacherously.

"I'm not running from anything. I'm simply trying to give my little sister a future. The one she deserves. The one our mother would have given us if she'd lived." Jo had had enough of this conversation. "Dinner's at six-thirty." She started down the steps, but she felt his firm hand grasp her arm. His touch startled but intrigued her, and she halted. Looking into the depths of his eyes, she tried to see his villainous ways, but there was nothing—only purity, in clear blue, gazing warmly at her.

"You know there's a reason for that alcohol flask, don't you, Jo?"

Jo crossed her arms. She assumed as much, but she wasn't willing to relent. She wanted an explanation.

"I think you and I have a lot in common."

"I doubt it," she answered curtly, but her heart didn't agree with her snappy mouth.

"Still, you agreed to a year with the Lintons. You're not going to back out on your promise when your sister gets here, are you?"

"I promised. I'll be there for a year."

"No matter what?"

"Within reason," she answered.

"That's not what you promised. You should know me well enough to know I wouldn't ask anything of you that would compromise yourself."

"On the contrary. I don't know you at all, Glen. You play cards, carry liquor, and have the face of a Boy Scout leader. I haven't figured you out at all."

He laughed aloud. "There's nothing to figure out, Jo. I'm just a simple carpenter's apprentice going to work every day and trying to make a future for myself."

"Somehow I find that hard to believe." And she did, too. Hardworking carpenter's apprentices didn't carry liquor in their lunch boxes. Glen made her swear she'd keep *her* job for a year, yet by his very actions that day, he could have lost his own position.

"Winthrop said the ladies—"

"Winthrop says a lot of things, Jo. The sooner you learn to ignore most of it, the safer you'll be. If he ever gets too close, you come to me, do you understand?"

Jo laughed. "Winthrop's a gentleman, Glen."

"Gentlemen ignore the hired help, Jo, and it's worse when they don't." He skipped the steps beyond her, never looking back. Jo simply shook her head. *They lived in America, not in the caste system of India.*

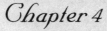

Chapter 4

Glen and Jo rode the streetcar to work silently the next day. She felt his disdain, and he probably felt hers, so they both opted for silence. Glen apparently thought she was a foolish girl who couldn't handle herself with the likes of Winthrop Linton, and Jo thought he sought his place in the bottom of society too readily. Submission was not something that came easily to Jo, and she found Glen's easy example of it pathetic.

The great house looked so spectacular from the front, it was hard to fathom such darkness dwelled within. Jo shivered at the memory of Mrs. Houston's cold reception and Mrs. Linton's outright refusal to acknowledge her. Winthrop drove up the street, honking the horn of his Duesenberg at the unholy hour. Once again, the young, enigmatic Winthrop appeared perfectly attired after his long night.

"Good morning, Glen. Good morning, Miss Mayer." The young man tipped his hat chivalrously, and Jo couldn't help her sideways glance at Glen.

"If gentlemen ignore the hired help, someone forgot to tell Winthrop," she whispered through clenched teeth.

"Winthrop is an exception. He's from a different

generation than his parents. *He* believes in the American dream, but his parents are still in the Victorian age. He's watched many of his friends die from the postwar flu epidemic. Money is not a separator to him. Trust me, Jo, it's not that way with his parents. It won't do you any good to be mingling with the likes of Winthrop. His mother would have you shot down faster than an enemy biplane." Glen smiled as well, giving the impression they were having a perfectly amiable conversation.

Winthrop slurred inaudibly and stumbled forward. Glen rushed to catch him, and Jo realized that young Winthrop was decidedly drunk. His eyes were glassy and he wore a careless smile. He tried to say something else, but she heard only sputters of sound.

"Jo, go get to work! Mrs. Houston will be expecting you!" Glen shouted. Jo averted her eyes, which is really what Glen meant. She scrambled up the back steps and entered.

"Good morning, Mrs. Houston." Jo gave a slight curtsy.

"Good morning, Josephine. There's coffee brewing if you're of a mind to drink it." Mrs. Houston had already assembled the elegant breakfast for the family and kindly had left a few scraps of bacon for Jo next to the coffee. "You'll be working hard today so be sure and eat up. We can't have you withering away to nothing." Mrs. Houston maintained her solemnity, but she must have had a heart. To consider Jo's hungry and tired state defied that callous front.

Jo inhaled the rich coffee aroma and took a cup from the cupboard. "Thank you, Mrs. Houston. The coffee smells divine. It's so frightfully cold out there. I didn't think Michigan had much competition for its winters, but that ocean fog just cuts right through a person."

"Drink it up quickly. I'm going to teach you to serve today. You can practice on Winthrop. Most likely he'll be needing coffee this morning, and he's not particular if you make a mistake." Mrs. Houston clicked her tongue. "Perhaps after some practice you'll be ready to serve Mrs. Linton tomorrow."

"Yes, of course, Mrs. Houston."

The older woman assembled a perfect tray, complete with orange juice, a coffee cup, two eggs, and three strips of bacon. "Now, there will be a sideboard in the dining room. Set the tray on the sideboard and serve the coffee first. There's a silver pot waiting over the warmer. Serve from the left. Pick up from the right. Winthrop takes his coffee black. After he's been seated with his coffee, you may set the warm plate in front of him. Don't bother to ask him what he wants, he won't be of a mind to care. If he needs anything you don't see in the dining room, come back to the kitchen, and I'll help you. All right?"

"Yes, Mrs. Houston." Jo's confidence waned. She would have actually preferred scrubbing bathroom fixtures to being thrown into proper serving techniques. Of course, her mother had taught her manners, which fork to use, and all that, but actually serving for an upstanding San Francisco family was beyond her mother's skills.

Jo watched the orange juice shake and sputter as she headed toward the dining room. "Head up, Josephine," Mrs. Houston called.

Jo straightened and followed voices into the elaborate dining room. The walnut-paneled room was laden with crystal electric lights, though the general darkness of the fog and day still dimmed the room immensely. Jo was shocked to see Glen sitting beside Winthrop at the great table. It didn't coincide with his "hired help" persona. She did as Mrs. Houston asked and placed the coffee in front of Winthrop. He and Glen were looking at plans for some type of building project—the same schematics Glen had with him on the streetcar. At least, Glen was trying to interest Winthrop in the plans, but the weary man only wanted to sleep. She placed the plate of food alongside the schematics.

"Would you care for coffee, Mr. Bechtel?" Jo asked sweetly. Glen nodded and she poured him a cup. "Cream or sugar?"

"No, thank you." Glen watched her for a moment, clearly hoping she'd leave. Something about his determination caused her own to muster. She settled in at the sideboard, rearranging items that didn't need to be rearranged.

Winthrop smiled his drunken smile her direction. Obviously, he had little interest in Glen's plans, or business of any sort. Winthrop just watched her dreamily. "She's such a peach," he slurred in Glen's direction. "I like good-lookin' women."

Glen nodded as if to tell her to leave, but she didn't. She lifted up the coffee urn again, hoping to refill Winthrop's cup. The poor man was in such a sorry state. His glassy eyes couldn't quite focus on her, but he gave her a sloppy smile anyway. Suddenly, Winthrop collapsed into his plate, his face a mass of yellow eggs when he finally turned to breathe.

"Winthrop!" His mother's opera-tinged voice bellowed.

"Help me get him out of here," Glen whispered. Jo

wiped Winthrop's face with a white linen napkin while Glen lifted the load up, throwing Winthrop's lifeless arm around his shoulder. "Get the door, Jo. The back door!"

Thinking Mrs. Linton would come in and find the unwholesome scene, Jo ran toward the door and let the two men out quickly. "What do I tell Mrs. Linton?"

"You'll think of something. Get the plans!"

Without thought, Jo rolled up the schematics and hid them in the sideboard. Just as she shut the cabinet, Mrs. Linton's shrill voice addressed her. "Is there something you're looking for?"

"I was just making sure there was enough silver on the table, Mrs. Linton. Teaspoons are a necessity." Jo cringed at the mistruth. Why was she covering for Glen? Mrs. Linton had to have some idea of her son's behavior if he came home in the morning every day.

"Tell Mrs. Houston I'm ready for my meal. *She* can serve. Did young Mr. Linton dine yet? He went to bed so early last night."

Jo's eyes rested on the plate of smeared scrambled eggs. The white of the china shone through where Winthrop's face had been, while much of the breakfast entrée rested on the crisply ironed tablecloth. "Yes, Mrs. Linton. He wasn't very hungry." Jo's eyes widened.

The older woman looked at the mess, and back at Jo. "Well, no wonder. What type of slop is that for breakfast? Please ask Mrs. Houston to come in here presently. I'm sure she can find something useful for you to do."

Jo nodded. "Yes, Ma'am." Jo would probably get her walking papers that very day, and then what would she do? This was all Glen's fault. He should have just left Winthrop to deal with the consequences of drink. Jo hurried back into the kitchen. "I'm sorry, Mrs. Houston. I'm afraid I ran into Mrs. Linton, and I didn't impress her with my serving."

"Never mind, Dear. I'll deal with Mrs. Linton. You start with the dishes. We'll work on serving again this afternoon before lunch."

If there is an afternoon for me, Jo thought solemnly.

"Psst. Jo!" Glen's roguish frame filled the doorway. "Did you get the plans?"

Jo put a finger to her lips. "Shh! Mrs. Linton is in the dining room. You're going to get us both fired."

"Jo, you've got to get those plans. Mrs. Linton cannot see them. Please," he pleaded. "If not for me, do it for Winthrop. You seem to like *him.*"

"Fine," Jo relented. "But only because I owe you both my job, and if you're up to something illegal, you ought to be ashamed for bringing me into it. I'll get them when I clear the dishes. Now get out of here before someone sees you."

He flashed his perfect teeth, with all the charm of a silent movie star. Jo pursed her lips, trying to remain unaffected by his captivating grin. "I owe you, Jo. I'll make it up to you, I promise. If Mrs. Linton asks where Winthrop is, tell her he's out back overseeing the building."

"I doubt Winthrop is overseeing anything."

"No, he's awake, and he's watching us build. I'm not asking you to lie, Josephine. I'm asking you to protect Winthrop. Give it a few weeks; you'll understand."

"Winthrop doesn't strike me as the type of man who needs protecting."

"He will, Jo. Just give it time. Thanks!" Glen planted a kiss on her cheek and shut the door without another word. Jo unconsciously touched her cheek. She should know better than to be affected by Glen's touch, but someone forgot to tell her pounding heart.

"Haven't you started the dishes yet?" Mrs. Houston's disapproving glare shamed Jo.

"No, Mrs. Houston. I'm sorry. I'm getting to it right now."

"Well, get snapping, my dear. There's no place for idleness in this household. Mrs. Linton opted for only coffee this morning. She's finished in the dining room. You can clear the dishes and put the table back to right. Then, come back and finish these dishes."

"Yes, Ma'am." Again Jo curtsied in deference. She doubted it had any effect on Mrs. Houston, but her working situation was precarious enough without being proud.

"And Josephine," Mrs. Houston continued, "the last girl was fired for associating with Winthrop. Make sure you keep out of his way, especially where Mrs. Linton is concerned."

"Of course, Mrs. Houston." Jo cleared the dishes from the table, filling the tray with the unused, elegant bone china. Jo sighed at the sight of it. *Bone china*. Marian and Mitch struggled for each day's provisions, and they still managed to feed her and Glen, too. Pot roast, no less. It couldn't be said that Marian didn't know how to run a proper home. It simply wasn't right that bone china went unused and prepared meals uneaten. All this waste sickened her. But she knew if she said anything about it, Mrs. Houston would have her gone before the day was up. The wealthy had room to waste.

Checking to her left and to her right, Jo opened the sideboard and took out the rolled plans. She was tempted to look at the contents but thought ignorance might be best. She was in enough trouble, and Claire was waiting in Michigan. Waiting for the money and the means to come to California.

Jo tucked the plans under her arm and opened the door. "Glen," she whispered. The hammering outside stopped, and Glen appeared.

"You're an angel," Glen said smiling, taking the plans from her. "I'll see you tonight. I may be a little late, but wait for me. I don't want you on the streetcar alone at night."

"I'll be fine," she protested.

"Wait for me," he commanded, and she saw something in his eyes she couldn't refuse. Everything about Glen Bechtel was a mystery. From what he was building out in the garden, to his liquor-toting lunch box. But for some reason, getting on the streetcar without him seemed dire. As much as reason pointed in one direction, her heart was taken in another. Glen's soft blue eyes and gentle touch with those around him made it impossible to believe he was up to no good even though all the evidence was stacked against him. Marian's good opinion had something to do with it. Marian wasn't easily taken in. She had a discerning nature.

"I'll wait," Jo answered.

"Good. I promised your sister I would not let you get on the streetcar alone."

Jo's heart plunged. Glen's chivalry went only as far as duty. "I'll wait in the kitchen," she added solemnly.

Chapter 5

Disgusted by the events of the day, Glen hammered with a vengeance. His aggression was well served by his job today. Winthrop Linton was an exasperating chap—too dainty to be useful, too strong-willed to be silent. Glen's jaw clenched remembering Jo's concerned look for the drunken Winthrop.

Glen would never understand women. Seems they were all taken in by those sweet, schoolboy looks of Winthrop's. Young, idealistic women had no idea the trauma that lay beneath his easy façade. Winthrop was a broken man; useless to his powerful father and yet trying to forge a place for himself before it was too late.

Maybe it was the money that fooled them. Women seemed to think money changed things—that it solved problems. The Linton household was a prime example that it simply wasn't true. Money just caused different sets of problems. Turmoil reigned in that household. Jo would see it quickly enough, if she hadn't witnessed it already with Winthrop's continual drunken state. Jo would soon relish her place in simple society. Not that he was without feelings for Jo. The school of hard knocks was no place for a girl of seventeen. Glen had admired men of means at one time, too. But never again.

Glen wished he could teach her the lesson without her having to see it for herself, but it wasn't his place. Glen promised Jo's sister, Marian, he'd look after Jo until she figured it out. An easier promise he'd never made. He'd feel responsible for any young woman in the Linton household. Josephine Mayer was special, though. He'd known that from the first time he'd laid eyes on her.

Glen was a man of few words. He didn't know how to describe the rush of feelings Jo sent through him. Jo wasn't a beauty queen, but she cast some kind of spell. She was an average woman of petite stature, yet solidly built for her young age, with dark brown hair always swept up into a neat bun. She had the lightest of green eyes. Something about her defied her average looks. Men were simply attracted to her. She had that magnetism that just made a man want to know more, as though an intriguing slice of heaven hid within. Certainly Winthrop was not immune, and neither was Glen.

He laughed aloud at the ridiculous notion of pursuing such a romantic thought. Josephine was a mere baby. Only seventeen and in need of a big brother's protection. She was too young to marry. He was too poor. Three dollars a day and a lifetime debt he couldn't shake. Courting was the last thing on his mind. Or at least, it should have been.

Glen drove the last nail of the day. One swift whack and the nail was embedded firmly into the redwood. He packed up his tools and headed toward the kitchen. He knocked. "You ready?" he asked as Jo opened the door.

She nodded. "Good night, Mrs. Houston."

"Night, Dear. See you in the morning. Don't forget about the party tomorrow night," Mrs. Houston called.

"No, Ma'am, I won't." Jo shut the door behind her and smiled up at Glen.

"Party?" Glen tried to hide his nervousness.

"Mr. and Mrs. Linton are entertaining business associates tomorrow. I have to work late tomorrow night. They said if it runs too late, Winthrop can take me home."

"No!" Glen shouted. "I mean, I'll wait for you. I have some extra work I can do. I have just one more thing to learn before I graduate to the next step. Step three of my apprenticeship."

"That's nice, Glen, but it's not necessary. The streetcar will have stopped running by then, and I've put you out enough. Mrs. Houston said the parties go well into the night."

That's not all they do, Glen thought. He took Jo's hand to help her down the steep walk, and rubbed her hand. It felt like sandpaper. She pulled her hand away, hiding it in her pocket.

"I had to shine the silver today," she explained. "The cleaning mixture was harsh on my hands."

He watched her in the fading sunlight, and they faced one another. Her pale green eyes filled with tears. Clearly, this wasn't how she imagined life. Glen unconsciously brushed a loose tendril of hair behind her shoulder. Her neatly arranged bun was now a mass of tangled confusion. She'd never looked more attractive—her vulnerability, her beauty, it all hung between them like an unspoken whisper of love. With it came the realization that she would be as irresistible to Winthrop tomorrow night as she was to Glen that very moment. Glen felt a shaft of guilt. He'd promised Marian to help get Jo work, but at what price?

"Jo, maybe this job is too difficult. Maybe you ought to think of looking elsewhere," Glen suggested.

"When would I go look for another job? I have to be there at six-thirty in the morning, and I'm not home until just about the same time in the evening. I need to focus on Claire, not myself. She has it harder than I do, Glen."

Only two days of work, and she was ravenously unhappy. Who could blame her? She looked bedraggled. Her hands were a chapped mess. The real Josephine Mayer was wilting away behind a disciplined servant's body. If she kept this up, she'd be an old maid before she was twenty.

Glen's guilt got the best of him. "I know, Jo. I'm sorry. I'm sorry I got you into this mess." He placed an arm around her, and they began walking again.

"Sorry? Glen, this is the only hope of work I've had in a month of being here. I have no experience, no references. I'd have nothing without your help. Neither would my sister, Claire. When she comes, Glen, it will be because you helped me. Even if I was too stubborn to realize it at first."

For the first time ever, Glen left his toolbox, his very livelihood, out in the work shed. He prayed they'd still be there in the morning, but he also felt a responsibility to have a free hand for Jo. Last night she'd been so bone tired she could barely lift herself onto the streetcar. Today, he'd be there if she needed him.

"I thought you were a spoiled child who was looking for easy work. I didn't realize you really knew what it meant to work for a living."

"Marian gave me no dreams about what it's like out here. I knew when I came that making the money for Claire and myself would be difficult. Life at home was worse, Glen, or I wouldn't be here. I just pray that my coming out here is helping Claire manage." Her voice dropped a bit. "I hope she's staying free of the strap."

Glen wondered what kind of woman their father married. Certainly Claire, at thirteen, would have outgrown the strap. Josephine's eyes were filled with apprehension. Glen knew life after the war wasn't easy; he knew many children who'd gone to work to help their families. It was different with girls, he thought. Young women should have been sheltered. He felt a bolt of anger toward Jo's father before remembering the man was only doing what he needed to do to provide for his family just like any other man in America. Work was hard to find, and war was looming in the rest of the world. The war to end all wars had done no such thing.

"Your father's only doing what needs to be done," Glen said in support.

"I know, Glen. So am I. Father and Agnes are bound to start a new family soon. After that, it will be too late for my sister. Claire will be expected to stay and care for the baby. She'll become nothing more than the family maid when that happens. I'm certain of it. Won't it be ironic?" Jo said with a sarcastic laugh. "My father will have hired a maid for his daughters, only to have his own daughter become the maid's maid."

"You have to look at Marian's life, too, Jo. Life isn't much different on your own. It's no picnic right now for the workingman. We scrape and struggle to keep food on the table while the rich get richer. They make sense out of all those stock numbers, and we are just thankful to have their scraps and to build their office buildings and houses."

Jo's eyes softened, and she faced him again. "I know, Glen. I don't blame my father one bit. President Hoover has big plans for this country. He said no American shall ever starve, and look what he did for the Allies. He kept them fed without ever rationing portions in America. I know we can expect things to get better soon, but until then, I feel responsible for Claire."

Glen admired her optimism, and he wished he shared it. In July of '28 he'd watched the Lintons panic over a big stock market drop. This gambling was a false economy, and he worried its days were numbered. When the rich suffered, the poor were bound to suffer more.

"I'm waiting for you tomorrow night, Jo. The party may go late, but I'd just feel better knowing you got home safely."

"But, Mrs. Houston said—"

"I don't doubt Mrs. Houston, and I don't doubt their good intentions, but all the same, I'd like to see you home."

She smiled. It was the first time he'd ever seen her smile in a way that he felt was meant for him. "I'd like that too, Glen."

Chapter 6

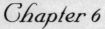

J o's hands trembled as she held the letter. *More bad news. I just can't take any more bad news, Lord. Please let things be getting better for Claire.* Jo ripped open the envelope on the crowded streetcar, ignoring prying looks from standing passengers.

Dearest Jo,

How I wish I were older. How I wish Father would let me come to California and supply for me there. I took your advice. I'm trying so hard to make Agnes happy. I am doing the wash after my schoolwork and have even taken to preparing some of the family meals, but nothing seems to please her. When Father is off the railroad line and here, things are almost worse because he does not give her enough attention. Or so she tells the ladies at afternoon tea. Grandmother Faith has been here a time or two, and I've been very careful to shelter her from the true happenings here. Her health is very frail, I'm afraid. I'm dreadfully sorry for my lamenting. I know things are tough for you, too. It

*is just that I'm so anxious to see you and Marian
and especially to see precious baby Davy. I miss you
all and long for the time when the Lord sees
us together again.*

Love, Claire

*P.S. Mother's wedding chest has miraculously returned
to the house. Agnes keeps it in her room. She's taken
down the pictures of Mother, and I cannot seem to
find them anywhere. I'll find a way to get the chest,
Jo—if it kills me.*

Jo's eyes closed as she heard her name called. "Josephine! It's our stop." Glen roused her from the correspondence, and Jo stepped off the car at the last possible moment. "Is everything okay?" He took her hand, and she felt herself pulled off the street.

Jo's words surprised her. "I'm simply not making enough money, Glen. I think I need another position." Jo stuffed the letter into her apron pocket, looking to Glen for some kind of answer. As if he had one.

"Jo, you're lucky to have this job. They're not easy to come by these days."

"Oh, I know, Glen. I know." Jo knew better than to feel sorry for herself, but she battled to fight the tears in the back of her throat. Life was tough for everyone right now. Everyone but the rich. However, she knew Claire was enduring the strap at home. She could read between her sister's lines, and she knew Claire's quest for the wedding chest could only lead to more trouble. Some legacies, no matter how treasured, were best left alone. The Holy Grail of her family—that would be all that remained of her mother's gown and family Bible, but certainly Grandma Faith would understand.

"Is there anything I can do?" Glen stopped on the street corner and gazed at her. His blue eyes seemed to offer her everything, yet she knew he had nothing. Nothing except three dollars a day and a rent payment to his own sister.

Biting her nails, Jo tried to think of a way. "No, Glen. There's nothing that time and a savings account won't cure. My sister Claire will be here. I just have to be patient."

Glen reached over and gave her a small kiss on the cheek. "God will provide, Jo. His timing is perfect."

"It doesn't feel that way today." His kiss was gentle and fatherly, but Josephine felt so much more within her. She stirred at the sight of his concerned brow and suddenly wanted to kiss him. To let him know everything would indeed be okay. She couldn't explain why his gentle kiss and concerned words soothed her so, but they gave her courage. The more she looked into his sincere expression, the more she knew there had to be an explanation for the liquor. She should have taken that explanation when it was offered.

"Sometimes, God's timing doesn't always feel right." Glen smiled again. His perfect, rugged smile highlighted his strong features. "I'll wait for you out at the work shed. Come out when the party is finished."

"I will." Jo let his hand go and walked into the Linton kitchen, thoroughly aware of Glen's eyes following her.

Preparing for a party made the workday feel even longer. Minute details seemed so unimportant when Claire was suffering. Both Mrs. Houston and Mrs. Linton put every-thing to the test. Jo wished to burn their white gloves over the perfectly arranged logs on the fireplace. Everything had a proper arrangement, and Jo wondered if rich people noticed such details as how the fire logs lay.

"Josephine, did you get the glasses down from the din-ing room cabinet?" Mrs. Houston's voice called.

"Yes, they are on the table. Where shall I put them? In the kitchen?"

"Heavens no. We can put them in the bar now. I'll get the key."

Jo looked up for a moment, only to shake her head. She must have misunderstood. Bars were illegal in prohibition-ist America, and although the eighteenth amendment was controversial, it was still the law. "Mrs. Houston? Where did you say I should put the glasses?" Jo walked into the kitchen, wiping her hands on her apron.

"Silly me," Mrs. Houston laughed. "In the bar, Dear. I'm going to open it soon. The guests will be arriving, and we'll want to be prepared. Mrs. Linton will stand for nothing else. You did bring your clean uniform for serv-ing, right, Josephine?"

"The bar, Ma'am?" Jo was still lost in Mrs. Houston's first comment. Were the Lintons setting up a bar for the party? Would Jo be put into a real speakeasy? The thought sent her heart racing like an out-of-control streetcar down a steep San Francisco grade.

"Josephine, you didn't think a state-of-the-art mansion like this would be without a bar, did you? You're not uneasy about the drinking, are you? Certainly you know that refined people take to the privilege of mirth. Although, these days, we can only get that rotgut from Canada, so we have to mix it with juice. People of society have a right to their pursuits, and why shouldn't they? Simply because a few do not know how to enjoy such things in moderation and with decency?"

Jo was too naive; she had no idea people of "refinement" pursued what her mother had fought so vigilantly to end. "Mrs. Houston, they must be aware of the law. The Volstead Act declares that the purchase and consumption of alcohol is illegal." Jo straightened her shoulders. She may have been innocent, but she was not ignorant.

"For the common folks, perhaps prohibition is necessary. I can see why when so many are dependent on their working men for their livelihood, but for the upper echelons of society, Josephine, you must see that they have a right to their pursuits."

"Why? Are they above the law?" Jo heard the indignation in her voice and bit her lip to keep more angry words from escaping.

Mrs. Linton appeared, laughing while covering her mouth discreetly. "We have a temperance league member on our staff, do we? You know, young lady, if the police find nothing wrong in our actions, neither should you. Rest your conscience, Dear." Mrs. Linton opened a locked closet, and to Jo's astonishment, a fully stocked speakeasy appeared. Bottles of every size and color filled Jo's view. She felt in the pit of her stomach a sickly, filthy feeling.

The room was newly built behind a great mahogany wall. Glen's apprenticeship had probably been spent building it. *The plans,* she thought. *The plans he was hiding. Were they for another speakeasy elsewhere?* Was Winthrop involved in building more of these dens of iniquity? Worse yet, was Glen? This must have been why he asked for her year's service.

Unwillingly, Jo walked somberly into the small room. It was a miracle she hadn't noticed it before, for the stench told of its oft use. Polished to a shine, Mrs. Houston herself must have seen to its care. Gold faucets and mirrored shelves reminded Jo of her mother's words: Sin is usually wrapped in a pretty package, never forget that.

Winthrop appeared at the doorway, and for once, he was strikingly sober. Jo's eyes must have appealed to him for assistance, because his comment suggested they had. "Mother, I don't think it's proper for Jo, a young woman of genteel upbringing, to work this party." The use of Victorian language was not lost on Jo. Clearly, Winthrop made a profession out of deceiving his mother. And it obviously worked. "Why don't you hire one of the men from the club? I bet Jo has never even heard of a cocktail, much less served one."

Mrs. Linton's outrage at Winthrop's suggestion was obvious. "Because, Winthrop, Josephine is our employee, and as such she is expected to work our social gatherings." Her stuffed chest stuck out just a bit farther than normal. Jo had no idea why Winthrop would try to help her, but she appreciated it just the same and remained quiet, knowing the young man would get much farther with his mother than she. Winthrop wasn't deterred by her dominant reaction.

He shrugged. "It doesn't matter to me, Mother. I was just thinking about you. If you have any thoughts of matchmaking tonight, you might want to keep her out of the way. You know how Dad's associates can be around the hired help. The young *female* hired help." He stated the last with special emphasis. "Seems to me you've been in trouble with some of the wives before, especially when their husbands part with their money during the evening." Winthrop scanned Jo up and down. "And none of those women were anything to look at, whereas Jo here. . ." Winthrop began to take a glass down from the wall, when his mother slapped his hand.

"Don't touch that. You know better." Mrs. Linton opened her mouth to speak to Winthrop but snapped it shut quickly. Then she hobbled off, mumbling to herself. "I'm going to call someone from the club. I'm sure this simpleton has no idea of the latest cocktails anyway. Her serving skills are still appalling. What was I thinking?"

Mrs. Houston followed hurriedly behind the mistress of the house, and Jo was left alone with the youngest Linton. His lecherous gaze was gone, replaced by an apparent longing for the odd-shaped bottles in the bar.

"Thank you, Winthrop. I don't know why you did that, but I appreciate it. My mother would have been appalled if I worked such a party."

"No need to thank me, Jo. Glen told me the favor you did us yesterday, with the plans. I certainly appreciate it. Mother and Father would never understand my plans. They think I'm destined for the family steel business, but I have other ideas. Big ideas."

"What are they, Winthrop? Do you mind my asking?"

He laughed. "Nothing to worry your pretty little head about. Let's just say it's going to be very profitable. Say, Glen's planning on working late tonight; would you care for a ride home? Have you ever ridden in a Duesenberg?"

"Glen was planning to work late to see me home. I

think I'll try and catch him now." Jo looked to the door as if it was her escape from sin. The one God had promised to provide. Her hands trembled as she approached the door. Winthrop may not have done her any favors after all.

Winthrop grasped at her arm and cooed his words. "I'll get you home safely, Miss Jo. I haven't had any complaints yet." He grinned, then winked almost imperceptibly. "Besides, I saved you from working at our den of iniquity tonight."

"I suppose you did, but Glen made special arrangements. He promised my sister to see me home, and I'd hate for Marian to worry." The door was so close, she longed to lunge for it and find Glen. Yet the opening was fading from view. A virtual black tunnel darker than a miner's pit.

"You know, Jo, working the parties is in your best interest. The revelers often have a few too many cocktails, and then they tip big. You might have made fifteen dollars or so." Winthrop's face curved into a half-smile, and Jo felt herself swallow hard. "What were you saving toward?"

Fifteen dollars. That was more than a month's rent on her sister's flat. It was certainly enough to get Claire out to California. The tunnel disappeared when the door opened and late afternoon light streamed in, blinding Jo. Glen closed the door and stood in the doorway, his blue eyes staring warily at her.

"I finished up early." Glen looked at Winthrop, and then back to Jo. "I'm ready to take you home as soon as Mrs. Houston is finished with you. I won't be staying late after all."

"How did you know I wasn't working the party?" Jo

searched both the men for answers, but they seemed to be having a silent conversation that didn't involve her.

"I'll wait for you outside," Glen answered.

Winthrop said nothing of the ride in the Duesenberg, and so Jo ignored the offer and followed Glen outside. "Glen, Winthrop says I might make fifteen dollars in tips if I worked tonight." She didn't hide the hope in her voice, or what that money might accomplish.

"He did, did he?"

"What do you think, Glen? Fifteen dollars is a lot of money."

"I think you either have a conviction or you don't, Jo. I suppose it's your place to decide. I'll wait for you if you want to work the party, but I won't support you. I know what Marian would have to say about it, and I would never go against a woman who cooks like Marian."

"I do have a conviction; drinking is illegal!" Jo cried. "But fifteen dollars, Glen! Claire could be out by the end of the month, and I could have a place of my own."

"Where would you come up with the rent for next month, Jo? Did you think of that?"

"I make enough to support Claire and myself if we lived frugally; I just needed a stash to get us started. This could be the answer to my prayers."

"You could make a lot more than fifteen dollars, depending on what you're willing to do, Josephine Mayer."

Jo slapped him hard across the face. "How dare you!"

Glen grabbed his reddened cheek. "Convictions are something you stand by despite the cost, Jo. If it's worth fifteen dollars for you to forget your convictions, you go right ahead. I won't stop you."

"How dare you lecture me! You carry liquor in your

lunch box. Are you going to stand here and preach at me?"

Glen pulled his billfold from his back pocket and casually pulled out a twenty-dollar bill. It was more money than Jo had ever seen at once. "Take it. Don't worry, I earned it. It's mine fair and square. Take it and bring Claire out here before you do something you regret."

"Where did you get this kind of money?"

"I earned it, like I said. Now take it, and let's go. Tell Mrs. Houston you'll see her in the morning."

"I can't take your money!"

"But you're willing to take it from a gang of drunken, rich fools? Take it, Jo! Before you take it from someone who expects something in return." The disgust in his voice held her riveted. He turned and walked resolutely to his work shed. Soon, the consistent pounding emanated from the room, a constant reminder she was back at the beginning with Glen Bechtel.

Chapter 7

Jo fingered the bill in her hand as she slowly returned to the kitchen. She had what she needed to bring Claire to California, so why did she hesitate? She could pay Glen back with some of her savings, and give him the balance soon. So why this annoying guilt?

"You can leave now," Mrs. Houston huffed.

Jo stuffed the bill into her apron. "I'm sorry, Mrs. Houston. I didn't know alcohol would be served. I—"

"Just never you mind. Let me tell you something though, Missy, for your own good. Wealthy people live a life of privilege. We have no right to judge them. They are our bread and butter. The sooner you learn that, and get over this high opinion of yourself, the better off you'll be. You're a maid, not even a housekeeper, Josephine, and with that attitude of yours, it's all you'll ever be."

Jo looked to the floor. "You're wrong, Mrs. Houston," she said gently. "I don't think I'm better than anyone. I simply am trying to be the woman I promised my mother I'd be. I can't do that and serve liquor when she fought so valiantly to keep it from America. I can, however, scrub floors with dignity." A surge of guilt rose in her throat.

After all, Jo had considered the offer. She'd considered it seriously and may have given into the temptation had it not been for Glen's discerning words.

"It's a good thing you appreciate washing floors, Missy, because it's all you'll ever do." Mrs. Houston's hands left her hips as she prepared the last of the appetizer trays.

"Do you want me to leave, Mrs. Houston? For good, I mean."

Mrs. Houston only huffed, her patience clearly waning for what she considered Jo's self-righteous indignation. Mrs. Houston walked away without another word. For now, Jo had a job, but she had no idea how long it would last. Glen was right, though; a conviction was nothing unless you really stood for something. Jo mumbled a prayer and left it to God. She wouldn't be anxious for something she couldn't control. Embarrassed by her behavior in front of Glen, she longed to make her peace with him. To let him know she was ever so grateful for his reason.

The sun had long since hidden itself behind the hills of San Francisco. Darkness filled every crevice of the Linton exterior. Only a lone light in the work shed shone as a beacon, calling her to it like a lost ship in the night. Silence greeted her, and she wondered if Glen was still there, or if he was angry with her, too, and left. She approached the work shed and heard voices. She peeked around the door frame, her eyes wide at the discovery.

"I got her out of the party, Glen. I can't promise any more than that. My mother runs this house as she sees fit." Winthrop Linton's sober voice hit her like a fist. His sobering words, even more so.

"Your mother runs this house as you tell her to, Winthrop, and you know it. Jo needs this job, and she needs to keep her reputation. She is not your typical flapper with bobbed hair and naked knees. You can't drink all night with her and dispose of her presence easily. She's young, Winthrop, and full of goals and aspirations. I won't let you harm her."

Jo bit her thumbnail at the realization—she was the topic of conversation. She didn't know whether to run or listen closely. Curiosity won and she leaned in closer.

"It seems to me you haven't much choice in what I do." Winthrop snorted. "In case you've forgotten, you work for us, too."

"In case *you've* forgotten, Winthrop, I know your secret. You can threaten me all you want, but if you want your secret kept, you'll find a way for Jo to keep her job. Your money means nothing to me. You ought to know that by now."

"What do you care about her, anyway? You've got enough missies following your every move. What's so special about her? I daresay a few of the society women would come down a notch or two to have you for awhile."

Glen shoved his hammer into his toolbox, the loud clanking breaking the unbearable night silence. "I don't know what she means to me. Nothing so special, I guess. I just want her safe because she's my responsibility. I promised her sister."

"You're quite the promise keeper, aren't you, Glen?"

"Winthrop, I've been a friend to you. I know you can't see that from your viewpoint, but you need to get right with God. You think only money has power. Understand this." Glen ground his forefinger into Winthrop's chest. "I haven't kept your promise because I feel compelled by my employment. I can get carpentry work at the presidio. I've kept your secret because I care about your eternal future. You can scoff at that all you want, but I will leave if you pursue Jo. And your secret won't go with me. She's an innocent, Winthrop. Find another hobby before someone gets hurt. You've got time to make things right."

"I only offered her a ride home."

"Don't fool with me, Winthrop. We both know what your rides home mean. I'm going to get Josephine, and I'd appreciate my money."

Winthrop held out cash, and then snatched it back when Glen reached for it. "Did you make her promise to be here a year, Glen? Did she fall for your ridiculous requests?"

"Give me my money, Winthrop." Glen held out his palm, his face red with anger.

"Who's taking advantage of her really, Glen? She knows I don't intend to marry her." Winthrop reluctantly handed Glen another twenty-dollar bill. In return, Glen handed Winthrop a clear glass bottle with a honey-brown liquid inside.

Liquor. Jo bit her fingernail clear away at the ends. Glen did have liquor, and worse yet, he sold it to a drunk. Right in front of her eyes. What was all that talk about getting right with God? *How could anyone handing alcohol to such a troubled man be right with God?*

"You're taking advantage of her, Winthrop. Don't try to fool yourself into believing anything else. Your hero image in front of your mother, your concern for her welfare at the speakeasy. . .I know what it all really means. I've watched you before, remember? I think of Jo as a little sister, nothing more."

"I saw you kiss her, Glen. You're going to deny that,

too?" Winthrop's smile curved up one side of his face.

"I kissed her. It didn't mean—never mind." Glen latched his toolbox, shoved the twenty into his billfold, and headed for the door. Jo raced down the walkway near the entrance to the house.

She pulled the twenty-dollar bill from her own pocket—the one Glen had handed her earlier. What was the difference between this money, and her "tips" had she worked the party? It was blood money, and she didn't want it—and she didn't want this job. She'd learned that much this evening. She had no reason to keep her one-year commitment to a man that bootlegged liquor. She'd go back to Michigan and beg Agnes for her old room. She'd see to it that she and Claire were cared for under Agnes's nose. Even if she did have to endure the strap occasionally.

"Jo?" Glen's tone was normal again. Smooth and gentle, not excited and angry as he'd been speaking with Winthrop. Jo tried to regain her composure, to act innocent of the conversation.

"Yes?"

"Are you ready to leave? I am finished in the shed. Anything else can wait until Monday. I imagine no one will be too fond of the hammer tomorrow after the party." He smiled slightly, and his straight teeth appeared. Glen appeared to have everything to offer a woman, maybe not money, but everything else. He was charming, handsome beyond compare, and chivalrous to a fault. What a pity it was all a desperate illusion. She'd heard by his own admission she was nothing special, and she supposed it was true. She was seventeen, uneducated, with little talent and fewer means. Being no great beauty, her youth was her only asset, and it wouldn't last long. She could hardly blame Glen.

"Why did you keep Winthrop from driving me home? Did you think I was unable to handle myself? That I am so inept at life I could have fallen prey to such a drunken man?"

Glen looked behind him nervously, putting his hand in the small of her back and forcing her down the path. "Let's not discuss that here."

Once at the sidewalk in front of the mansion, she stopped him, placing her hand on his chest. "No, we need to discuss it. I am not staying for a year here, Glen. I'm not even finishing the week. I'm going home where I belong, to take care of Claire and deal with my stepmother like I should have done from the beginning."

Glen's jaw flinched, but there wasn't even the slightest twinkle of surprise in the blue of his eyes, which reflected the streetlight. He'd been expecting her resignation, that much was obvious. She pulled his twenty-dollar bill from her pocket again. "Here, I won't be needing this, but thank you for your generosity."

She felt him grab her hand, forcing the bill back into her pocket. "Take it, Josephine. You deserve it. Get back home and make a life for you and Claire, but get out of this city. It will corrupt you faster than a bootlegger's man."

His eyes avoided her, and she touched his cheek, her finger tracing his jaw. She wanted—no, she needed, a reason to believe that his words to Winthrop were a lie. They'd shared something in their kiss. She couldn't believe the alternative. "Is that what happened to you, Glen?"

He raked his rough hands through his clipped curls and specks of sawdust released themselves. Little pink shavings fell to his feet. He slapped his hands together. "No," he finally said. "It isn't what happened to me, but I've seen it happen to a lot of men. There are so many temptations, so little cash for the workingman. If you're satisfied with the simple life, it seems fine, but if you have an ounce of ambition, postwar America can be harsh."

"So what's your ambition, Glen?"

"To finish my apprenticeship and be a full union carpenter, then build myself a little house at the edge of the city near the streetcar. That's my dream. Ain't much, is it?" He laughed.

Jo felt as though she was listening to his very soul speaking. There was no façade, no foolish games playing out. Glen really was a simple man. *A simple man who dealt in liquor*, she reminded herself. But his honesty, the true blue of his eyes—in them she saw nothing but a man she wanted to know more about; to be with for a long time to come. The honey-brown liquid faded into the deepest banks of her memory. Something else was filling her mind.

"What is it you want, Josephine? Have your dreams changed since coming here?"

"Woefully so," she said while keeping her eyes on his. Her breath left her, and she waited for his kiss, but it didn't surface.

"Here." He handed her another twenty-dollar bill. "Take this and get home to Michigan."

"I–I don't want to go back to Michigan."

"You just told me you did. What is it you do want, Josephine?" He said her name in a whisper, and she knew he felt the sparks between them, like one of the electric streetlamps that reflected in his blue eyes.

"I promised you I'd work a year in the Linton household, and I know I sound flighty, but I'm going to work that year, Glen." How could she tell him her convictions all stemmed from the concern in his blue eyes, from her desire to be near him? She forced the twenty into his large hand, and he grabbed her wrist with one hand. She felt his other trace her cheek, and she looked up to see the emotion in his eyes. He bent toward her slowly, and they shared a kiss. First, a small gentle touch to the lips, and then something far more passionate. She anticipated more, still gripping the money in her hands, but throwing her arms around Glen's wide neck. She tried to kiss him again, but he pulled away.

"Go back to Michigan," he said sternly. "I have nothing to offer you. Those two twenties you hold are all I have to give a woman."

"I don't want your money, Glen. I want answers. Why do you work in this creepy house? Why don't you finish your apprenticeship elsewhere? Why did you ask me to work for a year in that mausoleum?"

"Because I made promises. Promises I have to keep."

Josephine stepped back, her shoulders straight. "Then I have promises to keep. I promised to keep working here, and I will, Glen. I'll make you bring me here every day, and I'll figure out what your secret is. I know how you've been looking out for me, protecting me. Something is going on, and I intend to figure it out."

Glen turned from her. "There's no deep mystery, Jo. You've seen too many Gary Cooper movies. I'm just a workingman of no importance whatsoever. Any secrets I have aren't worth two nickels rubbed together."

"Kiss me again and tell me that." She baited him, not allowing his eyes to leave hers.

He just cleared his throat, looking back at the house. "Let's go, Jo. Before we both lose our jobs."

Chapter 8

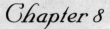

Marian, you must know where he gets this kind of money." Jo flashed the forty dollars in her hand. A king's ransom for the residents of Eighth Avenue, indeed. Jo moved her gaze to the sleeping Davy and lowered her voice. "I've seen him with liquor, Marian. Is he a bootlegger?"

Marian's hands kept busy. "Heavens no, Jo. He's probably just saved the money. He's a hard worker, and he's been working for a long time. Take it and send for Claire. Glen wouldn't have parted with it if he needed it, and he wouldn't have had liquor without a reason. I've fed that man two nights a week for years now. Not once have I ever smelled liquor on his breath. It's not the sort of thing you can generally hide, Jo."

"You think I should take it then?" Josephine's mouth dropped open. It was so unlike Marian to suggest charity. This was charity, wasn't it? "I thought you wanted us to work for everything we have."

"Glen doesn't want anything from us, Jo. He knows we have nothing to give, and he's been a good friend to us, especially to Davy. I wouldn't question a man who has a heart for children as Glen does. He probably feels for young Claire, alone in that house with a madwoman. Take the money; you can pay it back. We'll do what we can as well. Mitch has just been saying it was time to get Claire here, too. Her letters are sounding more and more desperate. It's just too bad we have to sneak her out here, rather than using Father's free rail pass. But Claire is so young, and Agnes would never let her come without a fight. Agnes would miss the live-in maid she's created."

"I'm going to wire her the money first thing in the morning, Marian!" Excitement fluttered in Jo's chest. Perhaps she hadn't accomplished things the way she planned, but Claire would be out of danger. The money was a simple loan; if Glen's conscience had something to worry about, let his heart be troubled, not her own. His image raced through her mind: his steely blue eyes, his intense work ethic, his three-dollars-a-day salary. None of it made sense, but she pushed such thoughts away. Ignorance provided her a clear conscience and her sister's safe delivery.

Since it was Sunday afternoon, Glen would be arriving for dinner soon. His church got out a bit later than their own, and she used the time to help Marian in the kitchen before freshening up at the sink. She wished there was a way to thank Glen for his generosity, but she felt he probably preferred her quiet gratefulness.

At his knock, she opened the door to see him standing before her with a black eye. The blue of his pupil shone brightly against the dark purple splotch surrounding his upper face. "Glen!" she exclaimed. "What on earth happened?"

"Come on outside, Jo. I don't want Davy to see me like

this. It will probably frighten him."

"Davy's sleeping," she explained. "Let me get you a cold compress to put on that. It looks dreadfully painful."

"No, just please come outside, Josephine. I want to talk to you." He looked around at Marian. "Alone, if you don't mind."

Jo followed him outside, intrigued by the nature of his visit, but fearful at the same time. If he was going to tell her the money came from an illegal source, she'd have to give it back—and she was so set on Claire's arrival. She closed the door behind her. They sat on the landing, as they now did every night following the dinners they'd shared in Marian's home.

"What happened?" She allowed her fingers to gently touch the swelling.

Glen flinched at her touch. "I'm in trouble, Jo."

Her stomach turned at the admission. "Do you need your money back? I have a few more dollars saved in the house—can I help you in any way?" She took his hand without thinking, only wishing there was a way she could dissipate his troubles as easily as he'd done for her.

"No, it's nothing like that, Jo. It's Winthrop Linton. This shiner was intended for him, and far worse, I suspect. Apparently he used my name to hide some business dealings from his father. He's dealing with dangerous men."

Jo shivered at the admission. Glen wasn't the dramatic sort. If he said dangerous men, it probably meant far worse than he was allowing. Thinking back to the recent Valentine's Day massacre in Chicago by bootlegging thugs, Jo was consumed by the thunderous beating of her heart. If there were any doubt left as to how she felt about Glen, it was gone now. The thought of him in trouble sent her mind stirring. She wanted nothing more than his protection, his safety. She'd do whatever to ensure it.

"What can I do, Glen? Please, tell me. Can I talk to Winthrop?"

"I want you to quit at the Lintons'. I'll help you find something else, but I want you out of danger, Jo. Once those men figure out I'm not the one they are looking for, they are bound to come looking for Winthrop, and I don't want you near there."

"But, Glen, I need that job to support Claire. Do you want me to go back to Michigan? Certainly Winthrop has kept his wits to keep his identity sealed."

"Certainly he has. Unfortunately, he's used my name to do so. I came to tell you we can't be in contact with one another anymore. Whoever these men are, they'll be watching. If they think you're important to me, well—"

She stumbled over her words. "*Am* I important to you?"

"Too important for me to get you involved in this."

"Tell me the truth, Glen. Are you selling liquor? Is this your mess and not Winthrop's? It won't change anything between us. I just need to know. Even if you did something illegal, I know where your heart is, by the fact you gave me that money."

He studied her face, the disappointment evident in his expression. "I'm a man of God, Josephine. I take that title with the utmost seriousness. I haven't done anything illegal, I promise you that. And as for us, there is no us. You've got to stay away from me. I'm moving out this week to protect all of you from whatever, whoever is out there. This is my bed. I made it that fateful day when I listened to Winthrop Linton."

"Tell me what you've promised Winthrop. What are his plans? What is his secret? Tell me, Glen, please!" She pleaded with him, longing to know what kept Glen at arm's length, and why he made her promise to work a year and now was begging for her resignation. Nothing made sense anymore. Least of all, her impassioned desire to kiss this man and gently touch the throbbing purple bruise around his eye.

"It is for your own good you know as little as possible. I'll explain your absence to Mrs. Houston tomorrow."

"I won't be absent tomorrow." Jo faced him, conviction in her eyes. "I'm bringing Claire out this month. I've already written the telegram for the wire. I need this job, Glen." Jo's nose prickled with the urge to cry. "If you can't give me a good reason to quit, I certainly won't."

"You don't need this job, Josephine. Go home and live with your stepmother. Surely your father or your Grandmother Faith I hear you speak of—certainly she could help you."

"No, Grandmother has an infirmity. She's had it since she was young, and it's only gotten worse with age. I can't worry her over such a small thing. I haven't even told her the wedding chest she passed to my mother has been taken." Jo shook her head. She'd long since decided her grandmother's health was too frail.

"Her granddaughter's well-being is not so small. Tell your grandmother, Jo. Or better yet, your father. Claire shouldn't be your concern. Not at your young age."

"What is happening to this world, Glen? This seems such a lost generation, with the women cutting their hair to obscene lengths, illegal alcohol is so readily available, and now, a man begins teaching we evolved from monkeys and are not of God. What's next? I just don't understand, Glen. Is there no truth left in the world? I want to bury my head in the sand and protect my sister's precious Davy from ever growing up and seeing the corruption we've created."

"Josephine, no. Don't cry." Glen leaned over and kissed her gently. Their lips met in a firestorm of emotion, and soon their kiss developed into a passionate encounter. The importance of breathing suddenly paled in comparison to his light touch. She allowed her hand to follow the structure of his face, to hold him before her, willing him not to leave her again.

"No!" He pulled away, just as he'd done that night on the Linton walkway. When would he admit he loved her? That they were meant to be together? She tried to kiss him again, and he stood. "The Bible says to be anxious for nothing. Take that advice, Josephine, and run with it. Run back to Michigan and live your fate." He headed up the street toward the streetcar, and she followed him desperately.

"No, Glen. Please don't leave!" But he was out of her sight before she finished her plea.

Glen rushed to the moving streetcar, dashing on it like some kind of Buster Keaton movie poster. Glen focused on the floorboards, ignoring the curious looks and whispered talk over his beaten appearance. He looked as though he'd been thrown out of some speakeasy, and he knew the hushed voices said so. This was the will of God? Glen shot a glance at the clouded sky.

Why, God? I heard Winthrop's cry for mercy, and I tried to help him. For what? Now I've lost Jo's trust, probably my job, and Winthrop's own parents think I'm corrupting their boy. I can't make him listen to me, Lord! Only You can do it. Only You can humble Winthrop to see his need, but will You? Or will You let me fall into this trap?

Glen rode to the end of the line and stepped off the streetcar without a destination. He had nowhere to be, nothing to do, but he couldn't stay with Josephine any longer. Josephine and her trusting eyes and willing heart. He couldn't even beat his anger out on the hammer today. It was Sunday. He walked toward the rocky cliff where the bay met the Pacific Ocean and looked at God's magnificence.

The wild surf beat the shore with one unrelenting explosion after another. God's power took on new meaning when watching the strength of the waves, the reminder that He was indeed in charge. The ferry to Sausalito sailed and returned multiple times before Glen knew what he had to do. It was time for Winthrop to quit hiding behind his mask. It was time his parents knew the truth and Winthrop prepared for the inevitable. The men who came after Glen had only offered a warning; the actual punishment would be far worse.

With renewed resolve, he rode the streetcar up to the Linton mansion. His presence would not be welcomed on a Sunday, but some things were more important than formal etiquette. Knocking on the door, he waited for Mrs. Houston. To his surprise, Winthrop himself answered.

"What happened to you?" Winthrop stepped back at the hideous sight of Glen's purple bruise.

"You should ask me what happened to you. This was intended for you."

Winthrop's small frame trembled as he opened the

door wider. "Come in. Go on into the study; we can talk there." His voice was hushed.

Turning, Glen witnessed the true Winthrop, the one behind the fine clothes and shiny Duesenberg. The Winthrop who cared nothing for people except as a means to get his way. Winthrop was more like his father than he'd ever know. The sight of him hurt Glen, even while filled with compassion for the sickly man. In the end, Glen felt a raw disgust.

In the past, Glen focused on the need, the spiritual dryness that the rich young man possessed, but today he could only see the sin, he could only feel the pride. Vanity emanated from Winthrop's pores, and he wasn't about to admit his need. Not to Glen, or God, or anyone else. The time had come for the games to stop.

"I'm done, Winthrop. I tried to show you God's love by helping you make something of yourself. But you've squandered my help. You've chased the almighty dollar, and I'd hoped it would impress your father, that you might be seen as some type of success before your time came. Now I know I've just wasted my time. You haven't appreciated a thing I've done for you, or you never would have given my name to those thugs."

An evil grin inhabited Winthrop's features. His lackluster chin and crooked smile came alive with malice. "I've seen you look at Josephine, Glen. You don't fool me for a minute. You've impressed her with my money. I saw you throw a twenty at her just last night. You see how dazzled she'll be by your measly three dollars a day. You've got no choice, Glen. Here." Winthrop held out the formal currency-like piece of paper which was so familiar to Glen.

"No, you get it yourself. I've done nothing illegal. I only

tried to help you. A useless cause, I see now. God knows your heart, Winthrop. Don't forget it. Even if you fool the entire city of San Francisco, you'll never fool Him."

"Do you think your God scares me? Your God is only a substitute for the power of money. I can buy and sell your God, Glen. He's only a figment of your imagination. A crutch for those of you who can't make it in today's world. We'll see how religious your little girlfriend is come Monday when she's fired."

Winthrop's threats held little power over Glen any longer. Glen had managed to pack away a tidy sum with his extra work. He had invested it in the stock market, made a killing on steel, pulled out the cash, and had enough to support a wife. Certainly not in grand style, but in the simple life he'd always imagined. He'd sent Josephine back to Michigan, but if she didn't go, he'd know God kept her there for him.

Now if only Josephine would trust him again, if only she'd be his wife, they'd find a way to make it. He'd tried to tell himself she was only a flight of fancy, too young to be a bride. But her kisses had crumbled that wall he'd built—her kisses and her stolen glances. When she could have been looking at Winthrop, in his impressive suits and fancy Duesenberg, her eyes always followed Glen in his simple denim jeans and wrinkled shirts.

Chapter 9

Mrs. Houston's coldhearted stare burrowed right through Jo's heart. Jo tilted her chin and returned the gaze blankly. There were no words, and none were necessary; Jo's employment was terminated. She curtsied before the older woman, not giving Mrs. Houston any more ammunition. Inwardly she winced as she slowly traipsed the walkway and the door slammed behind her. Mentally, she counted her meager savings at home in the coffee can. With no way to support Claire, Jo would have to focus on finding work, not on Glen. Failure decimated what she had left of confidence.

She couldn't return to Michigan now that Claire was on her way. She silently blasted Glen for leaving her in such a fix, but she was unable to stir up any anger. She knew he was only trying to protect her. Feelings of betrayal didn't surface, only an inexplicable longing for the muscular carpenter who had stolen her heart.

Summer ended quietly amidst the evergreen trees of San Francisco, and still Glen remained absent. She prayed for his protection every day. Finally, it dawned on her that Winthrop Linton might know where her love was and help put an end to her misery. Claire was due any day now, and Jo so wanted to share her arrival with Glen. One morning, after finishing the laundry and offering to go to the grocery, Josephine took the familiar streetcar route to the Nob Hill mansion in search of Winthrop, and, hopefully, some answers.

She drew in a deep breath and knocked on the front door, praying that Mrs. Houston wouldn't answer. Winthrop appeared. His face was white as stale snow and his weak features more sallow than ever. He splayed his bony, feminine fingers across the doorjamb.

"Well, Josephine. I see you couldn't stay away." He smiled, forcing her to gaze upon his small, sickly teeth.

"Can we talk somewhere privately, Master Linton?" She strained to use his proper title, to bow to his station in life, but it made her sick to her stomach. His adamant trust in himself and in his own power was more evident than it had once been, and his false confidence in his power over her made her want to laugh.

"I knew you'd be back. Not much work out there, Miss Josephine?"

She strode past him to the dining room, knowing he'd follow. Even in her long, green corduroy skirt, the kind everyone wore, she knew she interested him, and she'd use that to her advantage today. If she'd learned anything during her time in San Francisco, she'd learned she wasn't completely powerless. Certainly not to a weak-minded man like Winthrop Linton.

"I didn't come to speak to you of a job. My brother-in-law is doing fine financially, and we're managing just fine.

I came to speak to you about Glen."

"Glen?" Winthrop casually fixed himself a drink. "Do I know a Glen?" He tried to look down on her, to appear haughty, but Josephine stood to her full height. Although petite, she still towered over the spineless little man.

She walked toward him, forced the crystal glass from his hand, and plopped it on the shiny dining room table with a thunk. "Don't play innocent with me, Winthrop. I didn't come here for a job, and I don't want anything you have to offer. I just want to know what you did to give Glen a shiner. Besides hide behind his name, of course. Where is he? Tell me, Winthrop, or I'll tell those men at the apartment, the burly ones who have been looking for Glen, *who* they are really looking for. I think they would actually pay handsomely for the information." She watched his arrogant smile disintegrate into fear. "They might make my money woes go away completely, possibly?"

The familiar sound of a hammer caught her attention, a steady beat she'd know anywhere. Winthrop's anxious eyes gave way to recognition, and Josephine ran for the door. Winthrop tried to stop her, but his frail frame was no match for her determined self. She was at the door before he finished the thought. She flew down the steps to the work shed.

"Glen! Glen!"

The hammering stopped, and his steely gray-blue eyes met hers for the first time in months. Every emotion melted except one, and she ran toward him. He dropped his hammer and his muscular arms came around her tightly, clutching her in an embrace she once only dreamed about.

"Josephine!" His hands ran through her hair desperately, and he pulled her face back, looking at her momentarily, before she felt his firm lips on hers. All sense of decorum was lost as she returned his kiss frantically, searching for a way to tell him how she missed him. Her kiss grew firmer when words wouldn't come.

"Well, isn't this cozy?" Winthrop's voice tore them apart and Josephine's eyes threw daggers. Winthrop. The man who'd kept them apart all this time, who'd stolen precious moments from their love affair.

Before she spoke, Glen put a hand to her mouth. "Winthrop, I told you how I felt about Josephine from the day you first fired her."

"Winthrop fired me? I thought it was you, Glen. To protect me, remember?" Jo's face twisted in confusion.

"Is that what he told you?" Winthrop laughed, that obnoxious, weasel-like giggle she'd heard one too many times when he came home in the mornings, drunk. "How many women have heard that line and believed it?"

"That's enough, Winthrop! I've lived this lie of yours long enough. Leave us." Glen stood to his full height. "We have some things to discuss."

"Not at my expense you don't. You're not telling her the truth, or I'll—"

"You'll what, Winthrop?" Glen's eyes narrowed, and Winthrop cowered behind a brick pedestal decorating the garden. At that minor show of strength, Winthrop left them alone, retreating for the safety of his mansion.

"Where have you been, Glen? We've been worried sick. Even baby Davy looks for you when I take him outside." Her concern soon grew to feelings of betrayal at being left behind. "How could you just leave us and come back here—when you had me fired from a job I swore I'd keep a year?"

"Sit down, Josephine." She found a place on a dusty sawhorse and did as he asked. His expression was grave, his words slow. "I was prepared to leave town, to let Winthrop get himself out of his own mess, but then God spoke to me. Clear as day, He said I wasn't done here. I heard Him tell me not to desert Winthrop in this time of need. I couldn't go, and I couldn't explain it to you for your own good, but the time has come."

"Yes," she agreed.

"Do you know what this is?" He pulled an official-looking slip of paper from his back pocket. It had the appearance of currency but was headed by the title line "Original Prescription Form for Medicinal Liquor" and was attached to a stub reading the same. On the bottom it read in block, dollar-bill letters: National Prohibition Act.

"A prescription for liquor?" Fear rose in her like an untamed fire. "Are you sick, Glen? Is that why you had the liquor in your lunch box?"

"Not me, Jo. Winthrop. It's cancer. First they thought it was tuberculosis, but his cough subsided, and now they feel it is cancer. They gave him a year to live, just about the time when you started."

"That's why you wanted me to stay?"

Glen only nodded and continued. "He's been in a lot of pain, and they've given him prescription liquor to fight it. I've been picking it up for him at the drugstore so his parents wouldn't worry. I've been hoping my witness would show him that God's love wouldn't desert him. That's why I'd hoped to keep order in the house during his bout, but that was not to happen."

"Glen, there's enough liquor in his house to keep him drunk for years. Why would he need a doctor's prescription?" Jo shook her head, trying to make sense of the nonsense. Winthrop, although pale as a sheet, appeared in fine spirits when sober.

"His parents don't know about the illness. He's been building a neighborhood of small tract houses for the working folk with my help. That's how he planned to make his money from the allowance his parents provide him with. He wanted to succeed before he succumbed to the disease—to prove to his parents he was more than just an ornament to take over his father's steel business."

"Why the thugs? He had to be involved in some nasty business to have those kind of men after him. You're telling me it wasn't the liquor?"

"No, Winthrop borrowed heavily to keep building the houses after the stock drop in July. He didn't go to a bank to keep his father from knowing. It turned out to be a bad decision. Luckily, I'd made a little money in the stock market and was able to help him out."

"So you're out of trouble? And you still deserted me?" Jo stared into Glen's eyes, looking for the deception she felt. His answers only brought up more questions. "How could you allow me to lose my job?"

"I was worried, Jo. Really. Those men meant business, and I wanted you safe. I figured the forty dollars would keep you set for awhile until you could find something else."

"I used that money for my sister, Glen, to bring her to California. She's finally able to come after months of arrangements. You left me with meager savings, and no earning potential whatsoever. How could you do that to me? To my family?" She stamped her foot, embarrassed by her childish behavior, but too upset to care.

"I was trying to earn enough money to buy one of the houses, Jo. I took my carpentry test, and I'm in the union now, thanks to Winthrop, and making eight dollars a day! I cut the lumber here all day for the project downtown."

"Well, that's just fine for you. In the meantime, I'm stealing food from Davy's mouth in that cramped flat! Not to mention Claire is—"

"So we could be married," Glen continued.

Josephine stammered, "Wh–what did you say?" She looked up in hopeful anticipation.

"I said I wanted to buy the house so we could be married, Josephine. I love you. Maybe I've done an awful job of showing it, but I want you as my wife. My sister told me you hadn't left for Michigan, that you'd sent for Claire. I took that as a sign you cared for me, too. Was I wrong?"

"No, Glen. I love you, too, but what about Winthrop? What about his threats?"

Glen looked to the floorboards and pulled her into the shed deeper. He whispered, "I'm afraid Winthrop isn't going to be with us long enough to make many more threats. Pray for his soul, Jo. That's what we must do, and we must try not to upset him. He plans to tell his parents this very night. I tried to leave so many times, but God kept holding me back, forcing me to stay. He needs me right now, Jo. I know it's hard to see with his obnoxious behavior, but he's hurting. He aches with physical pain but even more with spiritual darkness."

Glen's eyes filled with tears as he spoke, and Jo had never seen a more beautiful sight. How could she have ever doubted him? "I'll marry you, Glen. Whenever you're ready, I'll marry you."

"It won't be long now, my love. Give Winthrop no pity, only your prayers."

"I will; you can count on it. I'm going to the station to pick up Claire tonight."

"I'll be home to you soon. Claire and you will have a quaint little house within the next couple months, and hopefully Winthrop will have a room prepared for him by our Lord."

She embraced Glen with all her strength, overwhelmed by the fact that her family would soon be intact. The new family which God had fashioned of His own hand.

Jo arrived at the station, anxious and thrilled for her sister's arrival. She babbled incessantly while Glen just watched her happily. Running alongside the train, Jo searched the windows for a sign of her sister, but slowed her pace eventually when the appearance didn't come. When the last traveler disembarked, a shudder of fear overcame her. She ran to the conductor and was directed to the office.

"My sister was supposed to be on that train. Is there another train due?" Jo's voice shook. Glen smoothed his hand along her back trying to comfort her, but it was of little use.

"You Josephine Mayer?" The office man's chin jutted toward her.

"Yes, yes, I am." Jo nodded.

"Letter for you, over there in that trunk."

Jo turned to see her mother's beloved wedding chest, hand-carved and filled with memories, lying isolated in a forgotten corner of the station. "Glen, that's my mother's trunk! The one Agnes stole from us." Josephine shook her head. "But how did Claire get it, and where is my sister?"

"Let's go find out." Glen held her shaking hand. Jo was overwhelmed with tears at the sight of the old chest.

"This chest meant so much to my mother and my Grandma Faith." Jo reached and opened the chest. A letter lay on top of the treasures within, treasures which included the seed pearl gown worn by generations of brides before her. Jo ripped open the letter with abandon.

Dear Jo,

I'm sure you're wondering where I am by now, and the answer is, in case you haven't guessed, I'm not coming. Grandma Faith found out what I was up to and asked Agnes for the chest back, saying she was in need of memories of Grandpa. Even Agnes couldn't refuse her. I've decided to live with Grandma for now. She could use the company, and I could certainly stand to get away from here. She was very angry with both of us for not telling her our situation. Anyway, I used the money you sent me to pack the chest and ship it to California. Marian tells me there's a husband in your future, and I knew you had to have the dress. I only wish Marian had had it as well. Wear it and think of me, dear sister. I love you.

Claire

Jo wiped the tears from her eyes and fingered the delicate fabric of the elaborate wedding gown. "It's all too much!" She stood and Glen took her in his arms.

"No, Josephine, it's all from God, and He never holds back in good gifts."

"Like our little house on State Street?"

Glen smiled. "Yes, just like that. Now that the stock market has crashed, work will be even harder to come by."

"Poor Mr. Linton." Jo looked to the fancy chest below her, thankful her own treasures would last.

"Mr. Linton is just lucky Winthrop invested outside the stock market. Winthrop finally got what he wanted—his father's respect."

"And God finally got what He wanted—Winthrop's heart."

Jo snuggled into Glen's firm chest, knowing whatever lay ahead, she'd weather it all with Glen at the helm under God's direction.

Epilogue

Josephine wrapped her wedding gown in cotton and placed it carefully back into the box. As she did so, she added a letter as each of her predecessors had done:

To My Future Generations,
    Times are very hard as I write this letter. Most of America struggles to put food on the table, and we are, gratefully, unscathed by the Great Depression. I don't know if times will warrant anyone wearing this elegant gown again, but know whoever reads this letter as my descendent, I have prayed for you and the generations that come after you. This gown meant everything to me at a time when marriage itself was a financial stretch. It was a piece of my beloved mother given back to me. While the gown may go by the wayside, I pray that your faith in our Lord and a godly husband will not. May God richly bless you, my daughters, wherever He leads you.

Josephine Mayer Bechtel
Married August 14, 1929

P.S. Enclosed in this chest, I've added a piece of colored glass that is so popular in our day. It is not expensive, nor will it probably ever be, but it meant a great deal to me when Glen brought it home. The pattern is called cabbage rose, and the pitcher held a place of great honor in our home.

KRISTIN BILLERBECK

Kristin lives in the Silicon Valley with her engineering director husband Bryed, and their four children. When not writing, Kristin also enjoys reading, painting, and conversing with her on-line writing groups. She has four published novels with the **Heartsong Presents** line and two novellas in anthologies from Barbour Publishing. Visit Kristin on the web at www.getset.com/kristinbillerbeck

THE PERSISTENT BRIDE

by Gina Fields

Chapter 1

"Hey, Beauty. Here's a beast for you to tame."

Carly Simmons, Head of Social Services at Bradenton General Hospital in Bradenton, Georgia, looked up from the open file on her moderately cluttered desk. Susan Shelton, the head orthopedic nurse, stood before her, holding yet another file. Carly hadn't even heard Susan come in. But then Carly rarely closed her office door, and Susan *never* knocked.

With a forefinger, Carly pushed her tortoiseshell glasses up the bridge of her nose. "Good morning, Susan," she said, reaching for the file. "Did you have a nice weekend?"

"Not really." In the same breath, Susan commenced verbalizing everything that wasn't nice about her weekend.

Inwardly, Carly sighed. She had known better than to ask the pessimistic nurse about her personal life. Shutting out Susan's disgruntled voice, she opened the folder and began reading about her next prospective client.

Mitchell D. Reynolds. Age, thirty-two. . .

Consternation pinched Carly's brow. No current address. No telephone number. No place of employment. No relatives. Shoving her glasses up again, she looked back up at Susan.

"And my husband was no help, either," the nurse was saying. "All he did was—"

"Excuse me, Susan."

Fortunately, the nurse took Carly's overt hint and fell silent.

"Is Mr. Reynolds homeless?"

Susan hunched a shoulder. "Beats me. What you see in that file is all the information we could squeeze out of him."

Which wasn't much, Carly concluded. The files sent to Social Services contained only personal information and not a full medical report. "The patient data sheet says he was in an automobile accident. How badly is he hurt?"

"He has a cast up to his left shoulder and one up to his left hip." Susan examined her fingernails, as though talking about someone else's problems, instead of her own, bored her. "His leg had to have a pin put in it. He also has a couple of broken ribs and some cuts and bruises."

Carly grimaced. "Ouch."

Susan shifted her gaze to Carly. "Don't let his injuries fool you. He can still growl loudly enough."

"I take it he's not a very good patient."

"Ha! That's putting it mildly. The only thing nice about Mitchell Reynolds is his looks. If it hadn't been for that, I would have thrown him out on his keister an hour ago. Good thing his arm is in a cast, or he would have wrung my neck when I pulled out the bedpan this morning."

Smiling at the mental picture the nurse's words evoked, Carly closed the file and leaned back in her chair. "Thanks, Susan. I'll check on him in a few minutes. It definitely looks like he'll be needing Social Services."

"It'll be interesting to see if you can redeem this one," Susan said as she turned to go. "I put my money on the beast."

Carly forced the nurse's gibing remark to roll off her back. After working six years in Social Services, she was getting used to the jeering comments her coworkers made about the effort she put into her job. Most of her clients were on the poverty end of the income bracket. Some because it was the best they could do; others because they didn't care. Some of her peers tended to look upon the destitute patients as something less than human, which not only disappointed Carly, it puzzled her as well. Why would anyone waste time working in a hospital if they didn't find joy in seeing their disadvantaged patients better themselves?

Mentally, she shook her head. She supposed there were many answers to that question, but she didn't have time to ponder them right now. She had to figure out what to do about Mr. Reynolds.

Propping her elbow on the desk and her chin in her hand, she drummed her fingertips against her cheek and focused on the scant bit of information he had provided. Usually, before meeting a prospective client, she studied a file and gleaned information on the patient from the hospital staff. But in Mr. Reynolds's case, there wasn't much to glean, except that he had a name, an age, and a vicious growl.

How did she approach someone she knew so little about?

After only a few seconds' deliberation, she filtered a resigned sigh. "Head on, I suppose," she muttered.

Straightening her spine, she picked up the folder, stood, and marched for the door.

With each step she took, the nerves in her stomach jumped a little higher. Meeting people had always been hard for her. Her reservations at making new acquaintances had begun in grade school, where she was often referred to as "Geek," "Nerd," or "Tweety Bird" by her classmates. It was the same reason she had stayed in Georgia after graduating from college instead of returning to San Francisco to live near her parents. The city of her birth held too many unpleasant memories. In Bradenton, a small town in North Georgia, she discreetly blended into her surroundings. While her peers sometimes teased her about taking her job too seriously, they didn't call her cruel names or make fun of her. Mostly, they simply ignored her, which suited Carly just fine.

By the time she stepped off the elevator onto the second floor, her heart was pounding. When she stepped up to the door of Mitchell Reynolds's semiprivate room, she noticed her palms were sweaty. She wished Susan hadn't referred to the new patient as a beast. The brutish label had only served to put Carly's nerves on edge.

She drew in a deep breath of fortitude and released it slowly. Then she raised her hand to knock on the door. She couldn't do much about calming her jittery stomach now.

It was time to meet the beast.

Mitchell Reynolds lay helplessly in the hospital bed, his casted left leg supported by two pillows. His broken arm throbbed inside its own heavy cast. His cracked ribs burned every time he took a breath.

On the other side of the curtain dividing the semi-private room, the television blared with some talk-show host trying to yell above a screaming match between two sisters who were sleeping with the same man. Did people really listen to that stuff? Mitch closed his eyes. Apparently, his roommate did. Thank goodness, the elderly gentleman would be checking out soon. At least, that's what Mitch overheard the man's nurse tell him awhile ago.

He tried to block out the pain, the noise, and the cold, harsh reality staring him in the face. Last night he'd lost his last earthly possession—his treasured sports car. Last month it had been his condo. Two months before that, his job.

How had he fallen so far so fast?

The answer jabbed at his conscience. He shoved it away. All he had needed to get back on his feet was a little more time—and one lucky night at the game tables. But no one had wanted to wait; no one had been willing to give him a second chance. Instead, everyone he cared for and trusted had turned their backs on him.

Now, here he was, lying in a hospital bed with his entire left side shattered to pieces, without a stitch of clothing to call his own, or enough money to buy the plastic pitcher sitting on his bedside table. He would have been better off if the truck that had T-boned his car had hit him just a little bit harder and put an end to his miserable life.

Someone knocked on the door. He closed his eyes. If it was the nurse coming to poke and prod him again, perhaps she'd think he was asleep and go away.

The door creaked open. "Mr. Reynolds?"

The soft, inquiring voice was female, but not familiar. Mitch kept his eyes shut and forced his breathing to remain steady.

After a few seconds, he heard her ask the man on the other side of the curtain to turn down the television, which he did. Without the loud noise, Mitch could hear her faint footsteps as she approached his bed. Although he couldn't see her, he could feel her gaze upon him, assessing his injuries. . .and him.

A fiery dart of anger shot through him. Why didn't she do whatever she'd come to do and leave? Hadn't she ever seen an injured man before? Or was she curious to see what a "homeless" injured man looked like? He waited for her to slip the blood pressure cuff around his arm or to check his IV, but she did neither. She simply stood there, staring at him like he was a freak in some sideshow.

His rancor reached the boiling point. He gritted his teeth. If all she wanted to do was gawk, he'd give her something to long remember him by. In one lightning-quick move, he opened his eyes, raised his head off the pillow, and said, "Boo!"

She jumped back, releasing an ear-splitting shriek. Her arms flew up, launching the clipboard and folder she was holding. Papers from the folder fluttered to the floor, but the edge of the clipboard crashed into Mitch's forehead, then landed with a plop against his broken ribs. A forceful *"Ooooof!"* shot from his lips. Had it not been for the impeding casts, the pain would have folded his injured body in half.

Struggling to breathe past the intense burning in his side, he pressed his right hand to his pounding forehead and leveled the woman who had just knocked him senseless with an angry glare. She stood with her hands clamped over her mouth, her back hugging a wall that was somehow still standing, her hazel eyes stretched wide behind a pair of large tortoiseshell glasses that swallowed half her heart-shaped face. She reminded him of a scared mouse. Mitch hated mice.

His nurse, whom he'd silently labeled Susan the Torturer, came rushing in, skidding to a stop when she saw the shocked woman plastered to the wall. "Carly, what happened?"

The nurse directing her question to the woman she referred to as "Carly" only fueled Mitch's ire. "Get her out of here!" he said through clenched teeth.

The nurse eyed Mitch with something akin to suspicion, then shifted her gaze back to the woman. "Are you all right?"

Mitch saw red. Who was the patient here?

Susan's question seemed to pull Carly out of her dazed stupor. She dropped her hands from her mouth and peeled herself off the wall. "I–I'm f–f–f–fine."

Her stammering voice told Mitch she wasn't fine. She was still quite shaken, which should have pleased him. But, oddly, it didn't. For some reason, he felt the cord of ire wrapped around his soul loosen a bit.

She crouched and began gathering scattered papers from the floor but didn't offer to remove the clipboard from where it lay wedged between his plastered arm and broken ribs. With a little pain and effort, he could hand the board to her, but he decided not to. She was the one who threw the thing up in the air, causing it to fall on his head and ribs. Let her work up the nerve to come within biting distance of him. Not that he'd really bite her, but he could tell by the wary look on her face she thought he would.

Susan roughly plumped up his pillow, probably as payback for his earlier refusal to use the bedpan. He forced himself not to wince from the discomfort she aroused. She could fume from now until doomsday for all he cared. Nobody was going to get that cold piece of plastic under him. So what if she'd had to put forth a little effort helping him get up to go to the bathroom awhile ago? It was her job. She should be thankful she had one.

She gave his pillow one final punch. "Is there anything I can do for you before I leave, Mr. Bea—I mean, Mr. Reynolds?"

"I asked you to get that woman out of here while I've still got one good leg and arm left," he muttered under his breath.

Susan sent him a catty grin. "Sorry, but I don't have the authority to tell the head of Social Services what to do."

So, that's who the skittish woman was—the head of Social Services come to offer the homeless man a handout. He took a few seconds to assess her. His first impression had hit the target. She really did look like a mousy little thing with those alert hazel eyes, outdated glasses, and long, light brown hair pulled back in a ponytail at her nape. She wore very little makeup, no jewelry except for a simple gold-tone watch, and a drab beige pantsuit. She didn't look old enough—or competent enough—to be the head of anything, much less Social Services.

On her way out, Susan stopped and patted the woman's arm. "Let me know if you need anything. Gauze, bandages, duct tape for his mouth. . ."

The nurse's snide remark sent a ping of annoyance

through Mitch. He made a mental note to complain to her supervisor. Then he remembered who and what he now was, a penniless, homeless man—a bum. Who was going to listen to him? He tried to swallow the contemptible anger rising in his throat. It wouldn't go down.

The mouse pushed her glasses up onto the bridge of her nose. "Thank you, Susan. I think I can handle it from here."

After the nurse left, Ms. Head of Social Services finally met Mitch's gaze. Cagily, she studied him. "Hello, Mr. Reynolds. I'm Carly Simmons, he—"

"Head of Social Services. I heard."

She took a timid step forward, extending her right hand. He supposed he could at least return the social gesture.

"May I have my clipboard back?"

Feeling a bit chagrined at his misinterpretation of her action, Mitch pulled back the hand he'd started to extend and looked down at the clipboard leaning against his chest. He had already forgotten it was there.

"Please?" she added, her voice still sounding small, but not quite as shaky as before.

He abandoned his previous plans to make her retrieve the board herself and handed it to her.

She took a quick step forward, snatched the board, and took a swift step back. "Th–thank you."

Mitch's anger dwindled a bit, and, for the first time he could remember, guilt pricked a layer of his conscience. This woman didn't deserve the brunt of his short fuse. Sure, she'd stood next to his bed and ogled him. She'd even tossed the clipboard that had hit him in the head. But whose fault was that? He supposed he'd have to take the blame for yelling "Boo" at her. If only he'd known she was such a timid little thing.

"Um." She cleared her throat. "I'd just like to go over a few things with you, Mr. Reynolds." She pulled a chair away from the wall and sat down, opening the file in her lap. "According to the information we have, you have no current address."

"I'm between addresses."

When she looked up, her glasses had slid back down her nose. For some reason, the endearing picture she portrayed stirred within him a desire to smile, but the smile didn't quite make it to the surface.

"Do you have your new address yet?"

"No."

"I see." She turned her attention back to the file. "There's no place of employment listed, either."

Mitch was supposed to have started working with a construction company framing crew this morning. But, like everything else, circumstances had managed to rob him of that opportunity, too. "I'm also between jobs."

This time, when she glanced up, she pushed her glasses back up with her forefinger then pulled a pencil from behind her ear. "We have several different programs—"

"No, thank you."

"Mr. Reynolds, you didn't hear me out."

Was that a ring of irritation in her voice? She struck him as the type to cower with her tail tucked between her legs at the first blatant hint of refusal to accept her services. He noted the firm set of her delicate jaw and inwardly shrugged. He supposed even the faintest of heart had a frustration switch that could be tripped when hit hard enough.

"I didn't need to hear you out, Miss Simmons." He wanted to cross his arms in his own frustration, but he couldn't, not with this stupid cast up to his armpit. "If you are worried about getting your money, there's no need. As soon as I get out of the hospital and find a job, I'll set up a payment plan. It may take some time, but I will settle my expenses. I *do* pay my debts, Miss Simmons." That's why he'd grabbed the job framing houses—so he could pay off the debts the sale of his personal belongings hadn't satisfied. And so he could eat.

"That's very gracious of you, Mr. Reynolds. I appreciate your willingness to do your part. But in the meantime, if there's help out there, why not—"

Her persistence goaded his anger. "Because I don't need it," he snapped.

Tucking her pencil behind her ear, she leaned back in her chair and crossed her arms. "Mr. Reynolds, are you always this rude? Or did Susan put a burr in your blanket this morning?"

Her blunt response caught him off guard. Before he could gauge his reaction, he blinked in surprise. But he quickly recovered and drew his brows together in an impatient frown. "I'm rude when someone gives me a reason to be, Miss Simmons."

"No, you're not. You're rude because you think life has tossed you a dirty deal, and you're not only taking it out on everyone else, you're pushing away the very people who can help you."

Humiliation joined the rage roiling within his chest. "You don't know what you're talking about, Miss Simmons. I don't need you or your services."

Seemingly undaunted, she raised her brows. "Oh?"

Opening the file, she held it out in front of her like a choir book. "No home, no job, no relatives—or at least none you care to have us contact."

No, he didn't have any relatives he'd wanted to contact, except one. And he couldn't contact her without his greatest nemesis finding out where he was and what had happened to him. So, his whereabouts would just have to remain a mystery for now.

But that area of his life was none of Miss Simmons's business.

She snapped the folder shut and stood, holding both it and the clipboard by her side. Then, to Mitch's surprise, she stepped forward, propped her fists on the side of his bed, and leaned over him with her nose less than six inches from his. "The way I see it, unless you have a million dollars stashed somewhere, you need Social Services until you can get back on your feet. Then, if you wish, you can pay back every cent you owe to whatever program supplied the funds. But, let me assure you, with no income and no insurance, hospital administration is not going to allow you to lie here and grumble until you get back on your feet. And when they kick you out on your backside, then what will you do?"

Mitch found himself trapped between anger and awareness. Gold flecks burned in her piercing eyes, which indignation had turned a startling teal green. Her soft, rose-petal scent swam around his head. Each breath she released laced the air with the faint smell of spearmint. Their gazes locked for a frozen moment, and a strange, fluttery sensation, like a captured butterfly, rose in Mitch's chest. Then she drew back and stood, and an eerie chill whispered across his skin.

"I'll leave these." She slapped several pamphlets down on the bedside table next to a Gideon Bible. "Take some time to calm yourself, then read them. I'll be back tomorrow to discuss exactly which program will best suit your needs."

With that, she turned and stalked out of the room, leaving a dumbfounded Mitch looking after her.

After several stupefied seconds, he frowned in consternation. What had just happened here? Miss Carly Simmons had crept in here like a fidgety breeze, then stormed out like a tenacious tornado, leaving Mitch entirely speechless. And no one had ever left Mitchell Reynolds speechless.

No one.

Chapter 2

When Carly arrived home that evening and checked her mailbox, she found a postcard from her ophthalmologist letting her know her new glasses were ready. After ten years in the same frames, she had decided it was time for a change.

She retrieved the rest of her mail and pulled into the driveway of her modest two-story home which was graced by a wraparound porch, white clapboard siding, and mint-green shutters.

After parking at the side of the house, she stepped out of her twelve-year-old gray sedan into the brisk, March air. Slipping her purse strap over her shoulder, she strolled up her sidewalk while leafing through the rest of her mail. She'd received a couple of pieces of junk mail soliciting credit cards and a bill for her automobile insurance. Nothing out of the ordinary. But then there never was.

She unlocked the front door and stepped inside. On her way through the living room, she tossed the junk mail in a trash can and laid her purse, the insurance bill, and the postcard on the coffee table. She then wandered into her bedroom, where she collapsed backward on the pink-and-green flowered comforter covering her four-poster bed. Her arms flopped out to her sides, like the extended wings of an exhausted bird.

While she lay there, staring at the white rotating ceiling fan, her mind drifted back to that morning—and Mitchell Reynolds. She had never lost her temper with a patient before. In fact, she could count on one hand the number of times she'd lost her temper in her entire life. But his incensed raging had pushed her patience one inch too far. And it had all started when he'd opened his eyes and yelled "Boo!" The nerve of that man! She had left his room thinking he deserved the lump her clipboard had delivered to his head.

A deflating breath left her chest. As the day wore on, her roiling anger had dissipated, and guilt had crept in. The culpable little monster had even followed her home.

She rolled over, propping her chin on her folded hands, and watched a finch nibble the grain in the bird feeder outside her window. She hadn't set an example of God's love today. She should have been a little more understanding of Mr. Reynolds's rancor and frustration. How would she react if she woke up in a hospital bed injured, homeless, and alone?

Her brow creased in thought. Her instincts told her he had only recently fallen on hardships. She had worked with homeless people before, and he simply didn't fit the mold. His fingernails were cut short, neat, and kept clean. His thick, blond hair, while a bit unruly and long, bore the signs of a stylish cut. And his aristocratic face and athletic body had been taken care of, possibly had been a bit pampered.

A strange flutter rose beneath Carly's ribs as she

pictured the handsome patient, lying there with his left arm and leg bound in confining casts. Susan was right. He didn't have much of a personality, but beneath his cuts and bruises, he did have a nice face. . .and broad shoulders. . . and startling blue eyes. . . .

Realizing the wayward turn her thoughts had taken, Carly shook her head. Her job was to find a way to help Mr. Reynolds get back on his feet, not daydream about his male-model looks. But how was she going to help someone who didn't want to be helped? Filtering a despondent sigh, she sat up and slid off the bed. She'd ponder the answer to that question while she watered her thirsty houseplants.

She peeled off her pantsuit and replaced it with a green sweatshirt and worn blue jeans. While she was folding her pantsuit for the dry-cleaning stack, the phone rang. Abandoning the outfit, she picked up the nightstand receiver. "Hello."

"Happy birthday, Dear."

Carly's spirits lifted at the sound of her mother's voice. "Hi, Mom." Sitting back down on the bed, she crisscrossed her legs.

"Did you get your present?"

Carly glanced at her dresser, where the present still lay in a box with the lid cocked at a half-off angle. "Yes, Mom. Thanks for the dress. It's beautiful." And it was. The soft, peach-colored, knee-length silk garment was sleek and formfitting, but not too provocative. "I needed another church dress."

"Oh, I thought it would make a nice date dress."

Carly cringed. Her mother never failed to zero in on Carly's diminutive love life. Now that Carly had turned thirty, the interrogations could only get worse. "Yes, Mom," she said to appease her mother, "it will." If the dress wasn't out of style by the time she had another date. The last one had been over a year ago—and a disaster. Carly had shied away from the dance floor and refused to drink anything stronger than iced tea. Her date had brought her home early, leaving her with the impression he thought she was as square as a floor tile.

She wasn't eager to repeat such an experience. While time had granted her the ability to cover the pain of rejection, it hadn't lessened the sting.

"Are there any prospects, Dear?"

Her mother's question elbowed into Carly's dejected thoughts. "No, Mom. No prospects. How's Dad?" she asked, steering the conversation in a more pleasant direction.

"He's fine, Dear," her mother said, sounding a bit disgruntled.

"Is he there?"

After a few silent seconds, her father's boisterous voice reverberated in her ear. "Hiya, Sweetheart. How's it going?"

"Wonderful, Pop."

Carly had always gotten along well with her father. While practically everyone else in the world had made her feel like a misfit, he had always treated her like she was the center of his world.

They talked for awhile about the upcoming baseball season, how her job was progressing, and how much she loved the small church she now attended. Then, after a reluctant good-bye to both her parents, she hung up the phone. She might not miss the unpleasant memories of her life in San Francisco, but she did miss her parents. At times, she even missed her mother's well-meaning prattle about Carly finding "Mr. Right."

She stood and headed for the door but stopped halfway there and glanced down at the walnut chest sitting at the foot of the bed. Her great-great-great-grandfather, Ethan Cole, had made the trunk as a wedding present for his bride-to-be over 140 years ago. Inside the trunk was a meticulously fashioned wedding gown made by her great-great-great-grandmother, Charity Cole. Both the chest and the gown were heirlooms that had been passed down through five generations on the maternal side of Carly's family.

She kneeled and ran her fingertips across the ornately designed heart nestled inside the chest's flowing ribbon pattern. Ethan Cole had not only been a fine carpenter, but a talented carver as well. Of course, his feelings for his bride-to-be probably had a lot to do with the time and care he had put into making the chest. Carly could almost feel the love that went into each precise stroke of his decorative chisels.

She lifted the lid and inhaled the pleasant scents of the trunk's cedar lining, dried flowers, aged wedding-gown satin, and old paper mingled with various other sentimental items—all treasures passed down by brides and grooms honored with possession of the chest.

And it was left up to Carly, an only child, to carry on the family legacy. She fingered the lace and pearl-adorned bodice of the gown which age had turned a soft candle yellow. Would she ever march down a church aisle in that dress? Or would she be the end of a 140-year-old tradition?

As she closed the trunk, a gloomy spirit settled over

her. She knew there was someone out there for her—if it was God's will that she marry. But she wouldn't settle for anything less than mutual love and a shared belief in Christ. She certainly wasn't going to go husband hunting so she could pass down the treasured chest and give her mother the grandchild she so desperately wanted.

Turning her thoughts back to her job—and Mitchell Reynolds—she scrambled up off the floor. How was she going to help him without making him feel like he was accepting charity?

On her way through the living room, she glanced toward the coffee table, where her purse and automobile insurance bill lay, and there she found her answer. Even if Mitchell didn't have auto insurance, the company who owned the truck that hit his car would have. He was due a settlement. A slow smile curved her lips. Why hadn't she thought of that before?

Kneeling beside the low table, she dug a small notebook and a pencil out of her purse. She kept the notepad handy so she could list needs of her clients that hospital Social Services didn't supply; things like clothes, childcare, and help in finding a job or a decent place to live.

She had been so angry when she left Mitchell Reynolds's room that morning, she hadn't wanted to list his extra needs because she didn't think he deserved the extended effort on her part. But she had gotten over her mad spell and reminded herself he was just as human as the rest of her patients—in spite of his vicious growl. And now she knew exactly how she could help him land back on his feet.

Opening her notebook to a blank page, she began writing. And when she finished writing, she started to pray.

"Let me guess. You're left-handed."

Sitting halfway up with his bed at a forty-five degree angle, Mitch paused with the comb poised over his right ear and looked toward the doorway. For a moment, he thought he was seeing things. The voice belonged to the social worker, but she looked...different. She still wore her long brown hair in a ponytail at her nape. But her large, out-of-style glasses had been replaced by a small, stylish pair with rimless, oval lenses. A short navy jacket tapered to fit a narrow waist, and a matching straight skirt fell to the knees of two shapely legs. Had all that been hidden beneath a pair of gaudy glasses and a beige pantsuit yesterday? Or had he just been too angry then to see it?

She shifted her weight from one foot to the other, and he realized he was still staring at her legs. He lifted his gaze to her face and found her smiling—a friendly smile that said all was forgiven. But her amicable expression didn't fool him. Her cordial approach was most likely a tactic to get on his good side, so she could persuade him to accept her help.

With her clipboard trapped between her folded arms and her chest, she strolled forward. "Did I guess right?"

Her silky voice penetrated his suspicious thoughts. He searched his mind, trying to remember what she was referring to. He couldn't. "Did you guess right about what?"

"About your being left-handed."

"Oh." He blinked, then glanced at his right hand, which was still holding the comb over his ear. He cut his gaze back to hers, and, in spite of his resolve to maintain an austere distance, a sheepish grin toyed with one corner of his mouth. "Yeah, you guessed right. Does it look that bad?"

"It looks like my hair would look if I tried to fix it with my left hand." She laid her clipboard and a small notebook on the bedside cabinet. Then, to his surprise, she plucked the comb from his hand and started combing his hair.

He dropped his empty hand to his lap, telling himself the tingling he felt in his fingers was not the lingering effects of her touch. Let her comb his hair. Let her shave his bristly face and brush his teeth if she wanted. He still wasn't going to become her next charity case.

Her empty palm followed each stroke of the comb, patting down a wave here, tucking in a curl there. He should have had a haircut two weeks ago, but he had saved his last dollars for the most basic of necessities: gas so he could look for a job, soap, a razor, deodorant, and food.

Unbidden, her soft, rose-petal scent invaded his senses. When her arms circled his head, the heat from her body seeped into his pores, settling inside his chest like the warmth from a glowing ember.

He closed his eyes and relaxed under her gentle ministrations. Gradually, his bleak future floated to the back of his mind, and he allowed himself to rest in the moment.

All too soon, it seemed, she drew back, taking her pleasant warmth with her.

He opened his eyes to find her pulling his meal cart up to his bed. When the tray was positioned over his lap, she pulled out a small drawer from beneath the table and flipped up a mirror.

"There," she said. "What do you think?"

When Mitch saw his reflection, he forgot he even

had hair. His eyes were black, his left jaw was purple, and his right cheek bore eight stitches. His nose was twice its normal size. "Sheesh!" he said without thought. "I look like I've been run over by a truck."

She gave him a quizzical look. "You have, Mr. Reynolds."

A memory flashed through his mind. The traffic light turning green, him driving his car beneath it, a red dump truck coming downhill—*fast*. . .brakes screeching. . . The next thing he remembered was being pinned in his convertible by a huge tire, then he'd blacked out.

He'd awakened while the medical technicians were loading him into the ambulance. That was when a police officer had explained what had happened. But he'd had no memory of the accident until that moment.

An unsettling chill swept through him. The details had not been nearly as frightening coming from someone else.

"Mr. Reynolds?"

Her anxious voice filtered through his disquietude. He looked up to find her eyes full of concern, her forehead drawn with worry.

She touched his shoulder. "Are you all right?"

Slowly, he floated back to the present. "I'm fine. I just couldn't remember anything about the accident until now."

Understanding curved her lips. "It's amazing you survived. God was certainly looking out for you."

Was He? Mitch wondered. If God was looking out for him, why had he gone from a successful businessman to a homeless vagrant in less than a year? Why had his friends turned their backs on him when he needed them most?

Why was he lying in a hospital bed without so much as a pair of socks to call his own?

She pushed the cart to the foot of his bed, pulled the chair away from the wall, and sat down. "Did you get a chance to look over the pamphlets I left with you yesterday?"

"No."

Trapping her right lower lip between her teeth, she studied him a few thoughtful seconds. "Does that mean you're still refusing to accept any help from Social Services?"

"Miss Simmons—"

"Carly, please."

"All right, Carly." He paused, letting the name settle in his mind. It was a little unusual, but he liked the sound of it. "There are two things you can do for me."

Plucking a pencil from behind her ear, she pulled the clipboard from beneath the notebook and readied herself to write. "Okay."

"I need a phone book and a newspaper." He'd use the phone book to find an organization that would donate him some clothes, and the newspaper to search the want ads. Surely, he could find something to make some money until he could get back on his feet, even if it was stuffing envelopes for some organization that dealt with mass mailing.

Looking up, Carly raised her forefinger to her nose to push up her glasses, even though the new pair fit perfectly. Realizing what she'd done, she sent him a chagrined smile. "I guess it's true what they say about old habits."

Mitch smiled in return, which surprised him. He had forgotten what it felt like for a smile to come naturally.

Their smiles faded and a ponderous silence fell between them.

"Mr. Reynolds, if you'll give me your sizes, I'll be happy to check the county thrift shop and round up some clothing for you."

Mitch studied her stoical expression. Had her statement merely been a coincidence? Or had she guessed why he wanted the phone book? "I don't want you going to any trouble—"

"It's no trouble. It's my job."

Reluctantly, he gave a conceding nod. "Large shirt, thirty-two, thirty-four in pants, and a size ten in shoes."

She made a note. "Also, if I know what kind of job training you have, I can call the local employment agencies and find out what's out there."

Was she a mind reader, or what?

His mind jumped back to his final months on his last job, and he bit back a bitter laugh. "Considering my current situation, I don't think I'm going to find a job in my field of expertise anytime soon."

She hunched one shoulder. "Perhaps not. But it would at least give me something to aim for when I'm checking out the job market."

He thought about telling her he'd worked as a janitor, or in a fast-food restaurant, something that didn't require years of training and experience. But his professional profile, along with tidbits of his personal life, was on the Web. All she had to do was log onto the Internet to learn that four months ago he was employed by one of the biggest architectural firms in the South. And something told him she was resourceful enough to do just that. "I'm an architectural engineer," he admitted.

He expected surprise or shock. A look that said: *With all the development going on in this part of the country, what's an architectural engineer doing jobless, homeless, and penniless?* But her impassive expression revealed nothing as she made another notation on the paper attached to the clipboard.

Tucking her pencil back behind her ear, she leaned back in her chair and crossed her legs. The movement distracted him.

"Mr. Reynolds."

His gaze jumped back to her face, but he noticed his heart was beating a little too fast.

"Have your doctors told you how long your rehabilitation program is going to take?"

Her question ignited a spark of foreboding inside him. "What do you mean, 'rehabilitation program'?"

"Well, I can't speak for the doctors, but injuries of your nature usually require a lengthy rehabilitation program."

He shook his head. "Oh, no. I can't pay for a rehabilitation program. I'll just have to rehabilitate myself."

"Insurance will cover all your medical bills, Mr. Reynolds. Even rehabilitation."

"I lost my health insurance when I lost my job, Miss Simmons, and I didn't carry medical coverage on my automobile policy."

"Carly," she corrected. "The wreck wasn't your fault, was it?"

"No," he said, although he suspected she already knew that. In fact, he was beginning to suspect she knew a lot more than his sketchy file revealed. "But, I don't know yet if the man who hit me has insurance," he added.

"He does. He works for Bradenton Asphalt Company, and the owner of the company carries very good coverage on all of his drivers and vehicles."

Well, she certainly had been doing some homework, and he couldn't decide if he was grateful or irritated. "You've apparently called and checked all this out."

"Yes, I have."

"I don't recall giving you permission."

She regarded him for a speculative moment. "Actually, calling Bradenton Asphalt and inquiring about their insurance coverage didn't require your permission."

Knowing she was right didn't diminish his growing agitation. He'd already lost control over his life. He didn't need someone taking control of his mind. Thinking was about the only thing he could still do for himself. When that was gone, he really would have nothing.

Besides, all he'd asked her to do was bring him a phone book and a newspaper.

"It's my job to look out for my clients, Mr. Reynolds," she said, disrupting his ominous thoughts.

"Since when did I become your client?" he snapped.

"When you asked for my help."

"Don't I have to sign something to make it legal?"

She uncrossed her legs, then recrossed them in the opposite position. He forced his gaze to stay fixed on her face, which, he had to silently admit, wasn't hard on the eyes, either.

"Mr. Reynolds, gathering clothes, searching the job market, and investigating insurance coverage are not services actually provided by hospital Social Services."

"Then who provides these services?"

"It doesn't matter as long as your needs are met."

"It matters to me." He didn't want to become indebted to anyone else.

She met him with an unwavering gaze but said nothing.

"You?" he guessed.

Still, she didn't answer, but her silence told him all he needed to know. She was extending herself beyond her job requirements because she felt sorry for him, pitied him. Rancor and shame almost choked him. "First, you insinuate I'm your client, then you tell me Social Services doesn't provide the things I need. What, exactly, am I to you, Miss Simmons? A client or a charity case?"

Annoyance sparked in her eyes, turning them a brilliant teal green. "You're a human being."

Her words doused his anger, but not his shame. How long had it been since someone offered to help him simply because he was human and not because of what they expected to receive in return?

He glanced away, not sure how to react to her compassion. He didn't have a lot of experience at either giving or receiving unselfish acts of kindness.

"Well, I have other clients to see this morning," she said. "I'll let you know what I find out about the clothes and a job. I'll also see that you get a phone book and a daily newspaper. Between the two of us, I'm sure we'll come up with something."

He heard a soft shuffle followed by silence and knew she'd left the room. He turned and looked at the empty chair she had just vacated. Her pleasant, rose-petal scent still lingered in the room. His shoulder tingled like a cooling brand where she touched it in concern. The image of her delicate yet determined face when she'd told him he was a human being still hovered in his mind's eye. He had almost called her back to apologize for acting like a jerk—again—but something had warned him not to. Something that told him if he opened up to her, even a little bit, she'd slip past the thick walls of his reserve and take up residence inside his heart.

Yet, something else—an emotion he couldn't quite define—told him he might have just let something very special walk out of his life.

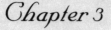

Chapter 3

T rying to shake off his befuddling thoughts about the social worker, Mitch reached for the plastic water pitcher on the bedside cabinet but paused when he saw she had left her small, red notebook there. Curiosity immediately took precedence over his thirst. Now, why would someone carry around a notepad labeled STUFF in fat, black marker letters? His hand hovered over the journal a few contemplative seconds, then, shaking his head, he grabbed the water pitcher. Whatever was in that little red book wasn't any of his business.

He filled a plastic glass with water and drained it in three long swallows. Then he adjusted his bed and his stiffening body—and tried to forget the notepad lying on the bedside table tempting him like forbidden food under a hungry man's nose.

After struggling with his conscience another futile minute, he picked up the notepad. What would one little peek hurt? At least it'd satisfy his curiosity. Besides, no one would ever know.

Propping the notepad on his uninjured thigh, he started flipping pages. Soon he realized the STUFF notebook was exactly that—a notebook with a list of stuff in it. Mitch suspected the people's names recorded on each page were Carly's clients, and the "stuff" listed was items they needed that hospital Social Services didn't supply.

Shaking his head, he smiled. Was this woman for real? Was there actually someone in the world who cared enough to reach out to others just because? Mitch had never known anyone like that. . .except his mother. But then she was one in a million.

Intrigued, he began to read.

Annie, 8: needs socks and underwear.
Homer, 81: asked for reference Bible; needs new
  glasses.
Josh, 6: wants video game player for room; wants to
  see his daddy (Ask Josh's mother. If okay with her,
  call sheriff and ask about supervised visit or a
  phone visit).

Mitch's chest tightened. Apparently, Carly Simmons and her copious generosity were for real. When she saw something someone needed, she took it upon herself to see they got it.

He kept flipping until he came to her last entry, and there his hand froze. His was the name written across the top of that page. Guilt jabbed at his conscience. Why would she even bother to consider his needs after the way he'd treated her yesterday? And today hadn't been much better.

Beneath his name, she had listed four things he needed: the second, third, and fourth items—clothes, a job, assistance with insurance claims—didn't really surprise him considering the conversation they'd just had. She had already figured out his immediate needs, and her thoughtfulness touched him. But it was the first notation on the list that moved something deep inside him—*prayer*.

Mitch's throat clogged with emotion. It had been a long time since someone told him she would pray for him. A very long time. He'd just finished graduate school and decided he'd heard his father tell him he'd never amount to anything for the last time. Mitch hadn't wanted to follow in his father's footsteps and become a third-generation lawyer. As long as he could remember, all Mitch wanted was to start with a pencil and a piece of paper and end up with a castle; to water a seed planted in his mind and watch it grow into the tallest tree in the forest. So with his father throwing in his face how much his college education had cost, Mitch had packed his car and set out to pursue his dream. But before he left, his mother had wrapped her loving arms around him and said, "I'll pray for you, Son."

And Mitch believed she had.

A pang of guilt shot through him. He hadn't kept up his end of the bargain, though. Before leaving, he'd promised his mother he'd stay in church and remain close to God. But soon he found what he thought were more entertaining things to do with his Sundays than attend worship services, usually at a casino or a card table.

At first, it had paid off, and he could soon repress the guilt that he was doing something that defied his beliefs. Then, he'd started losing, and that losing streak had cost him everything he'd worked his entire life for—including his dream of someday owning his own architectural and development company.

The heavy hand of regret bore down upon his chest. Where would he be right now if he'd remained loyal to the faith of his childhood? Not in a hospital bed without a penny to his name or a place to call home, he strongly suspected.

Like a twirling top, his mind spun back to twenty years ago, when, at the age of twelve, he'd prayed the prayer of repentance and asked God to come into his heart. All through high school and college, he'd managed to maintain a precarious grip on his faith, partly because he never wanted to disappoint his mother. She'd dealt with enough adversity living with a controlling man.

But as soon as Mitch had left the moral influence of his devout mother, he'd also left God. A sarcastic "Huh" left his throat. He'd once thought of himself as a strong-minded man. Now, facing destitution and an uncertain future, he saw just how weak he truly was.

Drawing in a laborious breath, he looked back at the notebook. A sudden desire to pray surged up within him, but would it do any good? Would God listen? Or, would He, like everyone else, turn a deaf ear to Mitch's struggle, to the needs that he, all at once, realized went beyond the material to the depths of his soul?

Deciding he didn't want to risk finding out, Mitch closed the notebook. He'd had enough rejection over the last years to last a lifetime. He certainly didn't need any more—especially from God.

He tossed the notebook back on the cabinet. What in the world had Carly seen in him that was worth praying for?

Carly stopped outside Mitch's door and drew in a deep breath of fortitude. She'd waited until the end of the day to retrieve her notebook, putting off another confrontation with the malevolent patient as long as possible. Their first two meetings had been disasters. He'd found fault in everything she said or did, and this morning, she'd had to make another quick exit before she lost her temper with him again.

She could understand his being upset—even a little angry—at his current circumstances. But she couldn't comprehend his taking his animosity out on everyone else.

Carly lifted her chin a determined inch. If he wanted to be a grouch, fine. But she wasn't going to let his distasteful disposition intimidate her again, as it had during their first two encounters.

The door was cracked open, but she didn't dare risk entering the lion's den unannounced, so she rapped on the door three times with her knuckles. Something clattered, then a rather bold word slipped from Mitch's mouth.

Carly grimaced. Just what she needed. The lion was already in a bad mood. She peeked inside the room and found him wiping something off the front of his hospital gown with a napkin. His meal cart bearing a plate of food was extended over his lap, and a fork lay on the floor beside his bed.

She tried to ignore the tightening in her chest. She was not going to feel sorry for him. *She would not do it.*

He reached up with his clumsy right hand to wipe his chin, which was stubbly with a two-day-old beard. The tightness in her chest rose to her throat. She clenched her teeth. No way was she going to let this man get under her skin. *No way.*

To her dismay, her heart couldn't quite grasp the conviction her mind was reaching for.

Noticing her, he glanced up, a sheepish grin dimpling his cheeks. "Seems I'm no better with a fork than I am with a comb."

Carly blinked in wary surprise. He actually sounded. . . nice. . .friendly. . .like her presence didn't repulse him. "I'll go get you another fork," she said, then walked to the nurses' station scratching her head. Was he, for some reason, trying to get back into her good graces? Had he decided he needed her help after all? She stiffened her spine as well as her resolve. If that were the case, fine. She'd fulfill her commitment to get him some clothes and investigate job opportunities, and she'd do whatever else her job required of her, but that was it. She certainly wasn't going to waste time on some ungrateful buffoon. She had too many other clients needing—and willing to accept—her assistance.

When she returned to his room, she handed him a plastic fork. "I hope this will do. It's all they had at the nurses' station." And she certainly wasn't going all the way down to the cafeteria to get stainless flatware.

"That's fine. Thanks."

When he took the fork, his fingers brushed her hand. A jolt of electricity shot up her arm. Static from the carpet, she concluded. When she stooped to pick up the soiled fork, she frowned in realization. The hospital didn't have carpet. All of its floors were tiled.

"What's wrong?" he asked as she laid the fork on the bedside cabinet.

"Nothing. Why?" she said a bit too quickly.

"You were frowning like. . ." He shrugged his right shoulder. "I don't know. Like something had you puzzled."

She forced a smile. "I was just thinking." *And please don't ask about what.* "I, um, forgot my notebook this morning." She stepped forward, picked up the pad, and stepped back. "Enjoy your meal." Pivoting, she scurried toward the door.

"Carly?"

She stopped. What else could she do, unless she wanted to be rude and ignore him? And she simply couldn't muster up the heart to do that. Pasting on a stiff smile, she turned. "Yes?"

"Ah. . ." He cleared his throat. "What time do you get off work?"

His question baffled her. Why did he want to know what time she got off work? "Ten minutes ago."

"Do you have anywhere you need to be?"

His second question further piqued her curiosity. "No place in particular."

"Could you stay awhile?"

His third question tossed her senses for a loop. Blankly, she stared at him, unable to react.

"I just thought, maybe, we could talk."

Talk? To each other? Them?

As she studied his hopeful expression, her addled mind cleared. Apparently, two days of staring at four white walls with no visitors and the nurses avoiding his growl at every turn were adding up to a lonely stay. He wanted someone to talk to, a sympathetic ear, and she was the nearest gullible Jane.

She crossed her arms, trying her best to convince

herself he deserved the isolation, but the words wouldn't take hold in her mind. That could be her lying there with nothing but four walls and a hospital bed to keep her company.

"Sure." She shrugged, feigning nonchalance. "Why not?" She pulled the chair away from the wall and sat down.

Mitch glanced from her to his plate, then back at her, unsure of what he should do next.

"Please, finish your meal while it's warm. It's a long time until breakfast."

"What about you?"

"I never eat this early."

"I can wait." He pushed the cart aside.

She stood and pushed it back over his lap. "No, you won't wait. If you think hospital food tastes bad warm, just try eating it after it gets cold. It's almost unbearable."

Mitch looked down at the stewed beef, rice and gravy, green beans, roll, and gelatin. Recently, there had been days he would have given the shoes off his feet for a meal like this. Poverty had a way of changing the way a man viewed things. A year ago, Mitch had been an ungrateful man. A very ungrateful man.

"I'm sorry."

He glanced up to find her still standing beside his bed, her expression repentant. She had read his mind, which didn't surprise him. She seemed attuned to others' feelings, even their innermost.

"That was a very insensitive thing for me to say," she added.

"You mean, to a homeless man?"

"To anyone." Clasping her hands in front of her, she averted her gaze downward. Long, dark lashes brushed her cheeks. "I suppose I take a lot for granted."

"So did I, once."

Her gaze darted back to his, then dropped to some point below his chin.

He narrowed his eyes. "Somehow, I get the feeling you already know that."

She hunched one shoulder. "You owned a nice car. I figured you couldn't have been homeless long."

Anyone with a little common sense could have figured out that. But from the way she avoided eye contact, Mitch suspected she knew more. A lot more. "How much do you know about me, Carly?"

She pursed her lips and slowly raised her gaze back to his. "I know you're originally from Michigan. That you have a master of architecture degree from the University of Michigan. Until a few months ago, you worked at Century Architect and Associates in Atlanta and lived in the metro area."

He waited a few seconds to see if she had anything to add. "Is that it?"

She studied the space high above his head, thinking. "Oh, yes," she said, looking back at him. "You enjoy tennis, racquetball, and skeet shooting." She thought for another moment, then shrugged a shoulder. "That's about it."

Either she hadn't called his former boss and learned why he'd lost his job, or she was too benevolent to mention it. "Where did you get your information?"

"Off the Internet. Century Architect still had your professional profile up on their web page."

So, they hadn't listed the reason for his dismissal. Then, again, why would they? Who wants to be associated with a compulsive gambler?

"You have quite an impressive résumé," Carly added.

Yes, his credentials did look good on paper. He was the most requested architect in the company until his slow slide downhill began affecting his job. But all that hard work had been in vain. Even if he did someday get back into architecture, he'd have to start at the bottom and work his way back up. He'd be taking orders from people a decade or more his junior. Not a pleasant thought.

Pushing aside his dismal thoughts, he studied Carly's pretty face. Considering the volatility of their first two meetings, why had she bothered to find out anything about him? If he had signed up for financial aid, she would have had to verify his lack of resources. But he hadn't signed anything requesting help from Social Services. Did she not believe he was really broke and homeless? Good grief! If he already owned clothes or had the money to buy more, why would he need donated clothes? And why would he be willing to take any job he could find?

Something told him she had already asked herself those questions and figured out the truth—that he really was destitute. Which brought him back to his first question. Why did she go to the trouble to find out about him? "Is part of your job researching people who turn down your assistance?"

She chewed her right lower lip a pensive moment. "No."

"Why bother, then?"

"Curiosity, I suppose."

He raised an inquisitive brow. "Curiosity?"

Her shoulders rose and fell on a deep sigh. "I just wondered how a man like you could end up. . ." She paused, like she didn't know how to deliver the last word.

"Homeless?" he supplied, an unanticipated bitter ring in his voice. Then he realized renewed anger was rising in his chest.

"Yes."

His body tensed with acrimony. "It happens to the best of us, Ms. Simmons. Who knows? Your number could come up next."

She stood there, seemingly calm and unaffected by his sudden burst of aggression. Her soft, hazel gaze bore into his, leaving him feeling raw and exposed, like she could see past his surface to the center of his being. And he feared what she saw wasn't pretty.

"Whom are you so angry with, Mr. Reynolds?" she finally asked, her voice mellow with something akin to compassion.

He knew the answer to her question, but wasn't quite ready to voice it.

"Your old boss?" she went on. "An old girlfriend? God?"

"Try all of the above," he said in rebellion to the truth.

"Mr. Reynolds, I don't know what happened to bring you to this low point in your life, and I'm not asking you to tell me. But I do know God's not responsible. In fact, He may be the only One Who can pull you out of whatever dark hole you've fallen into."

Something chipped away a piece of the ice encasing Mitch's heart. She was right. He was in a hole, a cavern so deep and dark he couldn't see where his next step would lead. Would God lead him out?

"I'll leave so you can finish your meal," she said to the back of his head. "Just let me know if you think of anything else I can do for you."

If she adhered to the lists in her notebook, she was already doing the thing he needed most. She was praying for him. But what good would her prayers do him if he didn't put forth an effort of his own?

He felt her slipping away, felt an odd coldness surround him and a foreboding fear grip him. Swallowing his pride, he turned his head. "Carly?"

Stopping short of the door, she faced him with her brows raised in question.

"Me," he said. "I'm angry at myself."

Chapter 4

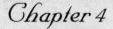

Mitch felt an odd sense of relief, like he'd just learned the diagnosis of a mysterious illness he'd suffered from for a long time. Even though he didn't yet know the prognosis, at least he knew the problem and could now seek a cure.

"Do you want to talk about it?" Carly asked.

He studied her obliging expression and wondered if the sincerity he saw there was real, or if she was just being polite. "I shouldn't burden you with my problems."

"Why not?" she asked, as though keeping misery company was also part of her job.

He shook his head. "I'm sure you have your own set of problems to deal with."

She threw her head back and laughed. The melodious sound seemed to bring a new spark of life to the depressing hospital room. "I have a sick sego palm, an inferiority complex, and a mother who can't wait to marry me off. Other than that, my life is pretty uncomplicated."

An inexplicable fear grabbed hold of him. "A mother who can't wait to marry you off?" he repeated, his voice rising with each word.

"Yes," she said, a soft smile lingering. "You see, I'm an only child, and my mother is dying to become a *grand*mother."

Mitch's heart jumped up and started tap-dancing on his breastbone. "What does the prospective groom have to say about that?"

Crossing her arms, Carly stepped farther into the room, stopping a couple of feet away from his bed. "That's the main problem. There is no prospective groom."

"Oh, I see." Tenseness Mitch had not been aware of eased from his shoulders. "Why do you have an inferiority complex?" he asked, suddenly eager to learn more about her.

Although a tender curve remained on her lips, a touch of wistfulness rose in her eyes. "Because during junior high and high school, I was the brunt of at least ten nerd jokes a day."

Surprise lifted his brows. "You?"

"Uh-huh." She gave a thoughtful nod. "I worked to make good grades. I never went out for sports or cheer-leading because I was too clumsy. I was very shy. And, even though I'm short, I wasn't much more than a walking toothpick back then."

Mitch forced his gaze to remain on her face instead of following the temptation to travel the length of her body. He'd already noticed she'd filled out in all the right places.

"Jocks found my lack of social graces pretty entertaining sometimes," she added.

"I find that hard to believe."

"Why?"

The nonchalant tone in that single-word question told

him she still saw herself as the skinny kid who was the object of cruel jokes. "Well, you're the prettiest nerd I've ever met."

A blush rose to her cheeks. "Thank you."

She accepted his compliment with grace but not without visible discomfort. And, somehow, he sensed she'd forced herself to maintain eye contact instead of ducking her head.

Tilting his head, he considered the decisiveness and persistence he'd witnessed in her the last two days. "You don't strike me as someone who lacks a lot of confidence."

"I'm getting better. Two years ago I started seeing a Christian counselor. Slowly but surely, I'm learning it doesn't matter what others think about the way I choose to live my life, as long as God approves."

The truth in her words struck an enlightening chord in Mitch. Wasn't that why he'd placed his first bet? Because he was seeking his friends' approval? If only he'd listened to the voice of his conscience then, while he could still hear it telling him he was headed down a destructive path.

"It took me a long time to admit I needed help," she said, her silken voice drifting back into his thoughts. "When I finally did, it was like being given a chance to start all over again, with the insight to change the things I did wrong the first time around. In my case, it was learning to like myself and not allowing others to intimidate me because I didn't fit in their social circle or follow their rules."

Mitch shook his head. "I don't want to learn to like the person I've become. I'm not even sure I like the person I was before I started gambling."

She narrowed her eyes, a knowing grin toying with the corner of her mouth. "Let me guess. You were a jock."

Yes, he supposed he was. He'd hung with the "in" crowd, excelled in sports, and thrown out his share of nerd jokes. Shame wouldn't allow him to maintain eye contact, so he turned his head and stared across the room.

"Mitch, I used to wish I could go back and erase every tear I cried over insensitive remarks made to or about me, or change the way I shied away from people. I even considered flunking a few tests so my peers would stop calling me 'Miss Four-point-oh.'"

Curiously, he turned back to her. "Did you ever allow yourself to fail any of those tests?"

Shaking her head, she pulled up the chair and sat down. "No. My grades were about the only thing I felt good about."

The only thing Mitch had felt good about over the past few years had been his skill as an architect, a talent and treasure he might never get to use again, unless he changed his way of living. And he wasn't sure he knew how to go about doing that—or if he was even strong enough.

"There's no shame in admitting you've failed at something, Mitch. And there's nothing degrading about asking for help. . .if you're ready for it."

"*If* I'm ready?"

"Yes. You see, that's key. You've got to be ready, and willing, to accept responsibility for. . ." She paused a second in thought. "For making that first bet, or playing that first card game."

Mitch considered her reasoning. Was he ready? He thought so. He certainly didn't want to continue in his current desolate state. But he wasn't sure he could resist the allure of Lady Luck when he found a job and got his hands on his first paycheck. Last night, he'd even placed an imaginary bet on a baseball game—and lost. "How did you go about finding a counselor?"

"I started with prayer."

"Prayer?"

She inclined her head. "Yes. First I asked for God's guidance, then I researched Christian therapists. When I felt comfortable enough to make a decision, I chose one and made an appointment."

He shook his head. "I'm not sure a therapist is the answer for me." How could someone relate to a gambling addiction unless they'd experienced it themselves?

Hunching one shoulder, she said, "Maybe it's not."

He cocked a brow. "Got any suggestions?"

She chewed her lower lip for a contemplative moment. "I know where weekly Gamblers Anonymous meetings are held."

"Where?"

"Here."

"At the hospital?"

"Every Thursday night, seven P.M., first floor, Meeting Room A."

"How does a meeting held in a busy hospital remain anonymous?"

"There's a back entrance to the meeting room."

At the thought of telling a group of strangers he had a gambling problem, trepidation clutched his chest. "I'll consider it when I'm mobile enough to get there."

"Oh, I can check with your doctor. If he gives the okay, I'm sure we can round up a wheelchair."

He raised his uninjured hand and wiggled his fingers. "I'm left-handed, remember? I don't think I'll be coordinated enough to get my driver's license by then."

"I can drive you."

Okay, now, how did he get out of this one? Allowing his gaze to roam her petite frame, he found his answer. She couldn't weigh an ounce over one hundred pounds. "Carly, with these casts, I outweigh you by at least a hundred and fifty pounds, and I need help getting out of this bed. I don't think you can manage."

"If not, I'll call for help."

He leveled her with a look of incredulity.

"We have plenty of nurses on staff," she added.

He tried to work up a fragment of aggravation at her unbending persistence, but all he felt was an emerging admiration for her and her tenacious spirit. With a shake of his head and a spontaneous grin, he said, "Don't you ever give up?"

"Not on something I believe in."

"And you believe these meetings will help me?"

"If you want them to badly enough. . .and I believe you do."

Mentally he shook his head. If she only knew how alluring Lady Luck could be and how weak he was. "You don't even know me, Carly."

She laced her hands over one knee. "I know it took a lot of courage to tell me you had a gambling problem, and I know you want to change your old way of life. Other-wise, you'd still be denying you need help."

Was there anything she didn't have an answer for? Anything she couldn't figure out? He might as well tell her he would go, or they'd banter back and forth all night. "All right. I'll go to the meeting under one condition."

"What's that?"

"You find me something besides a hospital gown to wear."

With an impish grin, she said, "I'll go through my closet and see what I can come up with."

He chuckled, which brought a splitting pain to his broken ribs. Wincing, he grabbed his left side.

"Mitch, are you all right?"

Suddenly, she was at his side, leaning over him, one hand on his shoulder, the other covering the hand he had pressed against his side. Her rose-petal fragrance wrapped around his senses. Her soft touch flooded his veins with liquid warmth. The worried expression on her face melted his icy reserve.

Their gazes locked, and a blanket of amorous tension fell over the room. His throat growing dry, he studied her delicate features. She seemed more beautiful every time he saw her. Not only on the outside, but on the inside as well.

A desirous need rose within him. He wanted to kiss her, sate the longing rising within him to taste the sweetness of her lips. But he didn't dare. She was more than a one-night stand or a casual affair. She was special—someone he would like to have in his life for a long time. But he had nothing to offer her.

An odd twinge of disappointment shot through him. Slipping his hand from beneath hers, he reached up and caressed her smooth cheek with the backs of his fingers. "I wish things were different. I'd really like to spend some time getting to know you when I get out of here."

Timidly, she smiled. "I don't think you'll be going anywhere for a few days. We've got time to get to know each other."

Shaking his head, he shifted his hand and cupped her cheek. "I don't mean on a client-caseworker basis. I'd like to take you out to dinner, walk around the block, sit with you on a front porch swing, and talk to you until midnight."

A look of surprise touched her heart-shaped face. She studied him as though he was a puzzle she was trying to put together. "You're not serious." Her voice held a note of disbelief.

"Of course I'm serious. Why wouldn't I be?"

Her surprised expression took on a pleased glow. "When you get out of the hospital, I'd like to do all those things with you, too."

Oh, no. He hadn't counted on her wanting to spend time with him, also. He had no assets, no money, and no home. What could she possibly see in him?

She stood up straight, forcing him to drop his hand away from her face. "You look like you wish you could take back your words," she said.

She was reliving the past, he realized. Seeing herself as the smart, skinny kid with the big glasses, and seeing him as a jock who was setting her up for a letdown.

Nothing could be farther from the truth.

He captured her hand and gently tugged. "Sit down here with me a minute, Carly."

Skeptically, she looked at the small space on the bed beside him. "Won't I hurt you?"

"I don't think so."

She gingerly sat down on the edge of the bed, facing him.

Instead of letting go of her hand, he curled his fingers around hers and caressed her knuckles with his thumb.

"Carly, I meant every word I said. I *would* like to spend some time getting to know you."

"But. . . ?"

He heaved a laborious sigh and tried to swallow the pang of regret lodged in his throat. "But, I can't even buy you a cup of coffee right now, much less dinner."

An injured look skimmed her face. "Do you think that matters to me?"

"It should. I've got a gambling problem that needs to be fixed. I won't allow you to make that problem yours."

"You won't *allow* me to make that problem mine?" she repeated in a voice ringing with annoyance. "Doesn't it matter what *I* want?"

He knew he shouldn't ask the next question, that her answer could make keeping his distance even harder. But, she'd opened a door, and he had to know what was on the other side. "What do you want, Carly?"

She thought for a moment, then gave a casual shrug. "How about we start with friendship?"

And then what? He wanted to ask, but kept the question to himself. Because, right now, friendship was the only thing he could give her. He mustered up what he hoped was a decent smile. "That sounds like a good place to start."

She withdrew her right hand from his, leaned forward, and poured water into two plastic cups. After handing him one cup, she picked up the other and raised it in a mock toast. "To friendship."

He tapped his cup against hers. "To friendship."

While he drained his glass, she pushed the tray back in front of him and insisted he finish his meal. And while he ate, he and Carly shared pleasant conversation.

Mitch was amazed at how easy she was to talk to. He sensed no judgmental attitude or preconceived opinions from her. Just an unbiased acceptance of him as a person, and a sincere desire to help him get back on his feet and overcome his gambling problem.

When she finally rose to go, he felt comfortable enough with her to make the special request of her. "Carly, could I ask a favor of you?"

"Of course."

"Would you please keep praying for me?"

She opened her mouth to answer, then paused, her eyes widening in surprise. "How did you know—?"

He grimaced. He'd just told on himself.

In realization, she looked down at the notebook she held in her hand, then back up at him. He expected accusation. Instead, he was met with question. . .and something else. Hope, maybe?

"You believe in God, then?" she asked.

"Yes." Guilt pricking his conscience, he lowered his gaze. "It's been a long time since I've lived like it, though."

A small silence, then, "You know, all you have to do is ask, and He'll forgive you."

He shook his head in reproach. "There's a lot there to forgive, Carly."

"It doesn't matter. All you have to do is come to Him with a willing heart and a repentant spirit. He's already there, waiting with open arms to welcome you back into His fold."

Mitch didn't see how that could be. Nothing in his life had ever been that simple.

She tucked her notebook in her jacket pocket and

picked up the Bible from the bedside cabinet and thumbed through it, opening it to a place near the back. " 'If we confess our sins, he is faithful and just to forgive us our sins, and to cleanse us from all unrighteousness.' First John, chapter one, verse nine."

Leaving the Bible open at the passage she had read, she laid it facedown on the cabinet and clasped her hands in front of her. "I'll come by and check on you in the morning." Leaning forward, she laid a hand on his shoulder and kissed his cheek. "Have a good night." With that, she turned and left the room.

With the sensation of her soft lips lingering on his skin, Mitch stared at the space she'd just vacated. She hadn't preached to him or pointed out his shortcomings and iniquities. She hadn't told him what he should or should not do. She'd simply told him God would forgive him, then backed up her words with His Word.

Mitch picked up the Bible and read the verse again, then he followed a trail of references to other verses that spoke of God's love and forgiveness. Once he was satisfied he still had one hope left, he bowed his head and began to pray.

Chapter 5

L et me make sure I understand what you're saying," Mitch said. "You're offering me the job."

"If you want it," the hospital administrator replied.

If he wanted it? Of course he wanted it. Rubbing his right hand over his jaw, Mitch studied the original hospital plans, the land plat, and the rough sketch of a proposed new hospital wing all spread out across his bed. Already, he could see the preliminary outline the administrator had drawn would never work but decided not to voice his opinion just yet.

But in his mind's eye, a blueprint began to take shape—a design that would make the most of every inch of space and even leave room for future development. Of course, he'd have to see the physical layout of the land, and—

"Well?"

The middle-aged man's voice interrupted Mitch's prolific thoughts. He looked up and realized the administrator was waiting for an answer. "Yes, Sir," Mitch said, trying not to sound like a kid who had just been asked if he wanted a new bicycle. "I'd appreciate the opportunity to oversee the development of the new wing."

"That's what I was hoping to hear." Mr. Carter extended his right hand.

Mitch shook it, sealing the deal. "Thank you."

"Oh, don't thank me." The older man pocketed his fists. "Thank Carly. She's the one who presented your credentials to me and convinced me you were the man for the job."

"I'll do that."

The hospital administrator shook his head in obvious admiration for the social worker. "That girl amazes me. She's like a puppy chasing a bone when she goes after something."

After Mr. Carter left, Mitch sat staring at the plans for the new wing still scattered on the bed in front of him, but his mind was fixed on Carly. The administrator was right when he said she was like a puppy chasing a bone when she went after something. Evidence of such was all around him. He had been moved to a private room at no extra cost. He now owned several pairs of gym shorts and large T-shirts, which was all he could wear until his casts came off. Several other outfits, including one business suit, hung in the small wardrobe at the foot of the bed. Toiletries to take care of his personal hygiene were tucked neatly in the top drawer of his bedside cabinet. Books and magazines on architecture and his favorite sports often trickled in with the daily paper he was still receiving.

There were other things she had done, things not readily visible but the effects of which would remain with him for a very long time. She had attended the Gamblers Anonymous meetings with him. She had accompanied him to worship services at the hospital chapel. She'd even started dropping by his room each morning before going to her office to share a devotion with him.

And now, she had managed to get him a job.

But this wasn't just any job. This was his first opportunity to handle his own project, from start to finish, which had been his career goal before a bad gambling habit had caused him to lose sight of his dreams.

He scanned the plat, the plans, and the paperwork in front of him. Before him lay a chance to start all over again—and he had Carly to thank for it.

Both excitement and fear danced across his skin. He couldn't wait to get started. Yet, a part of him feared he would fail, feared he would let Carly—and God—down.

Late that afternoon, Carly was clearing off her desk, getting ready to go home, when her phone buzzed, signaling an internal call. She picked up the receiver and sandwiched it between her ear and shoulder. "This is Carly."

"Carly, this is Susan," the head orthopedic nurse said. "Could you come by my station before you leave today?"

"Sure," Carly answered, not thinking much about the unusual timing of the request. The nurse probably had a new patient in need of Social Services and couldn't get away to bring Carly the information file.

She hung up the phone and headed for the door, leaving her desk in disarray. She would have to bring the new file back to her office and lock up, anyway.

When she arrived at the nurses' station, Susan met her with a conspiratorial grin. "Your presence is requested in room two-twelve."

Room 212. Mitch's room. A giddy flutter rose in Carly's stomach, like it did every time she anticipated seeing Mitch. She closed her eyes, berating herself for allowing her heart to become involved with a man who wanted nothing more than friendship from her—one who would probably walk away from her when the hospital released him.

For two weeks, they had spent a lot of time together, and he had treated her with utmost kindness, been a true friend to her.

In turn, he had become much more than a friend to her. She was falling in love with him, and with each passing day, it was getting harder to hide her feelings for him. Every time he laughed, or whenever their hands touched by accident, every fiber in her body would tingle like a lightning bolt had brushed her.

But Mitch? Well, he seemed oblivious to the well of romantic emotions building inside Carly. Apparently, even though they agreed to start their relationship as friends, she, against her rational will, had been the only one to step across the line and venture toward something more.

Someone snapped their fingers in front of Carly. She opened her eyes to find Susan's face directly in front of her.

"Hey, Beauty," the nurse said. "Now that you've tamed the beast, why don't you go see if you can cage him?"

"You've got the wrong idea about me and Mitch. We're just friends."

Grinning like a schoolgirl with a secret, Susan patted Carly's cheek. "Right. And I just won the lottery, even though I never buy a ticket." She grasped Carly's shoulders, turned her, and gave her a playful shove down the hallway. "Now *go* and see what that gorgeous hunk of mankind wants with you."

"All right, already," Carly responded in a rare exhibit of agitation. Why was Susan so eager for Carly to get to Mitch's room? It wasn't like she didn't visit him at least once a day. Sometimes more often if there was a need. And many times at Mitch's request. Why was the nurse making such a big deal out of something so routine?

Stopping outside Mitch's door, she knocked.

"Come in."

She swung open the door, took two steps inside, then stopped short. Any resemblance to a sterile hospital room was gone. Instead, the room was bathed in light from scented candles. The soft melody of an easy-listening tune glided through the air. The bed had been pushed against the opposite wall. And in the center of the room sat a small table dressed in white linen and adorned with a single red rose in a bud vase between two tall, slim candles.

But the biggest surprise of all was Mitch, sitting in his wheelchair, wearing a white dress shirt with one sleeve cut out to accommodate his casted left arm, a pair of black running shorts, and a black bow tie. He was an arresting picture of virile masculinity and boyish charm—and he took Carly's breath away.

An aimless hand fluttered to her chest. "Oh my" was all she could say. What did this mean? Dare she hope. . . ?

"Is that a good 'Oh my' or a bad one?"

"It's a surprised one."

He lifted an inquisitive brow that told Carly her response wasn't the one he was looking for.

"And a good one," she added with an assuring smile.

Her answer seemed to please him. "I hope hospital

316

cuisine will do. I've ordered what sounded like the best the cafeteria had on today's menu."

"*Anything* will be fine." She strolled to the table and reached for the back of the chair sitting across from Mitch.

"Wait a minute." He navigated the wheelchair around the table and pulled out her chair.

"You're getting pretty good at operating that thing," she told him as she sat down.

"I've been using the hallway for a practice track." He positioned himself on the side of the table flanking her left. "I think Susan's about ready to take away my keys."

Carly's lips curved with ease. The camaraderie between her and Mitch came so effortlessly. If only this dinner meant their friendship was leading to something more. "To what do I owe the honor of this special occasion?"

He met her gaze with a serious expression. "Carly, I wanted to thank you for everything you've done for me." His eyes scanned the table awaiting the arrival of the dinner trays. "I know this isn't much. . . ."

He fell silent, but Carly read clearly the message in his aristocratic face. *But it's the best that I can do.*

Reaching over, she grasped his hand. When he lifted his gaze back to hers, she said, "Mitch, I've not done all that much—"

"Yes, Carly, you have." He turned over his hand and wrapped his long fingers around hers, causing her breath to falter. "Mr. Carter came to see me this morning."

Her mouth dropped open in delight and surprise. "You got the job."

"If you're talking about overseeing the construction of the new hospital wing, then, yes, I got the job."

"Mitch, that's wonderful. Why didn't Mr. Carter say anything to me about it?"

"Because, I wanted to be the one to tell you."

A thin thread of disappointment needled through Carly's elation. So, this special dinner was in celebration of his new job. Not the first step toward a romantic relationship, as she had hoped.

"I don't know how you did it, Carly."

"Did what?" she asked, masking her disillusionment.

"Talked Mr. Carter into giving me a chance."

"All I did was give him your résumé."

"And twist his arm a bit."

Carly did have a tough time convincing Mr. Carter to consider Mitch for the job. But, at the same time, she believed in Mitch. Overseeing the development of the new wing would be a perfect opportunity for him to prove to himself—and to others—that he still had a lot to offer the world. Once he did, he'd be able to rebuild a prosperous and successful life—one she probably wouldn't fit into.

A lazy half-grin tipped one corner of his mouth. "You know what I've noticed about us?"

"What?"

"We spend a lot of time disagreeing about things that don't amount to much."

She shrugged a shoulder. "It keeps our friendship interesting."

"Oh, I can't imagine any time spent with you being anything *but* interesting."

Her pulse quickened. At the same time, her pragmatic side warned her not to read more into his words than what they really meant.

But her heart wouldn't listen. A glimmer of hope rose

inside her chest and fluttered against her ribs. Gooseflesh raced up her arm. Did he not realize what he was doing to her, caressing the back of her hand that way? And looking at her with those sapphire blue eyes, making her feel like they were the only two people in the world?

"Dinner's served."

Susan's boisterous voice shattered the enchanting dream Carly was slipping into. A cart bearing two covered dinner trays appeared next to the table. "Tonight's special is bland Veal Parmesan, unseasoned green beans, and sticky rice, compliments of the hospital cafeteria." Susan set one tray in front of Mitch and the other in front of Carly. When the nurse removed the dome lids from the plates, a cloud of steam rose from the food. Looking directly at Carly, she said, "You've got thirty minutes before I bring dessert."

Carly heard the underlying message in Susan's jesting comment. *Come dessert time, don't be doing anything you don't want interrupted.*

Carly targeted the nurse with a stern glare. "I'm sure that will be fine, Susan."

Susan cut a quick glance to Mitch and Carly's linked hands. Then, with a cheeky grin, she wheeled the cart toward the door.

"What was that all about?" Mitch wanted to know.

"What was what all about?"

"That comment about you having thirty minutes before she brought the dessert?"

Carly blinked. She couldn't tell him the meaning behind Susan's statement. What would he think? That she and Susan were working together on some sort of matchmaking scheme? Possibly. "Ah. . .it was an inside joke."

He arched his tawny brows. "And you're not going to let me in on it?"

"I. . .can't."

His skeptical expression told her he wasn't convinced. "Can't? Or won't."

She felt herself being backed into a corner, one she needed to get out of—*quick*.

She forced her shoulders to drop, feigning relaxation. "There we go again, arguing about something that doesn't amount to much and letting our food get cold." She ducked her head and spread her napkin on her lap. "I'm starved, aren't you?" Looking back up, she added, "Why don't you say grace?"

He narrowed his eyes, scrutinizing her like he was trying to analyze her thoughts. For a few suspended seconds, she thought he was going to challenge her. But she somehow held on to her wide-eyed expression of innocence, and he finally bowed his head.

Their meal was filled with conversation about his new project. While Mitch talked, his face glowed and his eyes sparkled. He used all sorts of architectural terms. Some Carly understood, since her father was a carpenter. But some were unfamiliar to her and she had to ask what they meant.

"Is the property accessible by wheelchair?" he asked as he pushed away his plate.

"Yes."

"Could I infringe on a few minutes of your time tomorrow? I'd like to look over the lay of the land, and I don't think the doctor will let me venture outside the hospital alone in this contraption just yet."

"Of course I'll go with you."

"It can wait until tomorrow afternoon, if that's better for you."

It probably could wait until then, but why put him through the anticipation? He already looked like a kid on Christmas Eve counting the minutes until Christmas morning. Her lips tipped. "How about first thing in the morning, after our devotion?"

"Are you sure? I don't want to interfere with your job."

"Of course I'm sure. Besides, helping you out *is* part of my job."

Something akin to disappointment cast a shadow across his face, then quickly disappeared.

Or had she imagined it?

For dessert, Susan served orange sherbet, a hospital regular.

"Why do I get the feeling Susan helped you plan this whole thing?" Carly asked as the nurse walked away.

"Probably because she did," Mitch responded with a wink, then the left-handed architect clumsily scooped his first bite out of the lightweight dessert cup with his right hand.

Carly kept stealing glances at him, wondering whether or not she should offer her help. She didn't want him to feel self-conscious or inadequate in any way. Then it dawned on her that her plate was still half-full, while he'd eaten everything on his and seemed to have ample room for dessert.

She trapped her right lower lip between her teeth. Did he simply have a big appetite? Or was he so grateful to get three meals a day, he didn't want to see anything go to waste?

Her heart twisted. What had it been like for him, counting pennies for a pack of crackers, living out of a car, shaving over a rusty service station sink? She couldn't imagine.

Noticing a bit of sherbet at the corner of his mouth, she unheedingly reached up with her napkin to wipe it away. When she did, he covered her hand with his own and met her gaze.

Something connected. Something emotional and enthralling. Something that stoked a sensuous spark between them.

Carly's world tilted. The air between them crackled with electricity. Nervously, she wet her lips. His gaze fell to her mouth, then rose again to her eyes. Slowly, he released her wrist and curled his finger beneath her chin.

Like a thirsty deer seeking water, she was drawn forward. Or was he urging her to lean toward him? She couldn't tell. She just knew they were both moving, both closing the space between them.

He was the faint smell of soap and shaving lotion, the heady scent of man. His breath, still cool and sweet from the icy dessert, filled her head with enthralling anticipation.

She was lost in the moment, trapped in a world beyond explanation, beyond anything she had ever experienced before. Yesterday, tomorrow, an hour from now. None of that mattered. Only the present. Only them.

The first brush of his lips was like a magic whisper. She trembled.

The second kiss, breath mingling with skin, was powerful.

Just before the third kiss, his hand slid to the back of

her head; hers rose to his clean-shaven jaw. Their gazes met, held a rapturous instant, then their lips merged in such synchronized harmony, the contact rocked Carly to her core.

She was on the brink of no return when his hand cupped her shoulder and he gently pushed her back. But he remained close, searching her face with a troubled expression.

Confused, she waited for him to speak.

After a long moment, he shook his head in regret. "I'm sorry, Carly. I shouldn't have done that."

A swift wave of disappointment washed over her. "You're sorry?"

"Yes." He swallowed, *hard*. "I don't know why I lost my head like that. Must be the pain medication."

Pain medication? She'd checked his chart this morning. He hadn't taken anything stronger than acetaminophen for three days. Nothing in that to make him "lose his head."

With the force of a tidal wave, the reality slammed into her. Friendship with her was okay. But he didn't want to become romantically involved with her, a natural-born misfit—especially since he had a chance to get his old life back.

Humiliation scalded her cheeks. How could she have let this happen? She had known better than to fall for a man like Mitch. Even at his lowest, he was charm and sophistication, prestige and good looks. She, on the other hand, was shy and ordinary, unassuming and plain. Painful experiences had taught her the two types didn't mix.

As calmly as she could manage, she returned the napkin to the table. "Um. . .I guess I'd better be getting home.

It's getting sort of late." Really, it wasn't. But she couldn't stay another minute. She was too mortified at responding so eagerly to his kiss. Too hurt by his rejection.

He didn't protest her decision to leave, just kept his gaze fixed on his lap and said nothing. She stood and walked toward the door, focusing on putting one foot in front of the other. But halfway there, her humiliation veered sharply toward anger, and she stopped.

No! her mind screamed. Lessons from two years of therapy rolled through her head. She wasn't going to walk away with her head bowed in shame. *She* hadn't been the one to initiate the kiss, then push him away in rejection. She deserved more consideration than that, and he deserved to know what he had just done to her.

Curling her hands into fists, she turned and marched back to the table. He looked up at her in surprise.

"Exactly what am I to you, Mitch?" she asked.

"Huh?" he responded, apparently taken aback by her abrupt about-face.

"I said, 'What am I to you?' A convenient experiment to prove you can still charm the ladies? Another notch on your belt? A gullible misfit you think you can use to satisfy a carnal need then toss aside like a worn-out rag doll?"

"No," he countered, his forehead creasing in bewilderment. "I care about you, Carly. I care about you a lot." A taut moment of silence hung between them, then his shoulders drooped. "You're my friend, Carly. The best I've ever had."

She didn't think it possible for a breaking heart to soften toward the person doing the breaking, but hers did. She swallowed past the tight ache in her throat and blinked back the sudden onslaught of tears. "Then let me give you some advice. The next time you decide to have dinner with a female 'friend,' don't light candles, and don't kiss her. It can give her the wrong impression." With that, she turned and marched from the room.

When she got back to her office, she locked the door, sat down at her desk, laid her head on her folded arms, and cried.

Back in his hospital room, Mitch sat staring at the flickering flame of one of the candles sitting on the table. He had done the right thing, he told himself. Whatever was happening between them could go no farther. He may have a job and a chance at starting over, but one fact remained; he still had nothing to offer Carly. Not yet, anyway. And he wouldn't start a romantic relationship with her until he was financially secure.

He loved her too much.

Chapter 6

L et all bitterness, and wrath, and anger, and clamour, and evil speaking, be put away from you, with all malice.' "

Carly's silken voice glided through the hospital room as she read the final verses of the devotion. Mitch had been a bit surprised when she had shown up this morning, Bible in hand, as though nothing out of the ordinary had happened between them last night.

Well, *almost* as though nothing out of the ordinary had happened. She did avoid his gaze whenever possible, and the few times she spared him a quick glance, he'd noticed a shadow of pain had dulled the usual sparkle in her hazel eyes. Knowing he had put that pain there twisted the knot of guilt in his gut tighter.

He needed to explain why he couldn't rush into a romantic relationship with her. He needed to make her understand that if, instead of succeeding, he slipped deeper into the hole he was just beginning to crawl out of, he didn't want to pull her down with him.

" 'And be ye kind one to another, tenderhearted, forgiving one another, even as God for Christ's sake hath forgiven you.' "

After reading the final verse of Ephesians 4, she fell silent but didn't immediately look up.

Would now be a good time to apologize for last night? She appeared so. . .thoughtful. Maybe she was meditating on the Scripture. Or maybe she was praying in silence.

Or maybe he was stalling.

He gave his head a begrudging shake. What was he so afraid of? That she'd feel rejected like she had in high school? Or that he'd learn she wasn't mutually attracted to him, and he would be the one to feel rejected? He released a dismal sigh. Perhaps he feared both. Either way, he had to try to make amends. He couldn't live with the knowledge that he had hurt her, even unintentionally.

Suddenly, she raised her head. "I owe you an apology, Mitch."

Confusion pinched his brow. "Me? Why?"

"I got angry with you last night." She paused, absentmindedly chewing on her right lower lip. "The things I said to you before I left were out of that anger. I know you would never take advantage of me, and I apologize for accusing you of doing so."

Mitch felt like a heel, one that had just stepped in mud. "Carly, you don't owe me an apology. But I do owe you one. Let me explain about last night."

"There's no need," she injected before he could continue. "You were right. There is something special about our friendship, and I wouldn't want anything to get in the way of that."

"But—"

"No 'buts.' " With a smile that appeared forced, she rose from her chair and laid the Bible on the bedside cabinet. "Let's get you into the wheelchair and out to the site of the new wing. The weatherman's predicting rain for later this morning, and we don't want your casts to get wet."

Accepting what little help he needed from Carly, Mitch positioned himself in the wheelchair. As she guided him down the corridor, he told himself he should be grateful their friendship was still intact.

But was it?

He sensed something between them now that wasn't there before, a wall she'd erected around herself, possibly around her heart, to guard against further hurt. Against him.

A flicker of apprehension coursed through his guilt-heavy chest. Would things ever be the same between them again? Or had he, by giving in to his desire to kiss her, alienated her for good?

Only time would tell.

Leaning on his cane, Mitch stood at a floor-to-ceiling acrylic window in the rehabilitation unit, watching heavy machinery move dirt in preparation for the foundation of the new hospital wing. If he didn't have an appointment with the physical therapist this morning, he'd be down there with the men. They had come highly recommended; Mitch trusted their judgment. But he preferred to be close to his work, feel the dirt crunch beneath his feet, and smell the pungent muskiness of the damp, red soil.

He rubbed his hand over his jaw. A lot had happened in the last six weeks. Mitch had spent a month in the rehabilitation wing, hired contractors to start work on the new hospital wing, and gotten his casts removed. And Carly had been the one to help him through each new adjustment. She had sought out and recommended top contractors, scolded him whenever he gave his physical therapists a hard time, taxied him back and forth to the hospital every day. She had even found an affordable one-bedroom, furnished apartment for him to move into when the hospital had released him last week.

True to her word, she had remained his friend, but she had also stayed hidden behind the wall of protection she had erected. Each time she started letting her guard down, he felt her pulling herself back, removing herself from the comfort zone they once so effortlessly shared. Every time their gazes were drawn together in the midst of dying laughter, she quickly looked away and steered their conversation in a new direction. Whenever their hands accidentally brushed each other, she quickly jerked away.

And with each passing day, a void in Mitch's heart grew, for he had to live with the knowledge that he'd let something very special slip away from him.

"Are you sure you're all right?" Mitch asked for the second time while Carly was driving them to the hospital one week later.

Keeping her eyes focused on the rainy road ahead, she pursed her lips and nodded.

Mitch knew better. She had been late picking him up, which was highly unusual for her, and she hadn't said a word, except to mutter a hasty "Good morning" when he had gotten into the car. She was also pale, and small beads of sweat were popping up above her upper lip. But, stubborn woman that she was, she refused to admit she was sick.

He turned his attention back to the rain pelting the windshield and the steady *swish-swash* of the windshield wipers. When he got to the hospital, he'd see that one of the doctors checked her out, even if Mitch had to hold her on the examination table himself.

As they approached the traffic signal at the hospital drive, the light turned red. The vehicle in front of them slowed, but Carly didn't. Visions from his own accident raced through Mitch's head. Instinctively, he pressed his hand to the dash and looked over at her. She was biting her lower lip—hard—and holding her right side with her right hand. "Carly, the light's red," he said as he extended his damaged left leg toward the brake, only to have his seat belt hinder him.

But something got through to her, and she slammed on the brake. Tires screeched, but somehow, miraculously, she stopped her vehicle short of hitting the one in front of them.

Mitch slipped the transmission into park and unbuckled his seat belt. Sliding over, he slipped his arm around Carly's shoulders. Her skin was now ashen, and the sheen of perspiration glistened on her forehead. Her knuckle-white left hand still gripped the steering wheel.

"Carly, Baby, what's wrong?"

"My. . .side," she rasped, like the Grim Reaper had ahold of her throat.

Mitch glanced down to the hand pressed against her right side and covered that hand with his own. Her skin was scorching hot to his touch.

Fever. Unbearable pain in her right side. Alarm lodged in his throat. He wasn't a doctor, but he knew the symptoms of appendicitis. He had the scar on his own right side to prove it.

"Sick," she whispered, reaching for the door, and, opening it, leaned over and retched. Another symptom of appendicitis.

Mitch switched off the ignition, slid back across the car's seat, and got out. He didn't remember his cane until he took his first urgent step with his left foot, but he didn't retrieve the walking stick. He couldn't afford to waste precious seconds. If Carly did have appendicitis, and her appendix ruptured, she could. . .

He cut off his terrified thoughts and focused on getting medical attention for her. He looked around at the gathering crowd, who merely glared in curiosity. "Somebody call nine-one-one!" he yelled as he hobbled up to her door.

"The hospital's just up the hill," someone stated.

Mitch glared at the lady who offered the obvious information. "I know that," he ground out. "But I can't get her up there." They were surrounded by a conglomeration of cars, people, and honking horns of those who were anxious to get where they were going regardless of the needs of a sick young woman.

He leaned over Carly and unbuckled her seat belt. Pulling his handkerchief from his pocket, he gently pushed her back up into a sitting position. "Carly, it's okay." He swabbed her forehead and upper lip with the handkerchief. She moaned but didn't open her eyes. Her arms now hung limply at her side. She was too weak to even hold her hurting side.

Leaning forward, he slipped his arms beneath her and picked her up, wincing inwardly when a sharp, tearing pain seared his weak left elbow. Gritting his teeth against his own discomfort, he limped around the car, weaved through the crowd, and plowed up the long inclining driveway leading to the hospital. "I called the hospital," someone called. "They're coming to meet you."

Mitch silently thanked the caller. At the moment, that was all he could do.

In the distance, the double doors to the emergency room swung open and out ran two nurses and a doctor navigating a gurney. By the time Mitch handed Carly over to the doctor, his entire left side felt like it had been torn to shreds, and his lungs burned like wildfire.

After laying Carly on the gurney, the doctor turned to Mitch.

Supporting himself with his hands on his knees, Mitch shook his head. "I'm fine. Take her in. I'm afraid she has appendicitis."

Without further argument, the doctor and the nurses pushed the gurney uphill.

Someone grasped Mitch's right wrist from behind, and a head popped up under his arm. "Come on, young man," an elderly man in overalls said. "Let's get you up this here hill so you can be with your lady."

Mitch mustered up a weary grin. "Thank you, Sir. You're an angel."

That evening, Mitch sat by Carly's hospital bed, waiting for her to awaken. He had guessed right; she had had a very sick appendix. The doctor said they had been fortunate. Another two hours and. . .

Mitch's throat tightened. He didn't even want to think about what could have happened. She was still alive. She was going to be all right. That was all that mattered.

He shifted in the recliner, clenching his teeth when his left arm, now supported by a sling, and left leg physically complained. Only when he knew Carly was out of danger had he relented to treatment. The doctor had admonished Mitch for carrying her up the hill and not waiting for help to come to them, pointing out that his "impulsive act of heroism" would set him back a few weeks on his physical therapy. Mitch had remained noncommittal. He didn't care if he lost the use of his entire left side, as long as Carly was alive and well.

She moaned softly and turned her head. Mitch flipped down the leg rest of his chair and scrambled up. He wanted to be next to her when she awakened, wanted to be touching her.

He eased down on the edge of her bed and curled his hand around hers. Her eyelids fluttered opened, and a weak smile touched her lips. "Mitch."

Her voice was raspy from lack of moisture. He picked up a cup of cool water he already had poured and placed the straw in her mouth. She swallowed twice then motioned for him to take the cup away.

"The last thing I remember is being terribly sick," she said. "What happened?"

Mitch smiled, brushing a strand of hair away from her face. "You had a very sick appendix."

Her eyes widened. "You mean, I've had surgery?"

He answered with a nod.

Her eyelids slid down and up slowly. "That explains why I've been feeling so poorly for the last two days."

"Carly," he said, his voice taking on a mild, rebuking tone. "Why didn't you tell someone you were sick?"

"Because I thought it was a stomach virus or something I had eaten. I was hoping it would pass."

"Neglecting your symptoms could have cost you your life."

One corner of her mouth tipped. "But you saved me."

"I just happened to be there. If you had been alone—"

"Shh." She shook her head. "All things happen for a reason. God knew I'd need a hero with me this morning, so He sent you."

Mitch's chest swelled with pent-up emotions. He certainly didn't see himself as a hero, but he was thankful that he was with Carly this morning. And he was grateful he had been given a second chance to tell her how he felt about her.

He raised her hand and pressed a soft kiss to the back of it. Then he laid her palm against his chest. She studied him with curious anticipation.

"Carly, I need to tell you something."

Wide-eyed, she nodded and timidly wet her lips.

"That night, when I kissed you, I didn't turn you away because I wanted to. I turned you away because I didn't want you to become involved with me before I got back on my feet and had more to offer you than I could as a homeless, penniless gambler. But, today, when I wasn't sure you were going to make it, I realized I may not have next year, or next month, or even tomorrow to tell you how I feel about you."

She pursed her lips. Her hazel eyes glistened with tears.

"I still don't have anything to offer you, Carly. But, if you're willing to wait a little while, a year or two, then, maybe, someday. . ."

Carly raised her hand from his chest and pressed her fingertips to his lips. "Mitch, I need nothing but you and your love. But I understand your wanting to get on your feet. You still have doubts about whether you're going to make it. I can see them in your eyes." She shifted her hand to his cheek. "I have faith in you, Mitch. So does God. We know you're going to make it. We're going to shower you with so much love, you'll never want to go back to your old way of living. So, yes. I'll wait, if that's what it takes. I'll wait forever if I need to."

Mitch's own vision clouded with moisture, and a lump of emotion rose to his throat. He covered her hand with his own and, angling his head, kissed her palm. "I love you, Carly."

"I love you, too, Mitch."

So full of joy he couldn't speak, he gazed at Carly in awe.

Finally, one side of her mouth turned up in an amused grin. "Well, are you just going to sit there and cry, or are you going to kiss me?"

Mitch decided to do both.

Chapter 7

One Year Later

itch stood at the front of the church watching the flower girl, Carly's niece from California, sprinkle a trail of rose petals down the aisle. Mitch's nephew, the ring bearer, followed. Beside Mitch, as best man, stood his father. Martin Reynolds still wasn't thrilled about Mitch being an architectural developer, especially in a town as small as Bradenton. But, the older man was coming around. And he seemed more considerate of Mitch's mother, too; something Mitch had been praying for for a long time.

Joining Mitch and his father as attendants were a man Mitch had met in Gamblers Anonymous and become good friends with, and another young man Mitch had met at the church he now attended with Carly.

Today, Mitch's joy cup spilled over, filling his soul with gladness and thanksgiving. The day he'd waited for, dreamed of for the past year, was finally here. Today, he and Carly would become husband and wife.

His mind scrolled back over the last twelve months. It was hard to believe so much had happened in so little time. In addition to completing the hospital project, he had started two more, signed contracts for four others, and was negotiating several that looked promising. Mitch had enough work to keep him busy for several years.

Last month, he'd received a generous insurance settlement from the automobile accident. With those funds, he was going to build a house with a home office and plenty of growing room. Until the home was finished, Carly's house would be plenty big enough for the two of them.

A contented smiled tugged at the corners of Mitch's mouth. Last year, when Carly had told him she and God were going to shower him with so much love he'd never want to go back to his old way of life, she had been right. Not once had he been tempted to hop into his car and drive to an out-of-state casino. He could even go into a convenience store and walk out without buying a lottery ticket. Amazing what God's grace and the love of a good woman could do.

The organ's volume increased, announcing the bride's entrance. The attendees in the sanctuary stood. Carly stepped up to the doorway with her father, into the yellow and rose sunlight filtering through a stained glass window.

Mitch's chest swelled with pride. She looked like an angel. No man ever had a lovelier bride than he. She wore her hair up in a mass of soft curls. Her lace veil hung from a crown of baby's breath and pink tea roses. Her candle-yellow gown, which had been passed down through five generations, fit as though it had been tailor-made to hug each soft curve of her small, shapely body.

The family tradition was for each bride and groom to add their own heirloom, along with a letter from the bride, to a hand-carved chest that had been passed down along with the gown. Then, at the appropriate time, the possessors of the gown and chest would hand down the heirlooms to the next generation.

Carly stopped at the front pew, handed a rose to Mitch's mother, and kissed her cheek. Then, Carly turned and gave her own mother and grandmother, who had once worn the gown Carly now wore, a rose and a kiss.

"Who gives this woman in marriage?" the minister finally asked.

Carl Simmons cleared his throat. "Her mother and I." His voice was raspy with emotion. He pressed his lips to his daughter's cheek, then, teary-eyed, handed her over to Mitch.

Mitch and Carly spoke their vows with ease and confidence. When the minister announced, "You may now kiss your bride," Mitch wrapped his arms around Carly and pulled her close.

"I love you, Mrs. Reynolds," he said.

"I love you, too, Mr. Reynolds."

Then the heirloom bride and her handsome groom sealed their union with a long, lingering kiss.

GINA FIELDS

Gina is a life-long native of Northeast Georgia. She is married to Terry, a pastor, and they have two very active sons. When Gina is not writing, singing, or playing piano, among a hundred home-making activities, she enjoys volunteering for Special Olympics.

A Letter to Our Readers

Dear Readers:

In order that we might better contribute to your reading enjoyment, we would appreciate your taking a few minutes to respond to the following questions. When completed, please return to the following: Fiction Editor, Barbour Publishing, Inc., PO Box 719, Uhrichsville, OH 44683.

1. Did you enjoy reading *Mother's Wedding Dress*?
   ❑ Very much. I would like to see more books like this.
   ❑ Moderately—I would have enjoyed it more if _____
   _____
   _____

2. What influenced your decision to purchase this book?
   (Check those that apply.)
   ❑ Cover   ❑ Back cover copy   ❑ Title   ❑ Price
   ❑ Friends   ❑ Publicity   ❑ Other

3. Which story was your favorite?
   ❑ *Button String Bride*   ❑ *Bayside Bride*
   ❑ *Wedding Quilt Bride*   ❑ *The Persistent Bride*

4. Please check your age range:
   ❑ Under 18   ❑ 18–24   ❑ 25–34
   ❑ 35–45   ❑ 46–55   ❑ Over 55

5. How many hours per week do you read? _____

Name _____

Occupation _____

Address _____

City _____ State _____ ZIP_____

If you enjoyed
mother's wedding Dress
then read:

Speak Now or Forever Hold Your Peace by Veda Boyd Jones
Once Upon A Dream by Sally Laity
Something Old, Something New by Yvonne Lehman
Wrong Church, Wrong Wedding by Loree Lough

If you enjoyed

MOTHER'S WEDDING DRESS

then read:

❦ ♡ ❧

A MOTHER'S HEART

*Four Historical Stories of Couples
Brought Together by the Faith of a Child*

One Little Prayer by Kimberly Comeaux
The Tie That Binds by Susan K. Downs
The Provider by Cathy Marie Hake
Returning Amanda by Kathleen Paul

Available wherever books are sold.
Or order from:
Barbour Publishing, Inc.
P.O. Box 719
Uhrichsville, Ohio 44683
www.barbourbooks.com

You may order by mail for $4.97 and add $2.00 to your order for shipping.
Prices subject to change without notice.

If you enjoyed

mother's wedding Dress

then read:

❧

Blind Dates

Four Stories of Hearts United with
a Little Help from Grandma

The Perfect Match by Denise Hunter
A Match Made in Heaven by Colleen Coble
Mix and Match by Bev Huston
Mattie Meets Her Match by Kristin Billerbeck

If you enjoyed

mother's
wedding
Dress

then read:

❧

LIGHTHOUSE
BRIDES

*Four Romantic Novellas
Spotlighting Lighthouse Heroines*

When Love Awaits by Lynn A. Coleman
A Beacon in the Storm by Andrea Boeshaar
Whispers Across the Blue by DiAnn Mills
A Time to Love by Sally Laity